TERRIBLE DEMIURGE

A novel about Loss, Search and the Secret of the Universe

Alfonso Asensio

 LT Books

Published in Japan by LT Books in 2022
TERRIBLE DEMIURGE
Copyright © Alfonso Asensio 2022
ISBN: 9798848748925

To

John "Jack" Holbrook Vance (San Francisco, 1916—Oakland, 2013).
Writer, creator and demiurge.
Who will never know this book exists.

"The place I am telling you about—said the demon placing his hand over my head—comes from the light and the gods, and here I am, in exile, far from them."[1]

---

[1] It has not been possible to confirm the authorship of this quote. The phrase, offered by the Man Under Contract, is imprecise, probably erroneous.

9

The Travelogue of Gavriel Artiel

13°24'N/103°52'E
Cambodia: The Sightless Paths

35°36'N/102°29'E
Tibet: The Wheel Ascendant

41°52'S/1146°01'E
Tasmania: The Chapel of Green

33°41'N/142°11'W
California: Diversions and Leaps

27°05'N/103°46'E
Japan: The Rumours of the Dead

--°--'N/--°--'E
Demiurge

Prologue

The life of the Man Under Contract—named Gavriel, gaunt, serious and of consumed expression—in recent years was centred around the following belief: there is a hidden space beyond this world, a fold of truth, and no one is allowed to glance behind the curtain which covers it.

But he also knew that the universe had, discreetly, left an opening through which those curious enough could look into the other side.

Gavriel—his name really had such a strange orthography, the legacy of a father and mother who wanted to give their son immediate notoriety—travelled through countries and cities looking for that opening, living sparingly, eating little. He thought of this Search as a personal manifest destiny, which was opaque but also certain, and strived to lose himself, anonymous, among the rest of the budget travellers who crowded the railway stations and dilapidated lodges of South East Asia.

Gavriel carried a notebook of illegible handwriting, and a list of names. He followed clues that only he could find thanks to a combination of intuition, reason and divine signals, and walked the byways of this world as if they were a map where converged everything he planned to use to reveal the greatest secret of the universe.

The Man Under Contract, as he would later be known to the parties involved in his story and to those deceased he left in his wake, endeavoured to look behind the curtain of reality, and this is the story of how he did it.

13°24'N/103°52'E
Cambodia: The Sightless Paths

Gavriel climbed the mountain.

Maybe that is not entirely correct.

Gavriel did climb the mountain but that came later, as an epilogue to the years he spent wandering through alleys and narrow roads, looking for a way to get there.

Long before that, Gavriel had left Phnom Penh, the capital of Cambodia, with his cap pulled low over the eyes and those eyes looking down at the ground. From there he had travelled to the border of Vietnam after deciding he would cross not by plane or train but on foot to leave as little trace as possible. He bought an anonymous bus ticket and, after hours of rattling on dilapidated roads, he reached the end of the journey. The last tank had crossed at that same place a few decades ago, at the end of one of the many intermittent wars between the neighbouring countries, and the five-hundred-metres-wide strip of land that separated the countries retained a certain desolate air. But even at the early hour at which Gavriel arrived, the traffic of bicycles and people carrying oversized pieces of luggage was intense. Gavriel marched from the Cambodian customs building on one side to its Vietnamese counterpart on the other and the architecture was as contrasting as the two states were. Vietnam used a sober construction of stern straight lines with the communist red star prominently raised; Cambodia, always inspired by the formidable Khmer heritage of the temples of Angkor Wat, showed softer curves: ogival towers and spires resembling lotus buds. An officer stamped Gavriel's passport, and he crossed the inter-border space, free and vulnerable at the same time. Half a kilometre later he departed Cambodia and the debacle of Siem Reap, trying, to no avail, to feel moved by the fate of those left behind.

He spent two days in Ho Chi Minh City, the much-maligned Saigon that the American War[2] had painted as a haunt of prostitutes and

---

[2] Since the familiar expression "Vietnam War" lost all meaning in the context of the country, this other name was how the conflict with the United States was nationally known. The Vietnamese had suffered so many wars that even that one, the most famous of them, needed to be adjectivized.

decay. What he found was a vital and expanding city which was ambitiously shaking off the scars of recent history and looking at a bright future. During those two days, Gavriel walked through night markets and the few archaic temples that resisted the push of urban redevelopment; he used up a whole morning visiting the expansive military museum, and, in the afternoon, he queued up at the mausoleum of the communist leader who gave the city its name. There, a mummified corpse with waxed and translucent skin was kept in a vacuum coffin, watching the decades go by in incorruptible dormancy.

From Ho Chi Min City he took another train and travelled to the actual capital, Hanoi, further north. He climbed the map in a vertical line, occasionally following the coastline but more often shouldering the thick vegetation of the jungle in an undulating and tiresome trek. The train was an ancient electric machine that stopped at unreasonable times. Twice he had to make a change no one had told him about, transferring from one carriage to another, from seat to seat, because the convoy had to separate with a loud clacking of gears and connections.

In the middle of the first night a railroad employee, wearing the pith hat that the North Vietnamese army had used during the war, shook him by the shoulder and spoke with urgency. Gavriel shook his head, not completely awake yet. He had been dreaming of the woman Maya, a ghostly set of fingers had him still wrapped around that dream.

"I don't understand," he said.

The man spoke again, waved his hands.

"I don't…"

"He says we both need to move. You should get your things," said a young Vietnamese woman in proficient English, getting up from her seat and picking up her bags.

She had a thick book with many little yellow post-it ribbons showing from between the pages.

They left the compartment and walked against the rocking motion of the old train. The railroad employee guided them through the overcrowded wagons and, dislodging a protesting man from his bunk, rearranged Gavriel into the liberated space. The woman sat down a few rows back and Gavriel saw her pull out her book and read by the glow of a small flashlight amid the snoring rumour of the passengers.

The following day, their connection for Hanoi was delayed and Gavriel descended with a large group of travellers to wait in a crumbling station, surrounded by deserted roads and lush fields, for the next train to arrive. With nowhere to go, he ate biscuits from a bag and read for the rest of the day. He noticed that the number of people dwindled, some walked out into the empty roads and others were picked up by vans and mopeds, and he worried if he was supposed to board the train somewhere else. Further down the platform sat the woman from the night before.

"Sorry, do you know when will the train arrive?" said Gavriel walking over to her.

"Hello," she smiled warmly. "Where are you going?"

Gavriel told her and she nodded. Gavriel glanced at the book in her lap, a dense-looking tome in English about business and tourism.

"I am on my way to Hanoi as well. We have to wait; this line is not very reliable, but a train will come eventually."

"And they?" asked Gavriel pointing to the other passengers who were leaving the open-air station.

"Don't feel like waiting, I suppose. They will probably try to go by road as far as they can."

And then, when Gavriel was about to turn around, the woman gestured for him to sit down with the random kindness of strangers. He did.

They spoke the rest of that day, sitting side by side and half-reclining on their backpacks. The studious woman's name was Tracy Le and she was, at twenty-two, a tourist guide in Ho Chi Min city.

"I am actually from one of the northern provinces. There is better work in the big cities, so I moved from there to Ho Chi Min but it's time to go back."

"So, will you stay in Hanoi?" asked Gavriel.

"Just for a few days, I will travel on from there and go home to Sapa. Do you know the place? Lovely hill country, great for trekking. All my family is there, including my nephew. It seems there are more tourist agencies now than there were a couple of years ago. I will need to find work," she patted the business book.

"Is that what you are studying for?"

"Yes, I am trying to finish my degree, improve what I can."

"Sounds like you have a very clear plan."

She laughed.

"Not at all."

At about four in the morning, as Gavriel dozed, a group of local families arrived with tremendous and animated uproar. They spread a thick carpet on the platform and sat down to prepare tea and cakes on a small stove. Tracy and Gavriel were the only other passengers in the platform and they accepted when invited to sit on the rug and share their food. In return, Tracy translated while Gavriel, often the only Westerner in lost corners of South East Asia like that one, responded willingly to the bombardment of questions that the new acquaintances sent his way about Gavriel's home country and the world beyond.

"They ask if you are going to Hao Long Bay," Tracy translated. "They say all foreigners go there."

Gavriel became alert. Hao Long Bay was one of the usual stops on the backpacker route which started in Hanoi; a magnetic site he had once considered significant. Once before had he found signs in a water/land configuration like that of the islets of Hao Long, a myriad of limestone pillars topped by jungle thickets in a labyrinthine arrangement. But that had been an exception, and this time none of the references pointed to anything similar.

"Why?"

Tracy blinked at the sudden intensity of the man.

"Well, it is a popular spot. I worked there for a while in the tourist cruises."

"Oh right. And? How was it?" Gavriel said, more composed.

"The whole crew run route after route, often resting just one day a month. We would pick up a group of passengers, about 30 people, navigate around the islands for three days organizing meals and entertainment, drop them at the harbour on the morning of day four and by noon, after cleaning and refuelling, we had another group coming on board. Competition between the sailing lines was tremendous and if our customer review rating fell, we would get salary cuts or get fired."

Their host family said something to Tracy and she replied in fast Vietnamese.

"They ask where we met. I said it was overseas, in America. Otherwise, they may think you are paying me for company; they probably think so already."

Gavriel was well aware of the nebulous line that separated courtship from prostitution in some of the developing countries of South East Asia where visitors and locals exchanged affection and funds in a wide range of degrees. He didn't know what to say that would not offend Tracy, so he remained silent.

At dawn, the train arrived, and they said goodbye to the Vietnamese family and their lively hubbub with reluctance. They moved north, the dulling hours of the trip grinding. Gavriel and Tracy spoke, ate and slept at synchronized intervals. Then, much later, the train rolled into the city of Hoi An, a picturesque coastal town that maintained its colonial-era buildings and streets in a fascinating well-kept state of conservation. Tracy stopped their conversation mid-sentence and pointed out of the window.

"Look, Hoi An. Very nice place, very classic. I was bringing tours here quite a bit last year."

Gavriel looked outside and when the train arrived at the platform, he stood up.

"I have to get out," he said aloud, moved by an impulsive rapture and following obscure signs that only he saw.

"You are getting out?" Tracy looked at him, then out of the window. "I thought you were bound for Hanoi?"

Gavriel could see the sleepy town beyond the station. This was not a scheduled stop for him but things were in motion, a complex conjunction of coincidences, references and constellations of data that he analysed in passing, guided more by impulse than by intellect.

"I am. But I must stop here. Just for a few days."

"Ok… well…"

With an impulse that was both genuine and calculating, Gavriel spoke quickly.

"Come with me," he said to the young woman he had known for two days.

"With you?"

"Yes, I need to stay here."

"I know, you said that. But why do you want me to go with you?" she spoke with an edge of sad realization.

"It's not that, not what you think. You know the city; do you want to be my guide? I will be happy to hire you."

She shook her head.

"I can't, my family is waiting for me, my nephew."

"You still can study, and you could save some money. It may be useful until, you know, you find a new job."

Tracy thought and said nothing but when Gavriel descended from the train, she went with him.

They ate together that first day, feeling awkward until it was clear to Tracy that Gavriel was indeed hiring her professional services and not buying her company. He asked endless questions about the history of the settlement, the establishing of a trading centre by Portuguese explorers, the opening of the Catholic cathedral and the long, soporific era of French dominion. He took detailed notes in a thick notebook with black-leather covers in minuscule handwriting.

Later, Tracy tried to take Gavriel on the usual tourist lap around Hoi An but very soon he was asking for detour after detour, forcing them to walk in a circuitous route that led nowhere. Tracy struggled to get him interested in the wide boulevards along the river, in the commercial arcade but Gavriel insisted on visiting obscure corners of temples, sepulchres and museums, barely paying attention to their historical plaques or decorations and scrutinizing minor friezes and decayed carvings.

Tracy watched the man all that day. For a few hours, he transformed from the congenial person she met on the train into an absorbed inquisitor. He scribbled in his notebook and asked questions as if he spoke from a remote place and she, who knew tourists and their many types (the curious, the bored, the restless) thought that Gavriel didn't fit into any of them. He was more like a stoical archaeologist, looking for the things behind things.

With the coming of dusk, he dragged her in a final mad rush, but whatever track he had glimpsed ended near a grandiose mausoleum at the churchyard and they returned to the hostel. On their way, Gavriel underwent his peculiar transformation and by the time they sat for dinner, he was, again, an agreeable well-travelled man on holiday.

"So, do you always travel alone?" Tracy asked. And then, "do you have a partner or somebody back home?"

Gavriel looked at his plate.

"And you? Anybody back in Ho Chi Minh?" he said.

"Kind of. I was dating an Italian man, Rober, But his company relocated him to Singapore."

"It is a great city. Do you plan to go and see him?

"Maybe. I probably need to settle down first."

"Of course," said Gavriel and kept on eating. Tracy waited for a moment.

"And? What about you?"

Gavriel moved his food around the plate with the chopsticks.

"There was a woman. Her name was Maya."

"Are you no longer together?"

"No, I don't know. She went away."

"Back to her country?"

"Uh-huh," said Gavriel.

It was the fourteenth of that month, and that night, while they were eating fish and noodles by the river Thu Bon, a procession of lights passed along the water. Residents and tourists floated paper lanterns lit by candles or raised balloons of the same material that peppered the sky with glows of red and tones of orange and enveloped the entire town in an unreal aura. Gavriel and Tracy attended the ceremony in fascination. The lights, together with the dreamlike quality of the century-old buildings constructed in precious woods, created a dream state that not only they sensed; all around couples joined hands and families embraced. Tracy felt the man standing very close to her.

"My name is not Tracy," she said unprompted.

"Sorry?"

"It is not Tracy. Well, not really, it is a nickname. I use it so is easier for clients to remember. My name is Trang."

Gavriel smiled and Tracy thought that, for such a well-guarded man, that smile was honest.

"Please to meet you, Le Trang."

They shook hands, comically formal. The paper balloons, still shining, flew north in a closed formation like that of the hermit ibis.

Later that night, Tracy studied her textbook until late to make up for the time they had spent looking at sights during the day. She pondered if it was a mistake to have left Ho Chi Min city and went to bed thinking how confusing the future looked. In his room, Gavriel moved around unable to rest. There were incomprehensible forces at play, and all he could discern were the peaks and clusters that emanated from them. If one were to reach the proper resonance, as Gavriel did through study and inclination of character, he could discover those dynamics of attraction that would lead, eventually, to objects or events of the same rank[3]. But he understood now that the stop in Hoi An had been in vain and spent a few more hours adding entries to his journal, a travelogue scribbled with all the information he had collected; a taxonomy of data that comprised notes and quotes from religious texts, archaeological commentaries, epistolary postscripts, press clippings and an amalgam of other references, which even included comments heard on passing at special places. Everything counted when dealing with the inclusive, integral and absolute nature of the Search.

---

[3] The methods and patterns of behaviour of the Man Under Contract are based on Carl Jung's theory of synchronicity and the work of biologist Paul Kammerer, an unhinged genius who ended up committing suicide in 1926 and wrote *Das Gesetz der Serie* ("all the events are connected"). Kammerer's experiments included, among others, sitting for hours to observe the attire of pedestrians in the street in order to derive relationships between them. The work process of the Man Under Contract was similarly confusing, fortuitous and intuitive.

They met the following morning and because the charm of the city had caught him, Gavriel proposed that they remained one more pleasant and unproductive day in Hoi An, drinking tea and waiting for the magic of the festival to recur, but it was not to be. The nights along the river were full of travellers, street vendors hawking knickknacks, and rowdy bars full of people that spoiled the memory of that first day.

Gavriel and Tracy got back on the train and didn't stop until they reached Hanoi. The weather changed, and it was raining torrentially when they entered the city. The streets had more character in the northern capital than they had preserved in Ho Chi Minh City, where real estate speculation and new businesses had destroyed much of the old neighbourhoods. Hanoi was busy; even in the rain, the hustle of mopeds and bicycles didn't stop. Galloping drivers sheltered under multicoloured plastic ponchos and defied the storm, speeding up in gay abandon.

The couple exchanged a clumsy and rather moving goodbye right there on the train platform, with promises to meet again before the woman left Hanoi for the northern mountainous town of Sapa. When Tracy walked away, Gavriel watched her go longer than he intended.

He took refuge in a cheap but clean guest house during the spell of rain which lasted all day and all night. Gavriel felt worried about being alone again; a lone man was too suspicious after what had happened in Cambodia, when even now people may be looking for him. He waited in his room until he could wait no longer and came to think he missed Tracy's conversation. Then, he was busy again and looked for clues in ancient computers and in travel guides scattered throughout the common room while the monsoon pounded the glass of the windows. At night he dreamed that a blind man pointed a finger at him. He woke up in the dark hours thinking about Jason first and then about Maya, and then could not sleep anymore.

With the sunrise, the weather abated. Gavriel toured the city as he normally did. But the efforts of the day were cursory, of low intensity. Hanoi was too urban and vigorous to find the inert quality required by the Search. Gavriel had realized by midmorning that he would find nothing there but continued his investigations with the inertia and the good habit of the conscientious detective. Crouching over a map, he thought about his next step. The telluric rules of the Search gave preference to high, mountainous terrain, and the traces left by the unfolding of religious ideas often pointed towards clues. What's more, during the American War there had been much movement of war material across the border thanks to the steady supply of cannons and rifles the cordial Chinese Chairman Mao provided to the Viet Cong and the communist Liberation Army. A quote came to Gavriel's mind: "Iron is a dynamic and conductive element; it's the way of all things." Where had he read that?[4] It did not matter; it was north, then.

That evening, he met Tracy for dinner. Gavriel waited at Hoan Kiem Lake Park where a long, lively line of bars and coffee houses illuminated the coming darkness with neon lights. People crowded the avenue, a car stopped near him and Tracy got off, looking relaxed in a flowing red dress. Her friends, four other young women, saw the western man waiting for her and teased from the vehicle in local dialect while she laughed and waved them away.

The couple sat down on the terrace of a brightly lit restaurant.

"You look like a local."

"Of course, I do, I am Vietnamese."

"I mean, you seem to fit better here than in Hoi An. There, I could have taken you for an American tourist visiting her long-lost family."

Tracy thought about that while the waiter served their drinks.

"You may be right. I am more suited for the north than the south. Vietnam may look like one country from the outside, but deep fractures still run through it. Not everything was solved with the reunification after the American War."

"Is that why you wanted to come back here?"

"Yes. That, and other things."

They ate in silence for a while. The French dominion had left a uniquely Asian bakery tradition in Vietnam which produced pieces of

------

[4] Robert de Chester, in his translation of *Liber de Compositione Alchimiae*, 1144. The Man Under Contract did not read the hefty volume but just a summary of it.

bread and pies as good as any available in Europe.

“When do you leave for your hometown?” asked Gavriel.

Tracy took some time to answer.

“Tomorrow. Today is my last evening in Hanoi.”

“There is something I wanted to ask you,” said Gavriel. “I plan to go to Sapa as well, towards the Chinese border. I wonder if you mind travelling together a bit more.”

The woman’s demeanour changed, and she appeared infinitely sad.

“Tracy?”

“That sounds good. Yes. I can show you the tea terraces. Free of charge this time,” she said in a tone that was now too cheery.

“Is that ok? I know your family is waiting for you, but it is just that I am going that way. I don’t want to impose or bother you.”

“You won’t,” Tracy said.

When Gavriel walked to his hotel that night, he regretted having put forward the idea. Spontaneous kissing was as rare as spontaneous violence in South East Asia, but he did wonder if Tracy had expected a romantic gesture from him. Yet Gavriel felt the spectre of Maya had entered the space between them and he could not help being continuously distracted by it.

Gavriel and Tracy left Hanoi. The northern hills rose gradually and Gavriel, a bottle of water in one hand and a book in his lap, swayed for hours with the movement of the vehicle. He had not found too many places in Asia that responded exactly to the exotic and remote image of the continent as it was firmly set in the Western mind: the Ryoan-ji temple in Kyoto, the Yellow Mountains in China. A few more, but not as many as the posters splashed across the walls of travel agencies worldwide would suggest. Sapa, however, was the idealized vision of rural Asia, with hills full of rice-field terraces. They passed farmers working in water up to their knees and wearing those wide-brimmed straw hats from the colonial adventure films, and the tourists on the bus turned to the windows in a frenzy of cameras and exclamations of wonder.

Gavriel stayed in a backpacker hostel. He became distracted by conversations with other travellers and often met Tracy to hike along the mountain paths and open trails of thick vegetation until, with tremendous effort, he sat down at last with his notes to decide what step to take next. The current path led him to the north and China, a place exorcised of spirituality. Was that right? He looked at the map carefully and scrutinized his notebook for hints. Because of the connection to Buddhism that he had been ruminating since Phnom Penh, Gavriel had convinced himself that he had to turn westward towards Nepal where, due to the combination of religious remnants and the orography of the Himalayan mountain range, he conjectured an Encounter. Even better, he could go all the way to Tibet and Lhasa, a holy threshold of all things Buddha. And yet no indication supported this idea. Lhasa, the old pious centre where the devotional energy of thousands of pilgrims had once marked a luminous point in the world, was now a husk without substance. Potala Palace was empty, its Lama exiled, its halls desecrated by Chinese agnosticism. Although pilgrims kept coming, the place was a corpse, and the Search needed a pulsating body. Confused, Gavriel folded the map and closed the notebook.

At dinner, he conversed with a group of young Israeli travellers who spoke about crossing the border from Vietnam to China and going north to the Yunnan region. They had just finished the strict, two-year military service back home and had been travelling avidly since.

"We have already passed through Thailand, Laos and Cambodia. Yunnan is the next stop," said one.

"From there we can take a plane to Shanghai and see the coast," said another.

All five looked similar to Gavriel. He was confused by the duplicated beards, cosmetic tattoos and uniform long hair. Also, he felt slightly out of place watching the group and their bond, born out of months of shared military hardship.

"But first we go to Shangri La."

"Shangri La?" Gavriel repeated. The implications of the name made his skin bristle.

"It's this place near the city of Kunming. The original name was Zhongdian but they just changed it. I imagine they want to attract tourists. They have a huge Buddhist centre."

"What about monks? Do they have active monks?" Gavriel insisted, although the conversation was already moving away from the subject.

"I think so," answered one of the five duplicates, somewhat abruptly.

Gavriel wrote down the name in his notebook and smiled. A pulsating body at last.

When he met Tracy the following day Gavriel was anxious. She, on the other hand, was in a jubilant mood.

"I think I found a job. Right here."

They walked out of the trekking path and into a small village. A few wooden houses stood next to the unpaved road and behind them, two large freestanding roof structures sheltered the collected tea leaves from the frequent rain.

"It is a small tour outfit but so very convenient, right next to my parent's house. In Ho Chi Minh my commute was terrible and…"

Gavriel stopped.

"I have to go on. To China," he said.

"When?"

"Soon, as soon as I can get a visa."

Tracy said nothing.

"I am sorry it is so sudden."

"It is not sudden, you are travelling. Travellers go away, foreigners go away."

"Tracy, I didn't mean…"

"Then why this? Why did you come here? Why Hoi An?"

"I have to go to China," was all Gavriel could say.

They walked back in silence. When they arrived in town, Tracy waved to an elderly couple who waited near a car. The woman held a little boy of about four who moved around trying to break free. Tracy's nephew, thought Gavriel.

They stood next to each other, shuffling their feet still in silence. Then Tracy put a hand on Gavriel's arm.

"I have to go, they are waiting for me. Will you call me if you pass through here again?"

Gavriel said he would.

Gavriel had to return to Hanoi to formalize his entry visa to China. It took a week to get it ready and, by that time, the Israelis, as often happened in the inconsistent world of the nomadic travellers, had already disappeared when he returned to Sapa. He moved on alone. In an hour he arrived at the border town of Laocai, at the other side of the border stood the city of Hekou on the Chinese side, where he would get on another bus to start a twelve-hour trip to Kunming. Gavriel was tempted to just board the bus and go but, pushing back the pangs of cowardice, understood he must call Tracy. He paid a few dollars to use a phone, waited with his finger hovering over the dial and then returned it with an apology and rushed to get a taxi to ride back to Sapa.

When he met Tracy that last time, it was outside of a backpacker café. She was holding the hand of a little plump boy. All three stood in silence and Gavriel understood finally. Her nephew's eyes, nose and mouth were too similar to her own, a little carbon copy of her features. But it was the way, too devoted, in which she caressed his hair, looking away but unable to control her hand, that told the whole story.

He said a few things. She spoke less. They went through the redundant goodbye in a slow, painful motion which was still very necessary. When the time for the last bus was close and he could not wait anymore they hugged.

"Goodbye Le Trang."

Back in Phnom Penh, Cambodia, the elevator that led to the morgue was at the end of the hall. Half an hour ago there had been a man of aggressive profile, formally dressed in a dark suit which seemed out of place in the humid Cambodian heat. When the man spoke, he did it by forcing some words out and, in every pause, he barely held back others, clenching his teeth. He was the father of a murdered young man; his name was B. Cohan and he was followed by a delegate of the American embassy in Cambodia and the chief of police of Phnom Penh.

From the morgue, the entourage moved to the upstairs floors. They entered the room with a sign announcing "J. Harris". The J corresponded to Jason, and Jason had been friends with Abel. Jason's family had never left North America and, without passports or much international experience, they could not organize a trip as quickly as Mr Cohan had done, so the Jason of "J. Harris" was lying on the bed alone, unaccompanied. The air conditioning hummed on the wall. Jason was blind and wore a thick bandage over his eyes.

The embassy attaché attempted the beginning of a sentence, but Cohan cut off the attempt.

"Jason …"

The invalid turned nervously. He didn't recognize the voice. Cohan's visit to Jason would be short, a minute to ask about his condition and fifteen more full of questions and reproaches. The chief of police ignored the conversation, the embassy attaché tried to calm Cohan, but the American (a stern New York Jewish captain of industry) had flown twenty hours to discover how his son had died and nothing but a piece of flint would have been less clement. When Jason started crying in frustration and fear, the doctor finally took action and evicted the visitors.

They re-entered twenty minutes later, all calmer, and, this time, the attaché stepped in and regulated the traffic of the conversation. Cohan clenched his jaw. Jason grabbed the white sheet with both hands. With long pauses in the story, the patient told how, during their vacation, they had met a man in a bar downtown; how they had met him again on the outskirts of Siem Reap; and how he and Abel had ended up lying, injured or dead, in the wet tangle of the jungle foliage.

There seemed to be all kinds of people in that venue in downtown Phnom Penh but, in reality, the groups were just three. First, the tourists, who were in Cambodia looking for a more genuine, truer alternative to the traditional excursions on offer in Thailand and the islands of Bali. Then the young Cambodian girls who, in regalia of short skirts and deep cleavages, were there looking for the money that the tourists had and willingly offered in exchange for any measure of transient love as it may be required. Finally, the street-level swindlers, who were on the lookout for prey and formed a compact but tiered group, ranked in a scale of malice from the sympathetic ruffian to the homicidal devotee. The bar, with its open counter and twenty-odd tables, was not a place of ill repute. In fact, it was listed in the *Lonely Planet* travel guide, reference and sacred text for budget travel all across South East Asia. But there, same as anywhere else on the continent, those who kept both eyes open and the bag secure under the table came out better served.

During the day the place served American sodas and Shingha Thai beer and had a large terrace which provided some shelter from the maniacal chaos of traffic in the avenue. But at nightfall the bar became too dark. Figures lost definition, and substances wrapped in brown paper with four folds quickly changed hands in the corners. Here as well were arranged semi-legal expeditions to the outskirts of the city where, for thirty dollars, you could shoot full blast an ancient Soviet-era assault rifle, a stout heritage of the Cambodian war of thirty years ago.

The man sitting at the third table was Gavriel. He only half read the book he was holding in his hand, an ageing copy of *The Demon*

Princes.[5] Gavriel was waiting and watched the door every few minutes, a reflex he had developed with passable efficiency. He looked at each face for a moment and then returned to the book. The clues had brought him to the city and the clues would take him away, but he needed to be alert to find them. All around, speaking in loud voices, sat couples and groups soberly planning escapades to remote sights, inaccessible temples and obscure local festivals, oblivious to the fact that their efforts to resemble travellers made them seem, more than ever, like tourists.

Gavriel had arrived at the bar at the same time for the past three afternoons. Those three days he had spent touring the tumuli and catafalques of the city in search of guidance and direction. But neither the palaces that remained in the capital as a dormant memory of the defunct monarchy, defenestrated in the Year Zero instituted by the communist guerrillas, nor the Buddhist shrines, with their relics, altars and ponds, bore any fruit. It was at the end of each day while resting at the bar when he had seen them, a rowdy group of young women with two American-looking men sitting at their table in the far corner. One of them waved his hands enthusiastically when speaking, the other was calmer. In the evening of the third day, Gavriel's ingrained detection system jumped and buzzed because that was what he did with his time, and the intense sense of the Search sometimes collected evidence that he was not looking for. One of the girls separated from the group and went out to make a call from the bar's terrace. Half an hour later she went out again. She fidgeted with the device absently until she saw two thugs dressed in colourful jackets and sunglasses who arrived riding mopeds. She made a discreet signal of recognition and then returned to the table with the Americans. Gavriel watched, intrigued, darting glances from his notebook to the street and back again. Shortly after, a white van with peeling paint approached. It stopped just across the street. Gavriel thought for a moment. Violent crime was uncommon in Cambodia, but there were always exceptions, and, in some cases, a quick shove and a quicker sprint were enough to ruin a happy trip. He hesitated, and finally the notion of *public pro*

---

[5] *The Demon Princes,* a novel by J. Vance. Like its protagonist, Kirth Gersen, the Man Under Contract had a list of names burning in his pocket and in his head. Seven of them.

bono won over his deeply seated indifference. He scrawled a note, stood up and took it to the table of the Americans. One had a prominent nose and the other a lax and docile appearance. He handed them the paper and returned to his table without saying a word. The sociable one read, looked at the street where the van was still parked, read again. Then both approached the bar and talked to the waiters urgently.

When the police car arrived, the van, the moped thugs and the four girls had disappeared as if by force of exorcism, surely in search of less vigilant prey. The two Americans stood in the safety of the centre of the bar, hesitant and nervous, and then approached Gavriel's table. The quiet American spoke first.

"Did you see that? They were waiting for us. If not for you ... How did you know?"

"Just chance.[6] I was looking out the door." He gestured, inviting them to sit down, and the Americans, who were still reluctant to leave the venue and brave the open streets, accepted. Gavriel introduced himself and they shook hands. The tall one was called Abel, the thin one Jason and, although they didn't know it, one would end up dead and the other blind.

Oblivious still to all of that, the three spoke amicably about their different lives while Gavriel pondered the impenetrability of the Search, eyes fixed on the shirt that Abel was wearing. It was a worn-out grey and had, across the top, a legend written in Gothic letters with the typography used on the label of bourbon bottles. *Creator,* it said, and right below it showed the xerographic image of a man with long hair playing the guitar, feet planted over the phrase *Demigods of Rock And Roll*. Gavriel looked at the letters with the effort of a clairvoyant, trying to see meaning beyond.

After ten minutes of conversation, Abel said, "At least let us buy you dinner."

The three knew that friendships in the travelling circuit were ductile,

---

[6] "There is no such thing as chance; and what seem to us merest accident springs from the deepest source of destiny": Friedrich Schiller, philosopher and pessimist.

often formed and dismantled with nomadic speed, so the offer was not significant. At the same time, Gavriel was aware that everything moved for a reason and, although the Search could be tedious, the clues ended up coming if he was patient. He read the shirt again. *Creator*. Gavriel accepted.

They left the bar and went into the street. There were no taxis in sight, but three mopeds approached them to offer service. In the crowded avenues of the capital, that was a sensible option, and they climbed after the pilots, taking care to place their backpacks in front of the body because the skilled pickpockets of Phnom Penh only needed some distraction and a knife to empty their contents in the recess of a traffic light.

They dined in the same pleasant camaraderie in which they had been drinking. In the conversation that followed, Gavriel learned that Abel Cohan was a New Yorker and Jason Harris from a small town in Illinois, next to the Great Lakes. He learned that they lived in Tokyo, working for a Japanese electronics multinational as lawyers. They were of similar age, but it was Abel who, by virtue of his inextinguishable energy, kept the conversation alive. Jason was quieter. He had a very narrow back and looked soft, supple. For Gavriel, it was all very pleasant. They parted after dinner with the usual promises to keep in touch. Watching the two friends leave, Gavriel waited for a moment. Nothing came. So with no portents or signs to guide him, he shrugged and walked back to his hostel.

What Gavriel didn't know that night was that Abel and Jason carried and shared a dense story. They worked together, had fun together and lived fifteen minutes from each other in an apartment block in the Tokyo neighbourhood of Aoyama-itchome. Their co-dependency was made clear on those occasions when one could see them engrossed in each other, speaking now excitedly, now calmly, often ignoring the rest of the company they were in.

Abel was bustling, funny, charismatic and cheerful. He was also terribly afraid of being alone during the long night vigils of his elegant apartment. His father was Mr Cohan, he of the stern profile and little patience who would arrive weeks later in the city to ask, screaming at the blind Jason, how his son had died. Cohan Sr had found in the religious eccentricity of his maturity an antidote to the remorse that forty years of abusive business practices and an abandoned family produced. So Abel, who had been relegated as a child to the arms of a somewhat distant mother and still felt, at thirty-three, rejected, was burdened with an ambiguous and well-disguised set of feelings towards others. His magnetic personality fascinated his bosses at work and he received promotions that might not correspond entirely with his professional merits. He also enjoyed great romantic success with the women of Tokyo, but none managed to fill that dry well that he kept inside, so he changed partners constantly and sought to find, in the glow of each new relationship, a poor substitute for the paternal love that had been ripped from him.

Jason had a different profile. Born into a large and not too wealthy family, he also suffered from the neglect of a fierce father, one of Irish descent who thought that displays of affection were a sure way to ruin a child. Jason was less interesting, overall, than Abel, and during his high school and college years he had lived a life devoid of glory. He dated several women, girlfriends of character like his mother, but none too attractive. To those he had shown affection, all the time thinking intimately and with some shame that they were not what he truly deserved. Everything changed when he arrived in Tokyo. Many Japanese women who were constantly exposed to the magic of Hollywood films accepted him happily for his exalted status as both a foreigner and an American. Jason was suddenly the subject of a type of attention he had never known before. He changed his name (he had used the diminutive Jay until then) and created a sophisticated and cosmopolitan personality to go with his new life. He rarely went back to see his family or hometown back in the US because every visit home reminded him of his dreary past, so distant from the glamorous Tokyo life he had built for himself. Jason did not have Abel's natural appeal but applied a mathematical approach to courtship and, by multiplying the ratio of his efforts, he achieved a net result and success with women that were not inconsiderable.

But the truth is that girlfriends didn't matter much to Abel and Jason. Sitting at the table in trendy bars, their weekly dates were not legitimate romantic relationships, but simply a framework which enhanced and added lustre to the friendship of the two Americans.

On more than one occasion they had been close to breaking the unspoken agreement by which their bond was maintained. Abel threatened to find a companion who could finally fill the perpetual deprivation left by his father, someone who would take Jason's place on his insomniac evenings. But, in the end, out of fear or neglect, he always returned to those seductions that were least demanding. Jason, on the other hand, had cycles in which his own conflicts surfaced, impossible to hide under the string of transitional romances, and he sequestered himself, mournful and taciturn, in his apartment, avoiding everyone until the spell passed.

In the end, they always returned to each other and, twice a year, as was the case when Gavriel met them, they took a flight to South East Asia on holidays. During the day they toured the nearest attractions and had lunch on sunlit terraces. At night they locked themselves up with rented women in one of their hotel rooms, and there the two Americans conducted a series of increasingly erotic exercises, pitting girl against girl, while they themselves refrained from intercourse for fear of venereal diseases.

Gavriel left Phnom Penh the next day. He travelled first by bus and then using an archaic ferry across lake Tonlé Sap to avoid the most rugged section of the road, full of potholes and byways. The ship was a deathtrap that leaked smoke and kerosene and where lifejackets and emergency exits were both missing. He went up north, surrounded by other tourists and Cambodian locals, until he reached Siem Reap six hours later. The city was frequented by travellers of the Cambodian circuit because of its proximity to the majestic ruins and restored temples of Angkor Wat. Once a small village of soporific pace, Siem Reap was now a small city of vibrant activity. Gavriel took a taxi from the jetty and found a cheap hostel near the outskirts, an old family house reconverted into a centre for backpackers craving adventure. The building opened onto a large courtyard with a quaint well in the middle, and shared elements with the myriad of similar guest houses which formed the travelling route of South East Asia: living rooms with dilapidated sofas, bulletin boards full of stickers advertising travel guides and adventure gear next to stacks of pamphlets for a myriad of tourist services. The common room, deserted now, was a mixture of cafeteria and lounge where visitors could have lunch and socialize. In the early morning, it would be full of guests devouring the meals that would keep them active during the long days of walking, photographing and discovering. Gavriel dropped his bag in a room that was as impersonal as any of the others he had encountered: a spartan box furnished with a boarded bed, a mattress, an old table and a mosquito net.

The Search impelled Gavriel to constant action, it was the *Vedānta Sūtra*[7] that had originally taken him to Angkor and he was convinced that it was in the religious evolution of the region where the key to the Search lay. The clues were herding him on and on, slowly but surely, as the signs moved from Hinduism to Buddhism. He waited no more and left the hostel. He took a quick meal in a place impregnated with the smell of cilantro and flavoured rice and filled in his journal with tight, precise writing while looking out the window. The midday sun was warm, and the air was filled with that heavy moisture, the oppressive mark of the continent that Gavriel could, however, not help but adore. The street was a parade of domestic life, full of women carrying packages, bicycles rolling in confusion and children screaming. He read his book, scribbled a few more notes, and then stopped a taxi scooter to take him to the ruins of Angkor Wat.

Gavriel toured the temples of the historical religious complex all that afternoon. He went through the wide gravel-covered avenues where the tourist buses ranged and cinema cameras cunningly edited when it was time to record exotic locations for movies. Although many of the structures were still covered by thick vegetation, Angkor was not nearly as remote as many travel agencies liked to present it. The main buildings (the galleried temple of Angkor proper and the disturbing Bayon) were packed with guides who raised flags and shouted through megaphones. There were men with carts that sold fizzy drinks and couples who looked at everything through the lens of a camera. Gavriel retreated towards the outer enclosure, looking for quieter corners. There the agglomeration disappeared, everything was quiet and walking down the paths between large stone slabs buried by roots one could forget that the temple was a UNESCO heritage site and one of the most famous places in South East Asia. He strolled past

---

[7] Also called *Uttara Mīmāmsā-sutra*, also called *Śārīraka Sūtra*, also called *Śārīraka Mimāmsā-sutra*. The canonic text of the Hindu Vedanta school of philosophy. It describes the relationship of the *Brahman* (the supreme cause of the universe, the higher state, the ultimate truth or, simply speaking, God) with the material world to which man is bound in a cycle of death and rebirth. *Moksha* is the process of self-knowledge that releases from that cycle.

deteriorating carved walls, masonry arches, discarded boulders. Parapets of dead stone were slowly strangled by the branches and trunks of living trees in a torpid duel which took an eternity to resolve.

Gavriel circled for hours, consulting his inscrutable diagrams and cyphers. The religious compound of Angkor and its satellite buildings had been built on the precepts of Hinduism and reverted to the analogy of the ascension to the heavens. Its architecture (steep stairs, sharp and elaborate prongs, narrow high buttresses) was a simulacrum that copied Mount Meru, the divine abode of the supreme Hindu beings. Everything was permeated with symbolism; the spiritual human dogma was frozen in stone and exposed for centuries there, bare naked and ready to be seen by those who wanted to. The diligent Gavriel knew that, before it drifted towards the conceptual calm of Buddhism, Angkor had been dedicated to the truculent deities of Shiva the Destroyer and Vishnu the Preserver, two of the three faces of the Absolute, the motor principle of the universe.[8] It was there where he looked for a connection that would allow him to move on, and yet he could not find it.

He passed through a gate, a dark space surrounded by figures chiselled in the stone. He found a sandy path limited by the stonework fallen in the decline of Angkor. A very old man sat in the doorway of a shadowy hall, selling beads and trinkets displayed on a cloth. He had a shaven head, slumped shoulders and eyes eaten up by cataracts. He reached out hopefully to display his merchandise when Gavriel approached but, seeing that it had little effect, he took instead a travel guide out of a canvas bag. The bluish tome was one of the most popular ones, seen in hostels and internet cafés across the continent. It read "Cambodia Guide, including Angkor Wat". The cover photo showed a man sitting in the doorway of a decaying stone hall; the same man, the same door. The old man laughed, showing his teeth and waving the book in the air, with his finger pointed first at the photograph and then at himself. Impressed by the coincidence, Gavriel searched for a dollar in the front pocket of his trousers. The blind hawker accepted the money and sputtered in Khmer while

---

[8] Such Absolute, or *Brahman*, represents the power of the true manifestation of the world and it is remote. It does not require idolatries and does not respond to human interaction, so worshipping it is an exercise in futility.

holding his hands to his forehead. Gavriel made to leave, but the man kept talking and, on seeing Gavriel move, he held his hand.

"Sorry, I don't understand."

The man spoke in a continuous stream, still holding his hand. Gavriel only got one word, one the man kept repeating.

"Raijin," he said and pointed with his finger. "Raijin, Raijin."

Gavriel looked at the old man, looked at the photo. "Coincidences are a telegraph from God," Maya's ghost murmured in his ear.

"Raijin?" repeated Gavriel.

The old man nodded, showing his teeth. Gavriel felt the texture of the world change.[9] The opaque lenses in the old man's eyes gleamed and the smile, which had been inane, became complicit and deliberate.

Down the trail now came a group of Asian tourists. They advanced in compact formation, like a human ship with the armoured artillery portholes bristling with cameras and telephoto lenses. At the prow, a man raised a small flag with the logo of a travel company. Seven or eight retirees trotted behind, men and women of an uncertain old age wearing vests full of pockets, wide-brimmed hats and suede masks to protect against the dust. Gavriel stepped aside to let them pass, and they marched through the doorway and into the inner courtyard of the temple. "Raijin,"[10] he thought. The Japanese advanced without stopping. The old man raised his hands, asking the group for attention, and even brought up his travel guide for greater effect, but this time he was ignored. He didn't seem to care. He smiled at Gavriel deviously, as if they shared a particular confidence, and pointed back to the path.

Behind the group, a northern European-looking couple walked, both

---

[9] The Man Under Contract described that in a more affected way: "The world is pierced, and, for a moment, what is on the other side can be seen in this." He was the only witness to the phenomenon.

[10] Japanese deity of thunder and storms, in addition to other things, as the Man Under Contract would later discover.

tall and blond. She wore shorts and thick mountain boots despite the heat. The man had a shirt with a large drawing of a fierce muscular figure standing atop a cloud and the legend *Raijin* written on it.

Gavriel turned to the old man.

"How ..."

The man was silent now. The white eyes were turned towards the blanket and the beads and the trinkets. Gavriel tried to interrogate him again, but without effect. If for a moment he had been the conduit of a higher instance, he was now only an old man of whom somebody, once, took a fortunate picture.

"We met again in a bar in Siem Reap," Jason said back in his hospital bed. Cohan sat on the edge of the chair and listened to him. The air conditioner had stopped working and everyone was sweating. "His name was Gavriel. He said his name was Gavriel. He had gone there looking for something."

Gavriel left the ruins of Angkor at nightfall. Past the main entrance, some men reclined on old scooters. There were few visitors left, and the opportunities for business that day had almost gone so, after haggling a little, Gavriel got one of them to take him to his hostel for a few dollars less than usual. In the interval that went from the activities of the day to the preparations for the night, the lounge was full of guests, mostly Western and Middle-Eastern tourists, with some Asian couples here and there. Gavriel changed shirts in his room and picked up his notebook. He went back to the lounge where he found a seat with some difficulty, ordered tea and sat down to write. He sought references to the name Raijin because the Search was a compendium of causes and coincidences, and its keys were always scattered, but all he could find were irrelevant religious entries.

All around him, the bustle of the room increased while the comradeship of the travelling circuit formed easy and fluid conversations. In the space marked by three armchairs, a group had gathered around a man in his sixties, big belly and long beard. He looked like exactly what he claimed to be.

"A hippie. Or at least I was, back in '68. Then the wife got pregnant and I had to find a job."

After forty years of bourgeois life, he seemed determined to recover the happenings of his youth. He told how he had already visited Angkor during his student years and the audience halted everything, listening to him.

"Back then, there were very few travellers here. Those who came made it through Vietnam just as the intensity of the war was increasing. There was no transportation and hardly any places to pass the night. We spent two or three weeks on the road between Phnom Penh and Siem Reap, buying and selling weed to the remaining French soldiers left over after the independence of Indochina and to the Americans who were here on leave. This was just a village, and I remember that we had to walk to the temple. There was no barrier at the entrance, of course. The locals passed through the courtyards of the temples to leave food for the monks. We went after them, a group of three. The trees were much thicker then and, except for Angkor Wat and Angkor Thom, not too many ruins had been cleared. Walking around the complex was like moving through time."

The younger travellers sighed in synch as a choir and they peppered the veteran with questions. They were, perhaps, resentful of the popularization of the routes that they themselves were frequenting and felt jealous of the old hippie. That was the dream of the dedicated globetrotter, to discover the isolated corner, to be a traveller and not a tourist, to see the real world behind the appearance.

Gavriel left the common room and, with the twilight, walked to the centre of Siem Reap. The word "Raijin" clanged in his head. In the avenues of the town, the terraces, illuminated with strings of bare bulbs, had a festive appearance, enlivened by the warm night and the bottles of Filipino beer. He looked for a place which had been recommended by the hostel manager and found space at a table on the terrace. When he reviewed what he had seen that day, he continually returned to the meeting with the street vendor, convinced that it was a precise and definitive clue. At that same moment, perhaps conjured by the network of providence and cosmic ordination that governed the

Search, two Americans sat down on the same terrace a couple of tables from him: Abel and Jason.

Gavriel, somewhat embarrassed, pretended not to see them and waited for them to be the ones who found him, but time passed, and neither noticed him. With a sigh, he got up and walked over.

"Cambodia is certainly smaller than one may think."

Interrupted mid-conversation, the Americans looked up with surprise. Abel was the first to recognize him. They invited him to sit more effusively than Gavriel expected. Maybe it was the sincere pleasure of having a new companion, or maybe it was just due to the monotony that always ended up settling on the two friends, even on trips like that. Because Abel and Jason, Jason and Abel, were running in an endless hamster wheel, trying to escape from the burden of themselves without understanding that could never happen.

They talked over dinner, shared anecdotes and travel tips, and, at the end of the evening, when it seemed that nothing said would help the Search, Abel spoke. "Anyway, we're at the Blue Haven hotel. We visited Angkor today and tomorrow we'll go here."

Jason handed him a bunch of sheets. They were computer printouts and had those incomprehensible rows of letters and numbers aligned at the top of the page. There was an article with the title "Angkor Wat Landmine Museum; Cambodia's best-kept secret".

"It's supposed to be the most interesting thing you can see around here. Besides the temples of course," said Jason.

"Why don't you come?" said Abel suddenly and without consulting with his friend. Gavriel noticed the look the other American gave him.

"I don't know if ..." Gavriel started to say while still reading. He almost refused the invitation but then, below the second paragraph, he saw: "Founded and maintained by Mr Rai Jin."

Rai Jin. Raijin.

Causes and coincidences.

The landmine museum was both a private property on a secondary road not far from Angkor and a hidden treasure in the path of the low-cost traveller. Outside the clearing of the enclosure, the jungle filled everything, dense and thick; inside, a man had created an experience that was simple and tremendously emotional, one that left none of his visitors indifferent. Originally, Mr Rai Jin had made efforts to promote the initiative with banners, posters and some discreet pamphlets distributed around the guest houses, while also asking for support from the tourist office of the city of Siem Reap. But it soon became apparent that no support for his idea would be forthcoming. Two conflicts with neighbouring Vietnam, a devastating civil war and four years of a paranoid regime under the Khmer Rouge had left the country full of landmines from which only certain travel areas were free. This was a very real problem that claimed victims daily and left a desolate landscape of amputated limbs in the geography of Cambodia. But the government was discovering the advantages of being a popular tourist destination and the last thing it wanted was to associate the image of its main source of income with the latent danger beyond the Phnom Penh-Angkor Wat corridor. Gradually, local leaders ostracised Mr Rai Jin, driving him away from the most frequented circuits and travel guides and using other measures of varying legal legitimacy. And yet, the significance of the message that hung from the walls of his museum was such that rumours and comments had filtered through those recesses where backpackers and travellers met and gossiped, and the landmine museum was becoming the most public secret on the Cambodian route.

Perhaps the word museum was not the best one to describe the crude wooden fence held together with string and tape or the pair of wooden shacks and buildings with flimsy walls that served Rai Jin as both home and workshop. Rather, it was an interactive exhibition with two parts. The most explicit one, in the first room, was a large display, a tangible catalogue composed of samples of deactivated land mines. Each had a little plaque with tightly written text describing the operation of the contraption and the effects of each detonation; a dismal journey through the demonstrated capacity of human inventiveness when it came to causing harm to others. The explosives, most of which Rai Jin himself had deactivated by hand, formed a line of rusty olive-green blocks of ominous appearance. The samples overflowed the room and spilt into the courtyard, where the flat round shapes mixed with the decommissioned housings of artillery ammunition and anti-tank rockets.

The other part of the museum was the one that made visitors move uncomfortably and chilled the soul. Rai Jin had been recruited at the age of ten by the Khmer Rouge militias, the communist-oriented party of dictator Pol Pot who, along with Chinese Maoism, Hanoi's Vieth Min and Kim Il-Sung's regime in North Korea, ravaged Asia in a crimson tide of ideology and blood since the end of the Second World War to the modern era. His parents had been killed by the same Khmer Rouge, and Rai Jin was forcibly recruited as a child soldier, roaming the jungles of the interior of the country with the guerrillas and carrying on his shoulder a rifle that was as tall as himself. He soon demonstrated unusual talent for working with explosives and was sent night after night to place bombs on the path of the government patrols. Rai Jin's little fingers kept busy in the dark, and often, when he returned at dawn to the fighters' camp, he could hear the "boom-boom" of his artefacts when detonating under military boots or civilian sandals. One day he was caught by the invading army during the war between the Kampuchea of Pol Pot and the post-American Vietnam. Instead of being shot immediately, he was forced at bayonet point to resume his job setting up death traps, this time against his former comrades. Lying in the grass or buried in the mud, the change in uniform did not alter the mechanics of his work. Rai Jin planted more than four thousand mines a month in a monotone cadence of tensioning cables and assembling fuses where, bit by bit, he left his childhood.

The nightmares that burned his consciousness as a child he now painted in a clumsy and somewhat puerile style on large boards that hung on the walls of his museum. Rai Jin was no artist, but those paintings did not need aesthetic proportions or golden rules. In one he recounted that day next to a river when his group was discovered by an enemy patrol and had to cower between the reeds while bullets whistled around. In another, he showed a mine exploding while guerrilla soldiers ran around like horrified caricatures with torn limbs and blood spluttering from the stumps. In that gallery of painted horrors, the visitor found torture, torn eyes, deaths from dysentery. In all the images the sky was tinted black with forceful brushstrokes; the eyes of the child-soldiers were round and furiously open, distorted by dread, and the mouths shouted out, dislocated and unreal like those of imaginary lions.

"This place is scary," said Abel, little inclined, as he was, to sensibility, be it artistic or of any other description.

A taxi left them at the entrance where they bought their tickets and went inside into the first room. Gavriel moved from one place to another, with little interest in the mines. Several visitors roamed the exhibition, taking pictures. Outside, half a dozen children and young Cambodians were playing football in the courtyard. Most of them were amputees who ran on crutches behind a ball to hit it using their rubber tips. A man with a childish face was talking to a Western couple to the side, Gavriel recognized him from the photograph of the printed pages. When the couple left, he approached.

"Mr Rai Jin?"

"Yes, I am, thanks for visiting." He spoke English with the fluency of good practice.

Gavriel was not a threatening-looking man.[11] He was not even a big man, but he did carry the intensity of the Search reflected in the eyes. Rai Jin, who was a survivor of a suffering life, recognized with a flinch the unusualness of that visitor.

"You have a very interesting museum."

"Thank you. Where are you from?"

Gavriel did not answer that.

"But your name, it doesn't seem Cambodian. It sounds almost Japanese. Is that right?"

"It's just a … how do you call that? A borrowed name, a moniker. I got it in my army days, because of a bootleg brand of cigarretes we used to smoke, you know? It stuck so I kept it."

There was a moment of awkward silence. Rai Jin looked around and jested good-humouredly with the soccer players, shouting in loud

---

[11] Other witnesses have described the Man Under Contract as "possessed", "alienated", "obsessive" and, in short, all attitudes related to the state of persistent monomania.

Khmer. Gavriel was still in front of him.

"Angkor Wat is a rare place. Spiritual, despite the tourists," said Gavriel.

"It has been a long time since I have visited. The museum keeps me pretty busy."

"I heard that there may be an atypical temple here, one dedicated to the worshipping of the blind god ..."

Rai Jin talked about other temples in the area. Gavriel did not really listen to him, attentive as he was to discover if the world showed signs of being pierced for the second time in a row.

"The blind god," he interrupted. "In its day it was called Saklas. Saklas the idiot."

"That doesn't sound like a Hindi name or Khmer. Are you sure it was here?" said Rai Jin.

"Well, I don't remember who told me. I thought it would be one of those interesting places to visit. Something outside the usual tourist range."

Rai Jin's refined survival system, which he had developed since childhood, was the only reason he avoided being carried away to the Pol Pot purge fields or blown up by a landmine's defective detonator. Part of what he had learned was to filter out what he heard, and that habit, which he had never been able to shake off, just as he would never be able to shake off the obsessive nightmares he put into his drawings, was now telling him that this man was lying. It could even be that the truth he was hiding was something no one would want to know.

"Sorry, I have to attend to the other visitors. But thanks for coming," said Rai Jin stepping away.

Gavriel watched him go. That didn't seem to be the connection he was hoping for. Had he been wrong? No, the coincidence was too precise. Although one should always be wary of the constant risk of apophenia[12], the signs and indications he worked with were the result of serial waves, recondite and inaccessible but much too real. If what had brought him here was not the person, then it must have been the place.

Abel and Jason finished touring the compound. The paintings in the second building where visitors walked with almost religious reverence had tempered their spirits and they kept an uncomfortable quietude. But upon exiting, Cambodia was again a warm and exotic place full of sites to visit. They saw Gavriel exploring the outermost part of the perimeter of the fence surrounding the museum. There was an opening in the metal mesh and, beyond that, a path that ran into a field of reeds and dense vines. Gavriel was about to move to the other side when the Americans approached.

"Hey, you better be careful. This country is full of mines," said Abel.

"And that there is the jungle already," added Jason, always suspicious.

Gavriel crouched and went through the opening.

"There's something out there. I don't know what it is but it's there, on the other side of the field."

"Something?"

"It's calling," said Gavriel, and with two steps he disappeared into the undergrowth.

"I didn't want to go. That man … I'm not an idiot. You could see it. That man, he was bizarre. I just wanted to go back to the hotel." Jason stirred in his hospital bed. "I had told Abel after dinner the night before, we shouldn't have invited him."

---

[12] Although a common phenomenon, the word itself is far too unusual and merits an explanation. Apophenia is described as the experience of seeing patterns and meaning in random events. There are not many things that can be said with absolute certainty about the Man Under Contract but that, to a greater or lesser extent, he was a sufferer of this particular condition is one of them.

"And Abel? What did Abel say?" asked Mr Cohan.

Mr Cohan had been nervously tapping his foot on the floor for a while. In the cloister of the hospital room, with the temperature rising higher and higher, the sound drove both the chief of police and the embassy attaché mad, but they took care not to comment on it.

Jason shook his head distractedly.

"What happened to me? What have they done to me? They tell me I'm blind. How can I be blind?"

Cohan stirred impatiently in the chair. "I'll help you with that, Jason, but first you have to tell me what happened. What about Abel? Did he want to go?"

"Abel? Yes, yes, he did. Abel had ..."

Abel had a penchant for chaotic situations, and that traveller with worn-out boots and an absent gaze was the most interesting thing he had seen since arriving in Cambodia. The trip was intended to be the best part of a year that had been deplorable for everything else. Work was taking a disastrous turn, with first a denied promotion and then the resounding failure of the project Abel had been working on for months, and he was feeling suffocated by a relationship with an attractive girlfriend with an irritating voice and expensive tastes for which he did not feel much affection. The lawyer thought that this vacation in South East Asia would be the vitalizing change he needed, but so far it had been bland; a succession of hotels and excursions that were becoming irrelevant. It was just a holiday at a time when Abel was looking for an adventure.

He went out through the opening after Gavriel and, with a little hesitation, Jason followed.

"Where are we going?" asked the American.

"There's a clue around here. Everything indicates this place, but Rai Jin doesn't know anything. We have to keep looking."

"A clue? What kind of clue? What are you looking for?"

At that point, Gavriel did not doubt that the presence of the two hedonistic Americans was preordained. They were part of the key that unlatched the way, cyphers in the equation and actors in the drama.

"There is a path here. Come on," Gavriel said.

"Hey, answer me! What are you looking for?" Jason asked again, irritable.

Gavriel replied, talking over his shoulder as he walked. "The secret of the universe, of course."

The path meandered, sometimes to one side, sometimes to another, but the vegetation did not permit them to see where it was going. As he had done many times before, Gavriel walked ahead, purposefully looking right and left. Signals and coincidences, sometimes indistinguishable, were milestones in each node of the Search. Each node required knowledge and scrutiny if it was to be overcome, and Gavriel's journey was an obsessive pursuit in such direction. Cycles in phases, phases in stages, stages in steps. The next node turned out to be a clearing in the jungle where a group of men loaded packages of methamphetamines into a rusted truck.[13]

The rings of Cambodian drug traffickers had been changing their habits over the past few years. From risky articles such as opium or heroin, which they painstakingly grew and then pushed through the distribution networks of the Golden Triangle (the infamous vice vortex which marked the geographical encounter between Thailand, Laos and Myanmar) they were moving into the production of synthetic substances. The crops of traditional narcotics had the disadvantage of being dependent on both soil and seasonality, and, with the popularization of the necessary chemical resources, it was already more profitable to set up a laboratory in some sequestered location and have a steady supply of product throughout the year. In Siem Reap, the preferred option was to make *Yaba* pills, magical

---

[13] The version of the facts seen here is not by the Man Under Contract. This is the story that J. Harris told Mr Cohan in the hospital's bed, and the substance of what he describes, if at fault, should be reproached to him.

bites, part methamphetamine and part caffeine, that were a source of unmeasured addiction and enslaved bands of children and adolescents in the poor neighbourhoods of the country. In addition to the local market, the drug had good acceptance among the younger foreign tourists and ended up making the Siem Reap/Phnom Penh/Bangkok route tucked into the bottom of their backpacks.

Gavriel remained still, very still, when Abel and Jason reached the clearing after following him down the path. The five individuals had chosen a secluded place to conduct their transaction, despite being a stone's throw away from the most famous monument in all of Cambodia. Away from roads and farm fields, protected by a phalanx of trees that grew in a tight circle, the only way to get there was by accident. Gavriel saw young men dressed in jeans, sandals and fashionably ragged t-shirts. There were tattoos, designer sunglasses, gold pendants and, on top of the hood of the truck, a dilapidated laptop computer for the bookkeeping of the packages and their cost. There were also five handguns tucked in five belts and several Soviet-era assault rifles. The contrast between the three tourists with their adventure-catalogue clothes and thick boots and the five Cambodians wearing full urban fashion in the middle of the jungle only made the situation more disconcerting. The task of counting, checking and stacking bales in that heat was burdensome, and it took the dealers a minute to discover the visit, one full minute during which the three intruders lingered motionless and fascinated at the foot of the path, seeing what should not have been seen. But finally someone looked up and gave the alarm. There were murmurs and jolts, and one of the men took a step toward Gavriel and the Americans, pulling out a long-barrelled revolver that he let hang carelessly from his fingers, not even aiming at them. He had a trendy haircut, asymmetrical, long in some places, short in others, and was missing several teeth. He walked with sunken shoulders, like a singer in a modern music video, and spoke in Khmer, very quickly, while pointing with the gun at the path, the truck and the inconvenient visitors. The rest of the dealers moved around, opening like a fan, and looked suspiciously at the gap between the trees.

Gavriel raised his hands and was going to take a step back when he saw the man on top of the convertible truck. He looked the same as the rest, a Manchester United t-shirt and counterfeit brand jeans. But running from his right forearm to his neck was a tattoo, a long lion-headed snake that zigzagged over the olive skin.

Abel and Jason wanted to turn around, but the fan had closed behind them and they were now surrounded. The man with the revolver and the broken teeth was certainly the boss and kept talking while the others laughed. Another approached and began to search Abel's pockets. The lawyer jumped but did not protest. Gavriel looked at the tattooed man who was ignoring him. The leader noticed his interest, shouted at the Tattooed Man and, suddenly irritated, approached Gavriel to give him a push that threw him to the ground. Then he signalled with the gun for the man to get down from the van.

"Hey, hey! You!" shouted Gavriel, prostrated. "That mark. Where did you get that mark?"

He spoke in slow English, pointing at his arm and neck like a mime. Jason looked at him with dread. He wanted to tell Gavriel to be silent, but he dared not speak. The Tattooed Man paid no attention. The leader with broken teeth sputtered even more quickly. Then he turned to Gavriel and shouted at him, raising the grip of the revolver as a threatening hammer. But Gavriel didn't keep quiet.

"Which symbol is that? Is it Samael?" he insisted, and then stopped. "Is it you? Are you the clue?"

The Tattooed Man jumped down from the truck. The leader spoke to him, shouting now, very close, pointing at the tourists. But the Tattooed Man shook his head absently. He stared at Gavriel, interested at last.

"Which one of them are you? Which one of them?"[14]

The leader stood over Gavriel and kicked him twice to quieten him. Covering himself with his hands and shrinking into a ball, Gavriel did go silent.

That was when the world seemed to be pierced. The clarity of the day blurred somewhat with the omen of the incomprehensible things that

---

[14] The Man Under Contract refers to the following: Athot, Elaios, Astaphaios, Iao, Sabaoth, Adonaios or Sabbataios. They are the seven names that he keeps in his notebook, and one he has already crossed out.

were to come. The attention of the Tattooed Man was now on the prostrate figure. Gavriel from the ground, the Americans, the drug dealers, they all turned to look when the Tattooed Man underwent a change, imperceptible in his anatomy but evident in his disposition. He straightened his back, filled the space and when he spoke he did not do it in Khmer but in Gavriel's mother tongue.

"You are so very full. Full of questions. Interrogating here and interrogating there. Moving stones and looking under them. Muttering names that maybe you shouldn't. Do you think we don't hear you? It may be full of tourists and photographers during the day, but this is a multilayered place. One where the world can be diaphanous."

The sudden loquacity of the Cambodian intimidated Gavriel.

"I ... I don't ..."

"Indeed you don't. You do not. So many questions you have, Gavriel. We know your name. We know your name and you are not welcome." He pointed a finger at his forehead. "Who marked you? Was it the Green Man? Was it the Soldier? It matters not. This is not going to be as easy as you think."

The leader interrupted, waving his revolver and shouting. The syllables hissed as they went through his broken teeth. He was increasingly nervous and asked for an explanation from the Tattooed Man. The Tattooed Man who he knew well, who turned out to be ambitious, who wanted his job and who now spoke in an unknown language with a foreigner just on the day they moved their laboratory and their merchandise. He aimed the gun and thought about shooting him, but the Tattooed Man just had to look at him to leave him paralyzed. He absorbed everything. He was a spectre who filled the clearing and kept all wilfulness suspended. The boss dropped the revolver and became, like all the others, captive.

"What do you want, Gavriel, little Gavriel who travels from one place to another, so busy?" asked the figure.

"I am looking ..." He swallowed once. "I'm looking for the blind god."

"Which blind god?"

"Samael. The principle that creates the world."

"Those are just words. A list of aspirations, an articulation of the true universe, but you don't understand what you say. The blind god is not for you."

The presence of the man was immense. It permeated the vines, accentuated the holes in the world. Gavriel, frightened by what he saw, wanted to close his eyes and ears, to recite a prayer asking for help.[15]

"What school is that from? I don't remember who said what. Too many dogmas and cosmogonies. What you want, you can't achieve that way. Think about what you're asking for. There is One who looks at you without being seen. You know that, right?

He moved closer to Gavriel who didn't answer.

"Right?"

"Yes."

"Very well, at least you know that, and you earn my mark." The Tattooed Man made a flourish with his fingers. "Say, then, his name. And remember, the architect builds, that's what it does."

Gavriel pressed his lips, reluctant. "Samael …"

"Not that one. Say its name."

"Saklas …"

"Not. That. One."

"Dem …"

Abel moved suddenly. At the end, hedonistic and fickle as he was, he proved to have the greatest willpower out of that group that had gathered in the Siem Reap clearing. Only he managed to look away from the fierce, overwhelming figure of the Tattooed Man. Abel, who

---

[15] "From falsehood lead me to truth, from darkness lead me to the light, from death lead me to immortality." Upanishad Hindu text.

enjoyed great intelligence, some courage and other wasted gifts, broke the immobility of the moment and did the only thing he could. He turned and ran.

The rest was a chain of actions. One of the dealers, eyes hidden behind sunglasses, shook off his lethargy, raised his arm and machine-gunned the fleeing American. A string of red holes splashed Abel's back and he fell. The Tattooed Man woke up in part from the entity that had kidnapped him. He reacted confused and, pulling his own gun from the belt, shot the man in the sunglasses. The ringleader saw this and, by aggressive instinct, unloaded the cylinder of his revolver. Half of the bullets hit the Tattooed Man and the rest reached the truck, the last one punching through a gas cylinder that did not explode but started spinning out of control when the pressure escaped from the leak, bursting packages and blowing pills into the air.

The remaining drug dealers were about to shoot, perhaps at the foreigners, perhaps at each other. But they scarcely had time to move before the body of the Tattooed Man, convulsed by the impact of the lead bullets, exploded, shining with a glow that was not entirely of this world.

The death of a western traveller in a South East Asian country was always a nightmare, and even more so if that country was trying to establish an internal tourism industry. Abel's death was on the front pages of the international newspapers on the first day, the television news for a week, and lingered in the comments of the digital travel forums for months. The police poured resources into the case, pushed by the US embassy, which in turn was being pressured by the father of the deceased. Mr Cohan had brought a personal entourage and was analysing all the data on the death of his son as if it were a corporate business campaign. A secretary coordinated his public appearances where he crushed mercilessly the reputation of police officers and diplomatic officials. Rumours of a third foreigner present in the group had already leaked.

"What happened to that Gavriel? Did you see him again?" Cohan asked in the hospital room of Phnom Penh.

Jason moved his hands to the blindfold that covered his eyes often, as if forgetting what he had there. "He told me not to talk about it, that there were things, worse things, that could happen and that nobody would understand."

Cohan opened his mouth grumpily, but before he could raise his voice the embassy attaché intervened, conciliatory.

"If there were other people involved, you must tell us, Mr Harris. This is a very serious situation."

"He came to see me the first day when I arrived at the hospital. He said he gave ten dollars to the nurse on call to let him pass. They had asked me questions and questions. They told me that my family was on their way, but they didn't arrive. Almost nobody spoke English …"

"That man came here? What did he want?" Cohan cut him off.

"He wanted to know what I had seen when the man exploded. I was watching him when he exploded. There was a great light."

The Cambodian chief of police rose from his chair. "It was one of the gas cylinders, the ones they used to cook the drug. It exploded," he said.

"No! It was one of the men! The one with the tattoo. His eyes shone and then he exploded!" Jason shouted.

The policeman, the diplomat and the afflicted father looked at each other.

"Did Gavriel tell you why the man exploded?" Cohan asked the ridiculous question in a calm voice.

"He said that he couldn't tell me everything but that he was sorry, that sometimes this happens to people. They get chewed by the gears of the world. He said it had happened to a girl."

"Which girl?" muttered the attaché, but Cohan silenced him with a wave of his hand.

"Go on, what else did he tell you?"

Gavriel spoke, sitting in the hospital chair where the air conditioner was still working, propelled by the dying rattles of its mechanical life. He spoke in a slow voice, very different from how he had spoken during the trip. He considered each sentence before releasing it. Jason shook his head and pointed towards Gavriel with the line of his hearing, with that gesture of the blind looking to compensate for lost senses.

"Ask me anything you want."

"The man, that man, who was he?"

"That's hard to explain."

"I know what I saw. The man was a man, but he was not. It was a Thing. It was a Thing, right?"

"Yes. A terrible thing."

Jason dropped his hands. He lifted them to touch the bandage. He let them fall again.

"And Abel? Is he dead?"

"Maybe. I don't know."

"And me … blind … blind."

The word sounded alien.

"You're blind because you saw something you should not have seen, the World behind the curtain of the world."

"What world? What curtain?"

"The real World, the divine World."

"Divine? Are you talking about God?"

"No, not God. God is incomprehensible. It is not possible to reach it, to really reach it, neither with faith nor with logic. No matter what religions or dogmas of salvation may pretend.

"But what if I told you there is an intermediate agent? It is one that has many names, and they all are different. For some he is an artisan agent, for others, he is a usurper of the divine principle. He can be found, Jason. He can be reached.

"That's what you saw. When the Thing exploded, you glanced upon the greatest secret of the universe."

35°36'N/102°29'E
Tibet: The Wheel Ascendant

The travelling route of South East Asia was not a modern invention, nor something new out of the era of budget airlines and fast internet connections.

It became somewhat popular in the 1960s as a pilgrimage of young rebels seeking enlightenment and the comfort of psychotropic substances. But even before, in the immediate post-war period, there had been young Westerners from good families who, influenced by the then prevalent orientalism sought to purge the horrors of the Pacific theatre and the Western Front with a tour to the devastated former colonies of Siam, Indochina, Burma and Laos.

Eventually, the hippie movement cemented the reputation of a journey that offered both dissipation and sexual liberation while, at the same time, exposing sensibilities to the little-known harshness of a life that over one hundred million people suffered. Travellers returned to their white-fenced houses after a year of living in the leprosaria of Sri Lanka and the brothels of Pattaya, ready to shout in outrage at the conservative Western policies that ousted the neglected continent.

The movement expanded. Inspired by the shameless gurus of the Beat Generation, young people eager to find spirituality and adventure exchanged the combed back hairstyle and the single-family houses of the American, Australian and European suburbs for sandals and hallucinogens.

The exacerbated social sentiment died with their generation, and by the 1970s the itinerary had transformed from a marginal journey into an initiation ritual for recently graduated university students, a momentary oasis and respite for those who were to leave the carefree life of the young and plunge into one of maturity and responsibilities.

The route was addictive. Now, same as before, a tribute was paid and stragglers could always be found there; veterans of the road who after many splendorous years of discovering people, places, cultures and their own personalities, could no longer acclimatize to any other type of existence. Here and there among the successive crops of backpackers which came and went, replacing each other, one could discover hoteliers and jungle guides who had decided one day to live in the perpetual exaltation of the journey, struggling to trap in a frame of amber that moment of absolute freedom that was born out of a backpack and a pair of boots.

Two days of uninterrupted transit by bus and van took Gavriel from the northern border of Vietnam to Zhongdian, in the Chinese province of Yunnan. For two more days, he investigated what turned out to be a false lead and walked annoyed through the cobbled streets, kicking at the garbage. The Shangri La Monastery was an active place that had become more a tourist attraction than a true religious centre. And yet, Gavriel had reason to feel optimistic. Like the emaciated monastery, there were parts of the historical Tibet that had been left, abandoned and engulfed, inside provinces of Chinese demarcation after Beijing annexed the small Buddhist theocracy back in 1950. Travelling to the special administrative region of Tibet, and its capital Lhasa, required a laborious process to obtain a special visa. But that political Tibet only comprised the U Tsang area, a small portion of the traditional territory and population of the highlands. The rest of the historical Tibet, the Amdo and Kham provinces, were segmented among different Chinese regions more easily accessible to foreigners: Gansu, Qinghai and Sichuan.

Still, the visit had been pleasant. In his wandering of the streets of Zhongdian, Gavriel found a very old shop, a curio deposit of almost tangible staleness, and, in the shop, a small box made of light wood lost in the piles of genuine items and vulgar reproductions. The box had neither labels nor prints, and he wondered if it may be a handcrafted object. The lid was engraved with two effigies, one of the moon, one of the sun, both distorted with lines in a simulacrum of perpetual motion. In an unusual impulse, he bought the souvenir and placed it in his backpack. That was one of the few objects that took up space without a purpose, and this one of the few occasions when Gavriel allowed himself to carry a banal memento.

After a month of wandering around China, Gavriel figured out where he needed to go: Labrang.[16]

Labrang was, with implicit permission from Lhasa, home to the largest active Tibetan Buddhist monastery and, unlike Shangri La, it had the credentials of a divine site. It was here where the current reincarnation of the Dalai Lama was born. The place attracted Gavriel with the inevitability of a lightning rod, and, after a full night on the road, he alighted from the bus at a place that was just a small, crowded recess on the main road, with his backpack at the shoulder and an eager stride. The clues of the Search glowed brightly at last.

The geography of the city was unknown to him. The only thing he had learned upon arrival was that the monastery sat on the Tibetan side of the town while the bus stop was on the Chinese side. The population was sharply divided between local Tibetans and the Han Chinese that had settled there forty years back, in waves subsidized by the Beijing government to change the demographic make-up of the region. Here and there were Hui Muslims with their white religious headdresses for men and veils for women. Although Labrang was one of the entry points for travellers aiming for the Tibetan highlands and tourists were a regular sight there, Gavriel received curious glances, and smudged-faced children shouted "hello, hello" at his passing.

He avoided the opportunists and vendors lurking with suspicious bargains near the station and randomly chose accommodation that put him within sight of the monastery's walls. The hostel was a three-storey building on the corner of a half-paved and dusty junction where motorbikes, diesel-powered trucks and herds of yaks passed. Gavriel got a room with a surprisingly comfortable bed and an outside bathroom he had to share with the entire floor. Out of the window, a collection of Buddhist pavilions climbed uphill until they reached the first rocks of the mountain that encased them against the river.

Calmer, free of the weight of the backpack, and not really knowing

---

[16] Labrang, called Xiahe in Mandarin Chinese, is a linear town stretched along the river of the same name. The Chinese district is located to the east and consists of blocks of functional buildings, government facilities and businesses with large windows of soiled glass, bordering a poorly paved road. The Tibetan district, to the west, is an amalgam of low houses that has grown organically between the river and the mountain range and stretches, wedge-shaped, to embrace anxiously the great monastery complex at the end of town.

where to start, Gavriel ended up sitting by the street, watching the parade of everyday life. Monks trotted up and down the avenue, of all ages and conformations but always in their striking uniform of burgundy habits and shaved heads. There was more. On the right, Chinese tourists arrived on the ten o'clock bus looking comfortable and wealthy, wearing rainproof jackets and climbing boots of genuine and modish outdoor brands and not the counterfeit copies that had flooded the country for years. They indolently wagged high-resolution cameras and other expensive devices, all flat and rectangular. On the left, shepherds marched with faces burnt by exposure to wind, sun and cold and wearing felt hats, while the younger Tibetans dressed in fashionable Americanized caps and white sport shoes. Occasionally, a group of nomads gathered in a corner, dressed in the thick *chuba* jackets of the plateau, which left the left arm exposed and the sleeve hanging down the back.

Gavriel watched the sun go down, somewhat bewildered by the atmosphere of rustic intimacy that Labrang maintained despite its considerable size, and then had dinner in a one-room restaurant. The place was a family business and he ordered pointing his finger at faded photos attached with thumbtacks on the wall. He asked the owner about the monastery.

"What monastery?" asked the man.

"There, where the monks live," Gavriel replied.

"You mean Labrang."

"I thought this was Labrang. Or Xiahe." Gavriel looked around. Those were the only names he had seen in the guide.

"That is Labrang. This is the town," the man replied.

"Are they called the same? Are they the same?"

"No, that's Labrang," replied the owner, shrugging his shoulders and closing the conversation with the absolute finality of the obvious.

It was nine o'clock, evening. The street was deserted and most of the lights had been turned off in the buildings. A vivid sense of loneliness settled over Gavriel, sitting as an intruder in the room with half a dozen empty tables while the family watched from the other side of the curtain that separated the kitchen. He thought of Maya again, and, to get her out of his mind, opened *The Demon Princes* and read. Upon returning to the hostel he greeted the owner who was entrenched, as he had seen him all day, behind the entrance counter. He was a native of the town and spoke English with an indefinable accent. The man played with one of the children that jogged freely around the building. It was a passing scene of domestic life, but Gavriel's feeling of isolation deepened and he felt disarmed by the indefinite sadness that he himself had created.

The next day he went to the monastery early on with his notebook in hand. The enclosure it occupied was a large expanse of land, full of stone pavilions, whitened brick stout houses, timber stores and other recesses for study because Labrang was a purposeful centre which combined houses of prayer and university halls where learned men delved into the arcane mysteries of the Buddhist religion. In addition to about two thousand monks, there were groups of civilian workers and supply crews that went tirelessly from one place to another, repairing stairs and collecting supplies. The life of the sworn monk was prayer and study, so the most mundane maintenance tasks were carried out by the faithful who came to work at Labrang, keeping promises and upholding penances. There was a large main building, easy to identify, which Gavriel kept as a reference to navigate the monastery because the rest of Labrang was a maze of well-kept alleys between garden walls where the visitor could go around and around for hours. For the rest of that morning, Gavriel was more preoccupied with not getting lost than with finding what he was looking for. He made sure to visit each of the temple pavilions, watching it all with eyes overloaded by the colour palette of Buddhist artisans. Next to the entrance gates of the halls and in the cobbled squares, the floor was covered with the thick leather and black fur boots used by the monks, which they took off before entering the buildings.

On the walls were paintings recreating the mythology of the Buddha and the process of reincarnation[17] and the images repeated the idea

---

[17] The principles (although not the intricacies) of the Buddhist teachings are simple even for the layman: The world is not what it seems and there is a higher plane of life that can be achieved through study and understanding. Men roam reality, living multiple lives until they learn and internalize this essential truth. If they succeed, they reach enlightenment (Nirvana) and leave the contingent plane. The Man Under Contract found this idea both striking and relevant.

from one to the other, with all the aesthetic wealth provided by twenty-five centuries of history. The concept of the Wheel of Life permeated everything; a circle which represented the vital stages of the human being in its passage through the world (birth, ignorance, the obfuscation brought by the sensory world and, finally, after many revolutions of the Wheel, perhaps enlightenment). It was surrounded and accosted on all sides by the ominous figure of *Yama,* the inevitability of recurring death for those who did not reach liberation from the cycle of suffering and resurrection. In the lower realms, painted figures of hungry ghosts with distended stomachs in whose mouths the food turned to ashes danced as animated reminders of all human addictions and compulsions. Next to them, indolent animals lying down signified the complacency and lack of curiosity that terminates the flame of human reason, flocks both happy and tremulous. In the higher realms, the inheritance of the Hindu religion that was the origin and source of modern Buddhism appeared in the form of *devas* and *asuras*, hedonistic and paranoid little gods, fully ignorant of the reality of the world and the need to escape the circuit of karma. And, at the centre of the Wheel, painted in shades of strong red, yellow and blue colours, beat the forces that allow it to continue rotating: greed, ignorance and anger. *A desolate landscape*, Gavriel thought, but only until he found, standing outside of the Wheel, the redeeming figure of the Buddha, a calm being who sat waiting for the blessed chosen few who would listen to his teachings, offering them escape from the world and the possibility of finally achieving transcendency.

He also walked the sacred path that circled the full perimeter of the monastery and where pilgrims circulated from dawn to late hour, turning the one thousand one hundred and seventy-four prayer wheels installed there at intervals. The belief was that turning the rolls of wood and copper with inscriptions and mantras painted on them made the beatitude of their messages rise to the sky as they spun. The devotees walked in a row, keeping the wheels in perpetual motion and obsessively singing the *Om Ma Ni Pe Me Hung* of their prayers; wheels inside wheels.

Gavriel ended up in the upper part of the complex, watching the first buses of Chinese tourists arrive. The relative calm of the monastery would be suspended for the rest of the day, so he decided to visit one of the minor lateral pavilions before returning to the hostel. Greatly confused by the proliferation of names, he found it impossible to remember whether he wanted to see the Hall of Immense Harmony or that of Perpetual Knowledge. He chose one based on the chromatic combination of the facade and, taking notes in his notebook, entered. The interior was dim, and he found the imposing door that gave access to the inner courtyard closed.

"I don't think you can get in yet. The monks are in class," said a thin, small man from the corner.

It was true that, from within the gloom of the pavilion, voices could be heard, and shadows moved under the doorway. Gavriel gave thanks, stepped aside and gazed up at the paintings at the entrance next to the huge wooden columns.

"First time in China?" asked the man. He was a Tibetan, with a dark complexion and a sparse beard.

"First time in Tibet."

The man laughed softly. "In this region, that constitutes a political statement."

"I thought the issue of Tibetan independence was resolved."

"Not for the Chinese government," said the man and quickly shifted the subject. "So, is Labrang what you expected?"

"I'm not sure yet. Here the border between the monastery and the town seems to disappear," said Gavriel, remembering the confusing conversation with the restaurant owner.

The little Tibetan man nodded. "Actually, in Labrang, the monastery is the town. The monks and the faithful pass from one to the other constantly and their presence sanctifies both. It is the Buddhist ideal, you know? A sacralized society."

His name was Jamphel. After a bit of standing conversation by the door, they both sat by silent agreement in a corner. Jamphel lived in Italy, working as a translator for a European non-governmental development agency. His uncle turned out to be one of the lecturers of the monastery and was the one teaching the class in the hall. He appeared shortly after, in the whirlwind of shaved heads and burgundy robes of the young monks who came running out the great gate. He was a man of virtuous appearance who wore the frock with the ease of long years. Jamphel and his uncle spoke quickly.

"My uncle would like you to join us for lunch."

The monk did not speak English but nodded and made a hand gesture of invitation that Gavriel took as sincere. The house of the religious was in one of the narrow streets of the temple. A wooden door gave entrance to a small courtyard surrounded by a wall, and to a residence, a narrow place with a couple of rooms and a glass gallery that delimited an open garden and where they sat. One side of the gallery faced the courtyard, the other was covered with an altar, floral offerings and photos of the Dalai Lama. They settled on embroidered cushions on the floor. While they spoke, deferential monks who attended the master brought for him a bronze mould and a bowl full of thick, rich-smelling paste made with yak butter. During the conversation, he dedicated himself to creating copies of the Buddha image by squeezing the paste into the mould, like a child in an arts-and-crafts class.

"The monks bury the figurines or throw them into the river to feed the fish," explained Jamphel. "The Buddhist theory is that everything alive has to be respected, and that butter moulded in the effigy of the Buddha extends its bliss to the world."

The old monk spoke in Tibetan and Jamphel translated. He was a picture of holiness. White-haired where some of the shaved hair showed, he spoke slowly and with a voice of resonant timbre and hypnotic cadence. Gavriel, who had never been in front of such a cliché, watched him, looking for signs. He was aware of how lucky he was to see this private piece of the monastery's daily life and how accidentally he had arrived there. *Coincidences are a telegraph from God*, he thought. They ate a frugal meal of vegetables, sticky rice and fruit, served by fast-moving and respectful cenobites.

"My uncle asks if you know anything about Buddhism, if you are interested in the monastery as a tourist attraction or if you understand what the monks do here."

"I have read a bit. I understand the principle of wanting to overcome the world through knowledge."

Jamphel acted as an interpreter, and his uncle began a lesson in Buddhist theology, accompanied by the clicking of chopsticks in porcelain.

"If I could only say one thing about our creed," the monk instructed, "it is that we must consider all living beings as we consider ourselves. After all, the world is transient but our actions condition other actions in a long chain from which we cannot guess the result."

"Is that karma?"

"Karma is only a moral law that governs the world, governs causality. Religion is not about whether there is one god, three or many. The guiding line that goes deeper than any other into the dogma of the faith is the exit from the perpetual cycle. We are trapped in the material world, the world of cars, homes and people we know. Every time we die we return to that same world."

The monk drank tea and continued.

"All beliefs are worthy of respect and consideration, but the biggest difference between our religion and the Western beliefs is this: If a Buddhist attains enlightenment, he is filled with peace and understanding. If a monotheist experiences the visit of God, isn't there a risk that he will feel tiny, impure, perhaps inadequate, facing such a divine presence?"

"Then only a Buddhist can transcend the world and see what lies beyond?" Gavriel asked, a bit too anxiously.

The monk drummed slowly on his temple with the tip of his finger. "Only a human being can."

Gavriel listened to the old monk's cadenced voice and the more dynamic translation of his nephew for about one more hour[18], then he and Jamphel said goodbye to the master and wandered back to town. Outside the temple walls, life did not care about the idealistic principles of the monks. In the light of a tea house serving late meals, which Gavriel would never have found without his companion, they sat down and Jamphel told his story.

When he was eleven, Jamphel had stolen some money from his parents and had joined a score of faithful and nationalist Tibetans to cross the borders that separated them from India, the place of exile of the Dalai Lama. It took him two months and twenty days to get there. Halfway through the trip, they entered Lhasa in secret, in the years when the city was under the most severe grip of the Chinese police. They paid their respects in one of the dilapidated minor temples of the city and continued through the Himalayas, following the guides who pulled the group and berated crudely any straggler. They travelled at night to avoid patrols and during the winter season. When Gavriel asked why not travel in better weather, Jamphel explained how hardened snow made it easier to move.

"In spring or summer, the thawing of the ice forms mud which hinders walking and makes rivers overflow."

They ate pancakes of *tsampa* flour and instant noodles that only needed hot water. They slept in the open, with no tents. Gavriel could not understand how it was possible to endure all that.

"I was a child. I didn't know much about anything," said the Tibetan, shrugging his shoulders as he didn't know how to provide better reasons.

Border police arrested part of the group but the rest finally reached

---

[18] Such Buddhist concepts fitted strangely well with the experience of the Man Under Contract, who was particularly attracted by the absence of presumption of divinity in its doctrine and the idea that, through human effort and intelligence, one can break the veil of the material world and reach the transcendent. The notion had lingered in the collective consciousness from the earliest days of structured thinking, from Hindus to Gnostics and Proto-Christians, permeating into the empirical thinking of controlled environments: mankind and its mind are the keys that open the World. The Man Under Contract was just another soldier in the immemorial ranks of human exaltation.

India. There they met with a community of exiled Tibetans who were organized politically and religiously around the figure of the Dalai Lama. Jamphel never referred to him as anything else than a very formal "his holiness". He met a distant relative who introduced him to the tour guide business. He learned English first, then Hindi, and those languages opened the doors to the NGO he worked with at the moment. He later married an Italian volunteer and settled in Naples.

"I return to Tibet when I can but too many things have happened in this country. My life is no longer here."

Slightly tipsy with the after-dinner liqueur, the two new friends said goodbye with a great display of emotion, patting each other on the back amidst solid promises of reunion. The link that the day had created between them was indubitable and, despite the wavy path of drunken men that they followed back to their hotels, sincere. A few hours later, the attention of one or the other was distracted with day-to-day requirements, the address scribbled on a paper napkin got lost and they never saw each other again. The meeting, however, would remain forever frozen in the memory of both, perfect and incorruptible among the flow of stories which pertains to travellers and their travels.

Even to a casual observer, the man who climbed the street on the way to the hotel in Labrang looked out of place. Ethnically, he appeared Han Chinese, but he had neither the resolute style of the Chinese residents in that Tibetan region nor did he wear the poorly assembled combination of dusty shoes, sweaters and suit jackets that, undecided between formality and comfort, they preferred. He had certainly not arrived all covered in fashionable outdoor clothing, in that exaggerated manner the wealthy national tourists from Beijing or Shanghai preferred. The man—Chao was his name—pretended to be another visitor but the pretence was not impeccable, and it frayed at the edges when, distracted, the accent failed him and strokes of native Cantonese jumped here and there. But Chao's imposture was most evident in the arrested looks he gave the ever-present policemen riding their patrol cars, the buses carelessly parked and blocking the sidewalks, the indolent service from the hotel personnel. Chao did not like mainland China, he did not like the Communist Party and he resented the fact that all that newly-minted economic power had fallen in hands that did not deserve it.

He had arrived two days earlier from Lanzhou, a city buried in the landscape of hills and semi-desertic peaks of the Tibetan highlands. It turned out to be a constrained place that breathed its own fumes when the wind did not lift them from the bend of the Yellow River it occupied. Lanzhou was industrial and devoid of charm, uncomfortable, with the streets crowded with cars where taxi drivers picked up several passengers at once, chaining multiple destinations in the same ride to maximize profit. Chao barely spent a few hours there and, irked, he hurried to get to Labrang.

Once there, he realized there was a limit on the time that a tourist could be in such a small town without attracting attention, so he started searching at once. The first day Chao toured the outer walls of the monastery with his camera, familiarizing himself with the place and looking for a recognizable face among the Western travellers of the main avenue. At midday he lunched twice in different places, unable to decide which one of those backpacker cafés gave him the best chance of finding his man. In the afternoon, he visited the hostels mentioned in the travel guide but, for the sake of discretion, he settled into one of the hotels for Chinese tourists that stood farther within the east side. At night, Chao returned to his room and called the Hong Kong office. Cecilia answered.

"It's me."

"Liam, I was about to go to bed. Everything all right?"

"All is good."

His sister noticed that not all was good. "You don't like it there?"

"It's interesting. The monastery is certainly worth it."

"But?"

"Beijing is ruining Tibet, as it has ruined everything else. In a couple of decades, there will be nothing Tibetan in this town."

He went on. Cecilia knew the nature of Chao's character and let him vent the frustration that the trip created for him. He was an old-school Hongkonger, one of those who grew up in a world that was not fully Asian but did not belong to Europe either. He had seen a beggared China from his comfortable side of the fence in Kowloon and had been as surprised as the rest of his cosmopolitan countrymen to witness the Middle Kingdom lifting its head, little by little and through the years until it reached the shadow of the proud buildings of the bay. After the China-Hong Kong reunification of 1997, and with the city full of fears about the designs of Beijing for the former British metropolis, Chao attended with his sister the first military parade of the Red Army through the streets near the harbour. That day, as in all the parades that followed, he felt no pride in being Chinese, only the deep nostalgia of the days when Hong Kong controlled the economic ambitions of South East Asia.

"And what about that man, the one with the contract? Any clue?" Cecilia interrupted. It was getting late.

"No luck today, but the town is small. I will continue tomorrow."

"Very well. I'll be at the office. Let me know if you need anything."

Chao hung up, looked out the window with smudged glass panes and wished he was back home.

He found his man the very next day, buying canned food and a walking stick in the open-front shops that bordered the avenue. He recognized him from the photographs and followed him when he returned to the hostel. Then he hurried to make a call. That night he watched the entrance of the building but saw nothing. He waited until the deserted street and the extinguishing of the lights made him look suspicious and returned to his hotel.

On the morning of the fourth day and at the reception of the hostel, he discovered that the Man Under Contract had left at dawn, very early. Through a street vendor who barely spoke Mandarin, he found out more: that the man had returned from doing the Kora, the pilgrim circuit of the monastery walls, had bought half a dozen loaves of bread from her and then left.

"Where to?"

The woman pointed vaguely towards the meadows of the Tibetan highlands that stretched out of sight of the town. Fearful of losing track, Chao entered the hostel that the Man Under Contract had left and, showing his license and a hundred-yuan bill, questioned pointedly the concierge, a middle-aged Tibetan who played with a child behind the counter. The man he was looking for, he said, had not been reserved about his plans and shared that he was to set on foot towards the town of Tongren, eighty kilometres cross country through the nomadic plains of the Ando region. This was a sea of grassland and mountain crossings that could be bypassed in five hours by using the new road that ran south of town, but the intermediate space, for those who chose the itinerary of the plateau, required between four and five days of vigorous walking. Chao stood there a moment. He could not go tramping into the prairie like that. Impossible.

"Is there a bus service?" he asked. He would take the road south and wait for the Man Under Contract in Tongren. Yes, that was the sensible thing to do.

The man behind the counter shook his head. "The road is flooded."

An hour later, Chao had visited the bus office, the taxi stand and the police station. The way to Tongren was indeed flooded and all traffic cut. The gravel road often got blocked by landslides, snow avalanches or, as in this case, rainfall. When he asked how long it would take to reopen, the police officer behind the counter shrugged negligently and cited one to two weeks.

Chao thought about giving up then, but it had taken money and effort to track the traveller to Labrang, and the fear that he would fade into the boundless grasslands was too acute for his professional conscience to endure, so he made a decision.

Chao returned to his hotel at a run, anxiously looked at his suitcase, but he hardly had anything suitable. He had packed his luggage in Hong Kong with the idea of conducting a search in towns and cities, He had even expected rides on rickety buses and some uncomfortable nights, but what he did not count on was the need for a four-day march outdoors. He went out again, bought a stout backpack, a sleeping bag at a disproportionate price and some preserved food of very unappealing appearance. The sports shoes and waterproof jacket he was wearing would have to do.

An hour and a half later, Chao went down the avenue due south-west, carrying his pack, a walking stick and a brimmed hat. He left behind the last houses of Sakar, a village at the foot of the hills that had prosperously merged with Labrang. He found his way between ramshackle houses and open ditches where septic brown water moved slowly. Children ran to the entrance of the houses to see him pass, surprised to find a tourist so far from the monastery. They were silent for a while and then, when he turned his back to them, they shouted "hello" and "ni hao" alternately. Chao was in reasonably good shape, but after two hours of walking uphill, he felt short of breath and both annoyed and uncomfortable. The road narrowed, the paved street gave way to a gravel road first and, later, a scar-like path of bare ground marked in the grass. He went up the natural drain formed between two cliffs where the rain, which began to fall as he was leaving Sakar and had since redoubled, had left the hillside muddy and slippery. Further on, he saw the pass that was the first step into the grasslands and gave way to the highlands of the Serchen Thang prairie. Chao had neither map nor compass but, using the navigation function of his phone, downloaded the topographic profile of the route. He fiddled with the device, but the more he went into the empty vastness of the steppe, the more the altitude and distance isolated him and he was soon without a signal. For many hours he didn't know where he was and navigated by the obvious landmarks of the terrain. Then he met a family, father, mother and small child, climbing the slope of that piece of the Roof of the World on a rickety Kawasaki motorcycle, who stopped, amused at his predicament. Chao asked for directions and oriented himself again. The shopkeeper who had sold him his backpack in Labrang had explained that with the spring thaw and during the summer months, he would find semi-nomadic groups guarding flocks of sheep and yaks, camped in the prairie with white and blue canvas tents. Chao hoped he could trust in their indications to find his way.

So far, the plateau was an unpopulated and vacant universe. There were no trees or shrubs, only extensions of grass waving over the low hills towards the horizon. He saw some scattered animals huddled together in the gradual climb to the plateau, also mastiffs and other dogs held down by chains at certain intersections but, after the family on the motorcycle, no other human being. It kept raining. Chao was not a man accustomed to rough weather, and the night he had ahead looked like it would be cold and damp without a tent to shelter in. He looked at the sky, grumbled and kicked the lumps of soil on the ground.

William "Liam" Chao was a detective, but not that kind of detective. He did not chase people in the wild like a marshal after outlaws in the Old West. His trade was missing persons, runaway children, fugitive husbands. He had a good eye to elucidate the route that a man who was haunted by debts could follow, and he had been serving his clients this way for more than fifteen years. But this case was different. The man on this contract was unpredictable. He changed direction at whim, and the plan he had followed since leaving Cambodia, if it was a plan at all, was not one of escape.

At sunset, when the light disappeared, Chao first tried to snuggle up next to a promontory that blocked some of the rain. Then he changed his mind and decided to walk farther in the semi-darkness, but there was no other feature of the land where he could shelter. The temperature dropped and his jacket had failed to keep him dry hours ago. Chao shivered. With the night closing on the plateau, he came to a thick canvas tent that stood in the centre of a flock where yaks lay sleeping next to each other. Smoke was coming out of the tin chimney. He knocked on the entrance post and raised his voice. A dirty-faced boy peeked out, disappeared, and a man with sun-beaten skin came out. The man looked at Chao with little surprise and, without saying a word, lifted the flap at the entrance of the tent and invited him in. Inside there was a complete and extensive family accommodated on cushions and blankets of yak wool around a burning stove. The adults spoke only Tibetan, but one of the children, covered in grime and with inquisitive eyes, attended a Chinese school in Rebkong during the winter months and, through him, Chao could thank his host properly. They offered him a good corner of the tent and several blankets in addition to milk, tea and fried bread. The strong smell of living, wet animal flesh sneaked in from the outside. The nomad patriarch was a Tibetan middle-aged man with white hair who spilt the first cup of tea in the hand where he wore a thick silver ring with the name "Lhasa" carved in Tibetan script and passed it over his head toward a faded photo nailed to the wood of the central post. The ablution was dedicated to the sanctity of the Dalai Lama, who looked at the family from the paper image through thick glasses and with a beatific smile. Chao pushed into reluctant hands a fifty-yuan bill as a token of gratitude until it was finally accepted and then, with the moisture leaving his bones, he went to sleep, listening to the breath of ten people around him.

The next morning dawned with clear skies. Chao had breakfast—cold sheep meat and hot water to which the shepherd added some milk and yak butter. With sheets ripped out of his notebook he made paper aeroplanes that he handed to the children. The patriarch smiled, grateful for the gesture, and the children ran from side to side throwing the folded toys and followed by yapping dogs. Chao picked up his backpack and said goodbye to the family. He began to walk a little livelier. The emptiness of the steppe was stimulating despite its monotony, and the imagination of the detective wandered from place to place, animated by the idle pace of the walk. He did not forget his obligations and watched the horizon through a pair of binoculars, the same pair he used to watch the stealthy walk of unfaithful husbands from the car in Hong Kong. The morning passed, but the figure of the Man Under Contract was not evident.

At noon, a sweating Chao crowned a new pass and finally saw opening majestically the infinity that was the great plateau of Serchen Thang. He could not calculate distances on the map that appeared on the screen that his phone showed him but the mountains to the north-west that delimited the grasslands were at least a full day's walk away. In between him and them, all was a sublime universe of rounded green hills which followed one another to the placid Serchen Chu river far away. That day would require him to walk halfway and then turn west. Chao remained on the crest of the pass, running his binoculars up and down the ocean of grass blades.

He saw the Man Under Contract a few hours later, far away. He knew it was him because of the rhythmic rocking his step had under the large backpack. He was leaving the great plain and aiming towards a valley that would take him to the next pass in the mountains, always upward in the ascending progression of the plateau. The only thing Chao could do was to look on as the point moved further away and then follow it with the reluctant agreement of his swollen feet.

He allowed himself just ten minutes to eat, cooked sausages and crackers that he swallowed with no joy or pleasure. He didn't need to reach the traveller, but he was worried that, if he arrived at Tongren much later than him, he may lose him again there. By early afternoon, the valley had narrowed considerably, and the figure had grown to the size of a thumb. He watched as the Man Under Contract halted at a camp of Tibetan herders. Despite the distance, Chao hid in a bend to observe and wait. Crouched there, he again appreciated the clean air and clear skies of Tibet but still wished he was back in his Hong Kong office.

The traveller stepped out of the canvas tent of the nomads. Chao saw him clearly with the binoculars. He said goodbye by waving his hand, and one of the women put a package of food wrapped in brown paper between his arms. Chao shouldered his backpack and started after him again, following through the vast expanse of grass and wind. An hour later he came to the same camp. He asked and was told that there were at least three hours left until the next mountain pass, Chadan Ka. He would arrive there just at sunset.

That climb, on the evening of the second day, was the worst of them all. The ground went up, ascending and ascending with no rest or truce. There was not even a path, only lumps on the hillside that looked like steps and that Chao climbed putting down foot after foot with an effort that left him with a bitter taste. It was an eternal staircase that he had to traverse, nailed down by the weight of the backpack while the top of the pass never seemed to grow any closer. With such a steep course, Chao drifted almost without noticing it to the right-hand summit, higher but with a more forgiving gradient. Up there was a landmark of sacred rocks called *mani*, a sort of stone promontory piled up by nomads and pilgrims that topped the peak and flanked the pass. From the stones arose a post, five meters high, held erect by the stacking of rocks, and from the top radiated a dozen cords like a spider's web, covered with Buddhist prayer flags, flaming furiously in the wind.[19]

Chao arrived at the *mani* and fell, defeated by fatigue. He could not even take off his pack and lay there, prostrated against the bulk at his back, breathing hard and feeling his legs burn. His phone miraculously returned to life after two days of negligent sleep and,

---

[19] Here it is, again, the Buddhist idea of extending the blessing of its message to the world. The flags are of diverse and striking colors (namely: blue, white, red, green and yellow in an established order representing the five elements of the primordial cosmogony) and are imprinted with the prayers that give them their names, and other mantras. When the wind lashes at them, it spreads their message of compassion and reconciliation

with a single bar on the reception chart, told him he was over four thousand metres high.

Someone moved next to him, the Man Under Contract.

"I thought about waiting for you right at the top but I could not stand the wind. Too strong there."

Chao looked to one side, then another. In Hong Kong, he had once been surprised crouched behind a door with a tape recorder in hand. The bodyguard of the person he was tailing, who was a man wealthy enough to have bodyguards, snatched the device and threw it out of the window, and the detective suffered more from the shame of being discovered than from the loss of the machine. That time, Chao limited himself to looking at the guard with professional detachment and, turning around, left. This time, he could do nothing but remain still and silent.

"My name is Gavriel, although maybe you already know that."

Chao did not move.

"I'm going to light a fire. When you're ready, let me know and we'll talk."

He turned, went to the other end of the *mani* and disappeared, hidden by the pile of stones. The sky was darkening, and Chao continued to sit there, held in place partly by fatigue and partly by indecision. If he got up, he would have to talk to the Man Under Contract, something that contravened the rules of the profession where the investigator should never contact the subject under investigation. That was a problem in itself, but what really immobilized Chao was the affront of seeing himself in the sudden reversal of roles from hunter to hunted. An orange glow appeared on the other side of the mound. Chao sighed and, pulling at his backpack with effort, got to his feet.

The Man Under Contract had lit a portable stove on which he boiled water for tea. He silently prepared two cups and handed one to the detective.

"Are you following me?" he asked abruptly.

"Following you? Why would I follow you? I am a hiker, on my way to Tongren."

Chao noticed the traveller gazing up at his jacket, too thin for the weather, and down at the sport shoes that the two days of traversing merciless ground had caused to burst at the seams.

"I saw you in Labrang, from the window. And now I see you looking for me here."

"And why do you expect someone to be looking for you? Have you done anything wrong?" replied Chao.

"You should know. Why are you here if not? Is it because of Cambodia?"

"I've never been to Cambodia," said Chao and it was true.

"That's not what I'm asking you."

"I don't know what you're asking me."

"Are you police?"

"No."

Silence.

"Who are you, then?" asked the Man Under Contract.

"Who are you?" answered Chao.

The Man Under Contract breathed tensely. He was not accustomed to these types of conversations. They were not common for Chao either, but they occasionally happened, and he knew that it was best to speak little and answer questions with other questions.

"Siem Reap was an accident. I didn't think it would happen like that," Gavriel said, inviting a more conciliatory tone. "Is that the reason? Did the embassy send you?"

"What happened to you in Siem Reap?"

"There are things … Sorry, I haven't asked your name."

"William."

"There are things, William, that are not entirely comprehensible. Cambodia was one of them. And it had happened before, you know? In Tasmania and elsewhere. And I know that there are people who can be injured. I understand that, but it's a risk that just has to be accepted. There's a lot at stake. You can't imagine how much."

William fidgeted in his seat, illuminated by the low light of the fire.

"I have no idea what you're talking about."

The Man Under Contract looked at Chao, narrowing his eyes, looking at him more carefully than he had in the previous minutes of verbal fencing. He was looking for clues to the piercing of the world.

"This … this is not a coincidence. Coincidences do not exist …"

"Of course they exist. They occur daily. Are you also a philosopher?" Chao said, belligerent.

Gavriel continued to look at him thoughtfully. "No, no, no. This is a clue. You are not here by chance. Maybe you are the clue …"

Chao remained silent, unsure how to channel the conversation. Gavriel waited, organizing his thoughts.

"Listen," said the Man Under Contract suddenly. "I'm going to tell you what happened with Maya.[20] Maybe that way you will understand what I'm talking about."

Gavriel started talking and this is the story he told.[21]

---

[20] Japanese female name. Also, in the Vedic Hindu tradition, the mirage of the physical world in which the True Being is stranded. It is a tangible environment but it fails to be real because it prevents human beings from reaching the superior strata they belong to. The implications of the name were not apparent to the Man Under Contract until much later.

[21] The idea of having the narration around the fire came to the Man Under Contract by inspiration of the emptiness of the plateau and the forced intimacy with the detective, but such resource is a primordial part of the human communicative process. The furious atavism of the moment partly explains the melancholy of the story which follows.

41°52'S/1146°01'E
Tasmania: The Chapel of Green

Gavriel met Maya on an island when he was yet to become the Man Under Contract.

It was a place of retreat in the South East Asian circuit where backpacking travellers stopped, a chance to rest on the path of perpetual pilgrimage. The beach was like many others in Thailand, Indonesia and Malaysia. It had an indefinable charm that came from the rusticity of the houses and the wharves made of rough timber planks. The water, the sand, the vegetation, all gave it the quality of a parenthesis, apt for forgetting previous lives and spending days of indolence under the sun and nights of wine and music in makeshift bars by the seashore. Food and beer were cheap. Even the local people, forced to work while tourists lay down on the sand, became infected with the lassitude of the place.

Gavriel's routine was simple those days. He read his books and filled in his notebooks hanging in a hammock; not forgetting what he was looking for, but neither letting it drive him as much as when he was on the road. This was before, at the time when the Search had not yet planted in him the fervour he later would have. He dived in the reefs and ate spicy fish. At dusk, he put on his only white shirt and went barefoot down to the bar stalls set up on the beach where chairs sank in the sand and lanterns hung from the palm trees. There were always new people, perennial travellers like himself, young (or sometimes not so much) men and women who had chosen to be in constant motion, repelled by the lives of cars and mortgages that awaited back home. Some covered the cost of living in those affordable countries selling photos and articles to travel magazines, others dealt with restricted substances, buying and selling at their own risk. There were groups of young tourists, liberal in issues of both sex and alcohol, who wanted to take a short dash into the bohemian lifestyle before returning home and closing the door to the last years of freedom. The mix of people was always changing and this, rather than confusing, was stimulating because conversations, and much more, came effortlessly in that incubator of uninhibited life.

Gavriel saw Maya walking through the sand with hands in her pockets. Maya had always lived in France and spoke English with a strong Gallic accent, but she was Japanese. Her father's company had moved the household to Cergy, near Paris, when she was only one month old and had thus managed to escape the stringent conventions of Japanese society. Gavriel, who had been to Japan several times, was struck by the contradiction of seeing the demure and tranquil appearance of Maya's features laid over the so un-Asian assurance she demonstrated when talking or swaying her hips.

That night Gavriel could not find the time to approach her, or perhaps he lacked some courage when he saw her come, flanked by her group of friends. Sheltered behind *The Demon Princes,* he merely looked up now and then with a certain yearning at the constant flow of suitors trying to woo her. The next day was easier. Gavriel had met an English traveller on the reefs that morning and they got on well enough to drop by the beach bar together at sunset. Encouraged by the company, he managed to get the attention of Maya and her group, two or three French women who had the annoying habit of reverting to their native language in the middle of each conversation. That night Gavriel and Maya said their goodbyes, mixing smiles and glances over the shoulder, and he returned to his dilapidated bungalow alone, the English accomplice lost, at some point, in the swell of the night's party. Three days passed and Gavriel was desperate because that was an almost unthinkable amount of time in the hurried pace of travellers who never stayed in a place longer than was strictly necessary. He delayed his departure, subtracting days here and there and finding excuses to spend time with Maya. He had the impression she was doing the same. Finally, a stormy afternoon left them stranded together, just the two of them, at the entrance to her cabin. The sky was of a turbulent sound and muted colour while darkness approached.

"And where will you go from here?" she asked in the growing spontaneity of the moment.

"I don't know yet. There are certain things I will need to do."

"Well now, that sounds mysterious."

"It's not really. And you?"

Maya approached. "If you were to ask me right now, at this precise moment, I would have to say that it depends on you …"

Later they lay curled up naked in the bungalow with chipped walls, the canopy covered with a mosquito net. They spent the hours until dawn modifying their plans so they could travel together for at least a couple more weeks.

Maya was halfway through a sabbatical year dedicated to seeing the world. After a whole life in France she had returned to Japan, a country she knew only from short stays during holidays, and found it was familiar and disconcerting at the same time. She had planned to settle there but the experiment was a disaster; no part of Maya's personality could fit into the strict formulations of Japanese society. She was fired from two jobs, and her social life agonized painfully until it died. Despite her appearance and the naturalness with which she spoke the language, she was too French, she understood, for Japan. She returned to Cergy and got an attractive position in an American multinational that closed a couple of years later. Without a clear idea of where she fit, she decided to use the dismissal compensation money to travel a few months before looking for a new job. Initially, she went to China but, after getting her diving certificate in Cebu, she had more interest in touring the diving areas that rimmed the southern coast of Asia. The months of travel multiplied and the desire to return to France was dying along the way.

That was why Gavriel proposed to visit the Great Barrier Reef in Australia. It was one of the most famous aquatic life centres in the Pacific, and Maya agreed with a bright smile, although the trip there, necessarily by plane, was going to put quite a burden on their finances. The suggestion was not spontaneous, of course. The signs pointed south and Gavriel had to follow them.

It took them almost a month to get down from Queensland to Melbourne, crossing the most austral inhabited continent from top to bottom. At that time, Maya seemed to have postponed her return to France indefinitely, and neither of them talked about life outside the narcotic rhythm that the continuous journeying gave them. The two weeks they planned on spending together grew and stretched. They camped on the beach like two hippies because the hotel prices in Australia far exceeded what they were used to paying in the economic Asian circuit. Eventually, they learned how to move with the tides of the surfer and bohemian communities that peppered the coast.

They had been together for a few months, but life as they knew it had the power of intensifying the flow of experiences and Gavriel, alone and lonely since he had started this crusade of his, could not resist telling Maya, in the privacy of a night in Melbourne, what it was he searched for.

Maya neither laughed nor did she leave. She did not, in fact, go through any of the emotions such revelation should have brought. She remained still, stroking Gavriel's hair in the dim light while he waited, silent and concerned about the burden of knowledge he had just put upon her.

They did not cross to the island of Tasmania until days later. That was the time it took for the woman to reconcile herself with what she had been told.

"Explain to me again why it has to be Tasmania," Maya said.

"With the details of *Timaeus*?" Gavriel asked, an ardent expression on his face.

"Yes, with all the details."

"You still haven't mentioned what that search of yours is about," Chao said, back at the *mani* that crowned the pass of the Tibetan plateau.

The Man Under Contract looked up in bewilderment, as if the detective's voice had woken him from the memories and the story he was telling.

"I'm talking about the only thing that matters, the secret of the universe. Let me finish. Everything will be clearer then."

He rummaged in the cavernous innards of his backpack, fetching more tea.

"What I described to Maya is the explanation Plato gives in the dialogue of *Timaeus* of the phenomenal world and how the universe is ultimately formed by the four classical elements. Earth because it is tangible, fire because it is visible, and between those two extremes, air and water, which refer to the law of mathematical proportions of

Pythagoras. The earth is solid and occupies the centre of the universe, fire is in the periphery. The two intermediate elements circulate between them.[22] The elements are in a relationship that is scrupulous, appropriate and precise, which binds and sustains the world."

The Man Under Contract put more water on to boil, and the shadows that the fire created jumped on his face. Chao thought that at times he seemed to be wearing a demonic mask.

"Initially I thought it was the island of Malta that best met the requirements of the Platonic description of the elements. It also has sediments from different civilizations, Phoenician, Roman, Arab, etc. like layers set one on top of another which give it continuity. But there was something that did not fit there. *Timaeus* speaks of the correct geometric proportions. Following the Greek indications, I realized the world is fundamentally mathematical, and so the proportions have to be respected. I had looked at many other places but none fit that balance. Only Tasmania fulfilled all the conditions: granitic mountains that grant solidity, surrounded by the flexibility of open sea, it sits in the confluence of three oceans, the Pacific to the east, the Indian to the west and the Southern to the south; and it is located in the path of the Roaring Forties, the wind corridor that descends all the way from the equator to Antarctica and accelerates through the ocean without restraint until it reaches the island."[23]

"But, what did you expect to find on that island? In Tasmania? I don't even know where it is."

"South of the Australian continent, on the edge of the very last sea.

---

[22] The theory is the result of the direct observations done by the classical philosophers, who saw stones fall to the ground, fire trying to rise in the flames, and clouds and water spinning and moving around without apparent pattern. They took the results of that scrutiny as a literal indication of the essence of the universe.

[23] Platonic geometry understands that the four elements are not the ultimate division of matter. They are, in turn, formed by an indivisible component: the equilateral triangle, considered the perfect shape because of its stability. Earth is formed by cubes of x12 triangles which explains its solidity, its immutability and its resistance to change. Fire is made up of pyramids of x4 triangles and the resulting figures, topped by a sharp angle, define its destructive nature. The triangles recombine, and the elements transform. The world is, therefore, a mathematical environment as indicated by the Man Under Contract.

What did I expect to find there? I wasn't sure. The island met the requirements of the elements but not those of the ideas. There's a map that follows the pulse of human thought, the paths of knowledge. Philosophy, religion, animism. But in Tasmania, there was nothing, no core of doctrine, no tradition of dogma or faith. I understood that whatever the island was hiding had to be something primal, ancient as the very origin of man."

"And the girl followed you there? Without saying anything?"

"She didn't say anything but yes, she trusted me and followed me there," lied the Man Under Contract.

In fact, Maya had said something. She had looked at him deeply and, embracing the irrationality of the idea, had taken his hand and muttered, "Very well, I believe you".

It was something Gavriel had never heard before and would not again until much later, from Chao himself.

Gavriel and Maya took the ferry from the pier in Melbourne and arrived at Devonport, a small coastal town of white houses hugging a bay in Tasmania. The character of the city had an Anglo flavour and reminded him of the small English towns on the coast of the British Channel. But in Tasmania the sun was shining in a sky dangerously clear of ozone and the horizon was blue. The seawater and the air of its coasts came directly from the South Pole and made everything pure and gelid.

"I'm cold," Maya said.

"We will have to buy some warm clothes. This is definitely not Thailand weather."

"I hate the cold. Paris was cold. That's partly why I have delayed in Asia for so long. Much better there."

They had tea and sandwiches in a coffee shop near the harbour, and then found accommodation in a hostel that the low season had left almost deserted. They spent two days touring Devonport and its surroundings but the city, undoubtedly of great charm, offered neither sanctuaries nor reliquaries nor any other sacred bastion that Gavriel could use as a handhold to begin the Search.

"We have to go further. The clues will not be religious or cultural. We have to look for the most primal aspects," Gavriel said, back in their room.

"And how do we do that?"

Gavriel opened a map. "The best thing that I can think of is the Cradle Mountain nature reserve. There's a cross-country hiking route that crosses from north to south, about seventy kilometres. I think it would take four, maybe five days to complete."

"Five days."

"Yes. We'll need camping equipment, supplies. I have read that there are wooden huts along the route that we can use if the weather worsens."

Gavriel took out his notebook and began to create a list. Maya observed him carefully.

"And you know that the clues you are looking for are there?"

"That's what I'm hoping for."

"And we go all the way there and find nothing?"

"Then I was wrong."

The woman was now watching the bay through the window. There was a tragic echo in her profile, an omen of things to come.

"Are you sure you want to embark on this? I know you like trekking, but the route will be demanding."

Maya turned, smiled, the echo faded. "I'm sure."

They spent that last night before the hike at a bar where Devonport's residents gathered to sing karaoke and drink with scarce moderation. The evening was somewhat melancholic, and not even the tender and intense encounter that followed in the bed of the rented room served to lift the gloom of their spirits. It dawned with rain, and they arrived by local bus at the entrance of the reserve. The Cradle Mountain route was very frequented by outdoorsmen and nature lovers, but its adversity and the cold and damp weather of the area meant many visitors stayed on the first leg of the trail and did not move further into the overnight reaches, accessible only by foot. Upon getting off the bus and taking the first steps along the path, Gavriel and Maya had the impression that they left the inhabited world to enter a separate, greener one. A ranger wrote down their names at the counter of the visitor centre.

"Make sure you check out as well when you finish, so we can know if you have had a mishap inside," he said.

Other hikers were waiting there; some groups and couples, dispirited by the unpleasantness of the weather, and lone travellers. Gavriel and Maya would find all of them again at dusk when the hikers, scattered along the trail, gathered under the shelter of the wooden cabins that marked the end of the day's walk.

The first day they trekked over flatlands where the wind ran cold and the rain kept falling. For a stretch, timber boardwalks installed by the rangers to prevent soil erosion helped them make good time, but soon the trail gave way to a narrow path lined up towards the mass of Mount Ossa, the highest peak in Tasmania. The mountain barely reached a thousand five hundred metres, but in that austral spring the island was like a great ship in the middle of the Antarctic wind and its water currents and Ossa, capturing all that inclement weather in its summit, sent it right down towards the hikers in the valley.

Maya, balancing herself on stiff legs, managed to approach the fireplace and sit down when they arrived at the shelter. Her lips and fingers were purple. The people who were already there, a Korean couple, some Germans and a Scotsman with a dense accent, made room for her. They settled around the stove and, little by little, she regained colour. The evening passed pleasantly, lit by candles and a burning fire where socks and boots dried. One of the Koreans had managed to load into a backpack filled to the point of bursting a bottle of liquor and decided that, rather than saving it for later, the buoyant mood of the company called for it to be shared that first night. When the travellers went to sleep one by one, Gavriel left Maya breathing softly on her pallet, put on his soaked jacket and went outside again. Tasmania was a large and sparsely populated island and, in the natural reserve, the noise and light of human presence were confined to the cabin. In the darkness, a varied fauna of wallabies, possums and bats came out to feed and maraud near the wooden hut with a certain disdain for the rattling of the people inside. It still rained, but the moon was shining through the holes in the clouds and it was surprisingly bright. Gavriel sought the shine of the fangs of Tasmanian devils, wishing and fearing to encounter one, but the infamously morose carnivorous marsupials were nowhere to be seen. With the compass in one hand and his paper charts of esoteric discernment in the other, he moved around, spinning in the spot, looking for references to guide him but found none. Only the mass of Mount Ossa crouching down the trail stood out. "Maybe …" he thought and went back inside.

The next day the rain stopped. The sun came out, the cold wind disappeared, and the path led the couple through a more rugged patch of terrain. Maya had suffered in the storm of the first day, but with the improved weather her spirit also recovered. Gavriel watched her with discreet fascination. Sometimes he thought that there was nothing extraordinary about her; that other equally intelligent, attractive and vivacious women existed. But he also knew that the synchrony of feelings does not care for precise measurements, and that although other women could, in fact, exist, the one he had found was the one for him.

They spoke about France and Nepal and the many other places they wanted to visit, building plans upon plans for an open future. The optimism did not last long. After breaking for lunch in a sunny grass patch, they went into a dense forest they did not leave until nightfall. As they walked, Gavriel felt consumed by the oppression of the trees, and it seemed that they would never come out into the light again. Maya walked like an automaton, not looking to either side. It wasn't just fatigue; a premonition grew inside her.

That night they were the last to arrive at the shelter. This cabin was much smaller than the previous one. There were no available cots or even free space on the floor on which to roll out the sleeping bags, so they had to set up their tent outside. They did spend the evening sitting around a small chimney of stone and sand, crowded with the other hikers to warm up from the night's cold that permeated the high ceiling of the hut. The Scottish man with a thick accent was telling a story, but the barrage of voiceless velar fricatives he used made it difficult to understand him, and the Koreans looked at each other perplexed. Gavriel and Maya found the sound of his voice bothersome so they withdrew early to their tent. It started to rain again.

Entrenched in the sleeping bag that isolated him from her, Gavriel knew that Maya did not sleep. Their intense breathing filled the air of the tent, still cold, and saturated the space with condensation. He wanted to break the silence, but his tongue refused and time went by in dreary stillness.

"Gavriel …" Maya whispered finally.

"Yes."

"Do you never lose faith? How do you know that you will find what you're looking for? I don't mean just here, I mean at the end of the road."

She spoke without turning, facing the wall of cotton and nylon where moisture from the rain and their bodies condensed.

"Maya, I know you have doubts. I had them too, but the things I've seen, the secrets that are out there …"

"I wanted to tell her that everything was within our reach, mysteries that were not of this world but another and that demanded from us zeal and absolute adherence. If we doubted, if our dedication was not absolute, we would fail. But I could not explain what I desperately needed to tell her," said the Man Under Contract crouched near the fire, at the Tibetan Chadan Ka pass.

"Was she afraid?" Chao asked.

"No, it wasn't fear. Nor lack of faith. Maya believed in me."

"Then?"

"She doubted. She doubted her place on that journey."

Gavriel thought the woman had fallen asleep, so long was she without saying a word. And suddenly.

"Japan always made me feel alien. France too, sometimes, due to my features, but the country was more multicultural and easier to fit in. Japan was worse. When I was ten years old my parents enrolled me in a public school during the summer months. In Japan, classes extend longer than in Europe and my Japanese was falling behind. A few days after I started, the other children realized that there was something about me that didn't match. This was in a small town of Chiba, very provincial, that did not understand well the world beyond the borders of the archipelago.

"One afternoon after school, some of the older children ganged up on me, asking who I was and where I came from. I told them I was from Chiba but, despite my Japanese appearance, they noticed something. My mannerisms maybe, the way I acted. My mother had recommended that I speak about my life in France, that it would help me break the ice, but I knew it was not so. Japan is a very homogeneous country and surprisingly close-minded once you leave the big cities.

"Surrounded by the other children, I told them that my parents lived in Europe. They started calling me *ainoko*, mixblood, yelling at me in chorus until a neighbour, an older woman, scared them away and took me back home. I cried when my mother opened the door. I ran into the living room but still managed to hear the neighbour say to my mother, 'That's what happens when you take a girl out from the place where she belongs.' Even today I don't know if she meant Japan or France and if she also considered me an intruder."

Maya turned in her sleeping bag with a slithering sound of skin on silk and faced Gavriel. "I fear that here I may be an intruder too. That this Search of yours does not want me."

While Maya was sleeping, Gavriel remained awake. Resigned to losing that night's rest, he reviewed his notes in the light of the flashlight and made a decision.

On the third day, they reached the foot of Mount Ossa. A man in uniform and carrying a huge backpack was waiting at the fork of the road where a smaller path separated from the main route, climbed to the summit and then returned. They greeted each other and shared their lunch with the ranger. His job was to walk the trail in both directions each week, loaded with supplies and a first aid kit in case some mountaineer had been injured or lost.

"It keeps me fit," he said with good humour.

Gavriel looked at the top of the peak. "Is it worth climbing to the summit?"

"It is. You get a good view and it's only a couple of hours walk. It would be harder to climb the original Ossa."

"You mean there's another?"

The ranger nodded while chewing on instant noodles. "We borrowed the name. The original Mount Ossa is in Greece. I don't know why we named it like that. Legend has it that a pair of giants, sons of Zeus or something, used the mountain as a ladder to reach Mount Olympus and enter the kingdom of the Greek gods."[24]

Inside Gavriel's head, the implications of what he had just heard circled in armed revolution. He asked a few more questions of the ranger but he seemed to have lost interest in the conversation and looked at the path, calculating the hours he had before reaching the next camp.

"Enjoy the walk. You have two or three days left on the trail," he said, shouldering his backpack and starting to walk.

Gavriel watched him go and looked up at the mountain. *There are always clues*, he thought.

---

[24] The two giants, Otus and Ephialtes, were the Aloadae brothers, sons of Iphimedia and Poseidon. Resentful at the treatment received from the gods, they wanted to storm Olympus and take goddesses as wives. They created a mountain staircase after placing Mount Pelion on top of Mount Ossa but never reached their goal. They were executed by Apollo.

The rest of the group with whom they had shared the route passed by while they waited at the fork of the path. Gavriel checked his store of provisions; there was enough, it seemed, for the detour he had in mind.

"There's something here, Maya. The Greek connection is too obvious to ignore.[25] The name is no coincidence. I'm convinced that this Ossa is where we need to be."

"As a coincidence, it's not the most impressive I've seen but I guess that's the way God talks to you, right? Like a telegraph."

Maya mimicked in the air the tapping of a switch, smiling smugly and not knowing that the phrase would stay with Gavriel for years to come.

They climbed halfway to the summit and stopped short of the forest line, just where the trees still offered shelter from the wind and allowed a clear view of the imposing mass of the peak. They planted the tent. No open flame was allowed outside the campgrounds in the reserve, but Gavriel risked the rangers seeing the glow with their binoculars by digging a hole surrounded with rocks. Using the abundant wood of the forest he lit a campfire. Maya hung their wet clothes on the branches of the ash trees that surrounded them. The sky was clear but, with the sunset, the wind turned colder than it did in the valley.

The routine of the days on the trail had got them used to finding the company of other hikers and the warm quarterage of the huts at the end of each walk. Now they waited alone in a forlorn landscape as the sun went down. Gavriel looked around attentively to discover if the world changed, if the piercing that showed what was on the other side had appeared. Something, indeed, seemed to have shifted with the revelation shared by the ranger but it was a faint impression, and

---

[25] The Man Under Contract was partial to the clues offered by the foci of religious activity around the world because their rituals and codes of behavior offered escape from the material world but, given a choice between creed and wisdom, he would default to the latter. Since the promoters of Hellenic reasoning were the first ones to establish that it was the power of the intellect (Sophia) that allows us to transcend reality and reach the supernatural, the Greek connection was, indeed, important for him.

Gavriel could not be sure if it came as a subjective reflex.

Night fell, and it was heavy and absolute.

"There's something strange in the air." Maya also seemed attuned to the abandonment of the Tasmanian wilderness and the huge shadow of the mountain behind her.

The sun had set beyond the tree line. The light of the campfire marked a circle of colour, and the usual parade of animals that arrived at dusk was nowhere to be seen.

"Yes, there is. But there's also a barrier. Do you feel it? Something separates us from it." Gavriel fumbled in the most hidden pockets of his backpack. "Aha, I bought this from a surfer on the north coast," he said with a nod of triumph.

In his hand he had two small bags of digestible plastic enclosing a portion of brown powder. "It's peyote."

Maya accepted one of the bags. "What does it do?"

"It is a psychoactive, used as a ceremonial drug in North and Central America."

"A drug?"

"Causes an altered state of consciousness. We will see things, perhaps visions. We better not start walking around or we may tumble all the way down to the valley."

Maya had taken ecstasy and other chemical drugs on the backpacking route through South East Asia. The feeling of euphoria followed by languor was familiar to her, but when she swallowed the peyote, she noticed nothing but a dry, bristly throat.

Hours later the only effects that Maya felt were just a tarnish on the edges of vision and the constant need to drink water first and then urinate. Gavriel, however, looked at the fire engrossed and thought he saw remnants of platonic solids in the shapes of the flames. For no particular reason, he waited for the fire to open, unfolding like a geometric puzzle, but the intuition that kept him in suspense did not come true.

Dawn arrived early in that latitude, and a very weak bar of light moved on the horizon after a sleepless night. A wallaby came out of the trees, walking on all fours. Maya watched it wander around the edge of the camp.

"The first one we've seen all night."

"What?" Gavriel gave a start, awakening from the reverie of the fire.

"The wallaby. Look."

The wallaby watched the camp with intense attention. Then approached the fire and spoke to them.[26]

"Comes a knight, Gwalchmei.[27] The Green Knight," it said, grinding ruminant teeth.

Maya, half-lying on the sleeping bag and caught in the lethargy of the narcotic, shook her head, trying to focus with pupils dilated by the vigil. Gavriel sat up. The wallaby turned around and, before disappearing into the trees, spoke again, turning its head towards them.

"Be prepared. The Green Knight comes."

Gavriel stood up, stumbling.

"The flashlight! Where is the flashlight?"

Maya passed it to him, and Gavriel shone it into the spaces between the trees. The effect of the peyote seemed to dissipate, and his senses regained sobriety.

"Maya! Maya! You saw that?"

---

[26] Wallaby: small marsupial mammal, almost identical to the kangaroo but smaller in size and resident of the Tasmanian forested areas. It lacks, of course, the gift of speech.

[27] Gwalchmei or Gualguanus, also called Gauvain, also called Walwein, also called Walewain, also called Waswain. The son of Lot. The Hawk of May. Administrator of the beheading blow: Gawain, the knight.

The woman slipped from the knot of her sleeping bag and came to Gavriel, staggering. "What was that? Was that the drug?"

Gavriel scanned the darkness. "No, no. This is something completely different."

Branches moved. Gavriel pointed with his light. A tall figure was hiding among the trees. Long arms, lithesome legs, green attire. From the dimness of a day that did not entirely dawn, he spoke.

"The debt is to be repaid, Gwalchmei. The chapel awaits."

Gavriel, ready now, jumped over the fire to follow the almost indistinguishable silhouette into the undergrowth of the forest. Maya shouted after him but Gavriel did not hear and would not have stopped if he had. The green silhouette appeared and disappeared, always far from his reach. It seemed to be wearing a rack of deer antlers on its head and moved with a soft and elastic step.

"When for the first time you came to me, you travelled through uninhabited forests and wild lands where the king's justice did not reach. Snakes and wolves and bears and bulls harassed you and, on the high rocks, giants chased you too," the voice rumbled.

Gavriel waved the flashlight to one side and another. He heard branches creak behind him. As he turned, Maya arrived, panting. She clung to his arm. Gavriel tried to find the clearest path to the voice but roots and rocks tripped him, and the darkness ate his light effortlessly. He took Maya's hand. The green figure was never totally missing, and among the rumour of the pursuit, they kept hearing its words, calling and asking for the restitution of the pending account.

"You survived because you served the Christian god; or so it was sung at your return. How do you come to me now, Gwalchmei? What is your merit?"

"We are looking for the blind god! For the blind god!" Gavriel shouted.

The dolorous and enormous figure appeared suddenly, a knight of furious green who wore an armour of flora and fauna: hauberk of moss, corselet of bark, high-helmeted head of antlered skull.

"Then look for the green chapel, as you did in the past. There awaits your judgement."

The voice left; the figure left. The world lost its magical dimension and, finally, it dawned. Gavriel and Maya found themselves in a forest clearing. Everything was normal.

That morning, and with a head clear of the last dregs of peyote, they decamped. Maya barely spoke, but the slow and absorbed manner in which she finished preparing revealed she did not fully understand what they had seen last night. Perhaps she thought Gavriel didn't understand either.

They climbed all morning, looking for a route to the opposite side of the mountain. The view of the valley followed them from the low reaches, and for hours they could see groups of hikers marching on the Cradle Mountain circuit in the distance. Then, as they turned around the mountain, looking for a spiral path that would take them high, the quality of the world changed about them again. It was not only the landscape and the air that became stranger; a new panorama appeared as they left the valley behind. Gavriel did not need the map to know that the tremendous cordillera that had sprung in the distance could not be contained in Tasmania. Despite the respectable elevation and inaccessibility of the interior lands of the island, what they saw was of an enormous scale, a succession of alpine heights that did not exist on earth. The world had unfolded and expanded, like a trick box that appears larger inside than when it is seen from the outside.

"But that was not a trick," said the Man Under Contract, sitting at the fire in very different mountains, Chao to the side and the night closed on them. "It was supernatural, the dominions of the blind god."

"Just like that. As if by magic," said the sceptical detective.

"It wasn't magic but yes, just like that."

"But how? How did you get there?"

"Don't ask me how. That doesn't matter. We got there, and that's what I'm trying to explain."

The Man Under Contract served more tea before Chao could refuse. His bladder bothered him but he did not feel he could move away from the light of the camping stove to urinate; the night was too dark on the plateau and the tone of the story he was hearing made him feel unprotected.

"And the giant creature with the armour of tree bark? Who was he?" asked Chao.

"Gawain's Ordeal," Gavriel recited. "I didn't know much about him until after that trip when I spent days digging around in the library of Devonport. It's a medieval chivalric tale, part of the literary body of early English Christianity.[28] The essence of the story, however, is much older, Celtic and even Mesopotamian. In the Arthurian version, the Green Knight is a bewitched nobleman, but in the primitive renditions his identity is more disquieting."

Gavriel and Maya walked all that day and left Tasmania behind. They spent the night next to a stream and continued on their way towards the mountain range, looking for the clues that the Green Knight could have left but, without the help of a hallucinogen or talking wallabies, they found nothing. Gavriel insisted on following a straight line and Maya looked back restlessly.

"How will we get back? This place is so vast."

Gavriel pointed to the distance. "Monte Ossa is still there, see? That flat peak. As long as we keep it within sight, we can find the way back."

---

[28] In the original romance, written in stanzas of alliterative verse, the knight appears before Camahaloth's court and challenges those present to strike an ax blow. The passionate Gwalchmei accepts and, although he decapitates the intruder, he stands up, collects his own head and summons Gwalchmei to visit the chapel where he will be the one to return the blow. The story that follows is a succession of the trials and temptations that define chivalrous virtue as a civilizing principle opposed to the chaotic disruption of nature.

They walked one more day, and then the food was finally over. That afternoon they reached a village. A frail palisade, already broken in places, surrounded the settlement but left a wide entrance space delimited by two thick posts.

Gavriel looked up. "It's here, here"

The posts were topped by carvings in the shape of snakes with the face of a lion, fierce-looking and with open jaws. In seeing the images, Maya felt a deep and inveterate fear; that was the symbol of the blind god and within were his servants.

The two travellers reached the edge of the fence and waited to be discovered. Inside, men and women moved between cabins of poorly finished timber and badly tanned skins. The ground was a quagmire of soft mud, discarded bones and ash. One of the children gave the alarm and the adults came, summoned by the shouting, with weapons and tools of sharp and dirty metal, and formed in front of the entrance into well-practised ranks. Gavriel stepped back. Sweating, he raised his hands and pointed at the leonine snakes.

"The blind god. We seek the blind god. Yaldabaoth."

There was no answer. The members of the tribe were short but broad-backed and strong. Mountain people. They looked at the sculptures and again at Gavriel.

"Samael!" he said.

Silence and weapons high.

"Saklas!"

"Saklas!" they shouted this time. "Saklas, Saklas!"

The men left their tools on the ground, touched their foreheads with both hands, and then took the two pilgrims inside the stronghold.

The tribe was made up of thirty men and twice as many women and children. They sat Gavriel and Maya in the interior of the wider hut, along with a dozen of the hunters, even though space was scarce, and knees collided with knees. The members of the tribe leaned close when speaking, smelling of herbs and sweat. Through the door, the windows and the gaps in the walls, the faces of the rest of the clan appeared. For half an hour Gavriel first and Maya later struggled to tell their story, gesturing and drawing on the floor of dirt. The hunters spoke a language of short, high-pitched sounds, like the chattering of intelligent birds. Except for "Saklas", Gavriel was unable to find any other word in common. When their hosts understood that they needed to eat, the leader, who was a man with a wrinkled face and a huge scar on his forehead, barked orders. While the men remained seated, the women threw themselves into a frenzy of activity that did not end until they served an indescribable panoply of food in the hut. Maya gave them some bagatelles in return, rings and bracelets. Although they accepted them, it was obvious that the tribe idolized the blind god, and just invoking its name was credential and safe-conduct enough. Inspired, Gavriel stood up, adjusted pieces of bark to his chest and pretended to have deer antlers on his head. The entire audience screamed. The chief stood and raised his hands to the forehead in that gesture of theirs.

"Midolto. Midolto ob Saklas," he said solemnly, and the tribe was silent.

Night came, a sudden change of light that was very different from the sunset in the true world. The tribe lodged Gavriel and Maya in one of the smaller huts and put out the fires. Still nervous, Gavriel sharpened stakes that he stuck in the mud floor in front of the entrance and then spent the night watching the hole with his hunting knife in hand.

Another grey and cold day dawned in the mountains. The tribe met with the travellers to eat porridge and drink bitter tea. Gavriel tried to get directions but the leader of the fenced town shook his head, refusing without answering. Resigned, the two pilgrims returned to their hut and came out with their backpacks in tow to say goodbye to the tribe, ready to leave and search for somebody who could lead them. The entire population waited at the entrance, and Maya walked in front of them self-consciously. Outside the palisade two of the younger warriors were ready with crooks and travel bundles. Without a word, they started on, ready to guide them into the mountains.

They walked three more days on steep terrain that was covered with gnarled trees with stout roots. At sunset, the guides from the tribe gathered fruits and small rodents from the recesses of the earth and with that they dined. They lit fires by snapping small pieces of flint collected from the ground and piled fern fronds on which to sleep. In return, Maya showed them the wonders drawn from the bottom of her backpack: flashlights, combs, binoculars. The Cradle Mountain valley and Mount Ossa were so far away that Gavriel didn't even remember what the first part of their trip had been like. All he understood now was the high peaks and deep cracks of that new world.

The guides were young, guileless and vivacious. When they were not pushing at each other, they laughed and whispered in a perpetual good mood, looking at the curve of Maya's bust while making appreciative gestures. Gavriel was unable to learn their names and just called them Tom and Jerry.

In the long evenings, the four of them communicated laboriously, sitting around the fire. Gavriel was learning things that he would later use away from there in other stages of the Search. The tribe[29] kept two mythologies in coexistence. One was the confused theology of the Green Knight, called Midolto, who was close and immediate. Another was a distant and sequestered presence: Saklas, an archaic god that could not be understood but remained real at the bottom of the human mind. Saklas was a tribal deity, one who protected his own and punished others, much like the Jewish Yahweh of the exodus.

On the fourth day, they reached a new settlement. It was different from the village of the tribe of the blind god. It had no palisade or wooden constructions, only cloth tents around open hearth spaces for cooking. The inhabitants were thinner and more agile than the two guides, a different ethnicity but still unrecognizable to Gavriel; neither Caucasian, African, nor Asian. Tom and Jerry gave great shouts before approaching the camp and waited at a safe distance, with dark iron knives concealed and ready in their sleeves. Sentries appeared, and only after intense scrutiny were they permitted to approach. They entered the camp. Gavriel saw that there were dozens of deer antlers crowned with sharp points on top of wooden posts.

---

[29] The clan of the blind god, which gave itself another name derived from a variety of nocturnal bats, was the closest enclave to the entrance of that land. The Man Under Contract and his companion were not the first visitors they had received and, unlike other groups, considered their religious duty to chaperone them in the search for the Green Knight.

The guides talked for a long time, crouched on the floor with representatives of the new group. They were men with severe faces and ashen paint around the eyes. They exchanged skulls of small birds in a ritual of opaque meaning to Gavriel. In the afternoon, the conclave ended, Tom and Jerry got up, hugged Gavriel and Maya and left, leaving them in the care of the new tribe on the road to the green chapel.

The hosts were not as welcoming as the snake clan had been, but they were still treated with deference. Gavriel tried several names for the blind god but none was recognizable. Inspired by the antlers, he drew on the ground a tall figure with an animal-skull helmet and moss armour. If the tribe recognized the Green Knight, they gave no sign of it. The gathering around the bonfire that night had more of atavistic ritual than celebration. There were gestures that Gavriel recognized, the sharing of water and food, the marking with soot on the forehead, ancestral labels that said the same thing in other places and other cultures: we recognize you, we welcome you. Other rites he could not decipher. One of the more burly warriors spat water on Maya's right foot, and one of the youngest girls on the left. These were references to the veiled religious creed of the group, dynamics of social hierarchy for which he did not have the key.

When night came everyone went to sleep. The tribe gave up a large tent woven with raw materials for the two pilgrims to use. The entrance was a blanket fastened with a bone pin. Gavriel took his knife and the flashlight again as a protective measure, but four days of travelling and lying down in the open made him fall asleep immediately. He woke up suddenly, shaken and with a heavy weight on his back. He heard screaming and saw Maya and robust shadows in the penumbra of the tent. Hands held him face down and covered his eyes and mouth. Between the fingers were gaps through which he distinguished the small and thin figure of Maya turning on the floor. Someone perched on her, and Gavriel heard the snorts of a man trying to pry open the woman's legs. Then there was a noise of torn fabric, and Gavriel went mad with anger and helplessness. They had taken the knife from his right hand and, desperately, he clicked the switch of the flashlight in his left. A burst of white light filled the tent, and the hands that held him jumped, leaving him free.

It was not the light itself that frightened them; rather it was its colour. The tribe did not use oils or alcohols; all their illumination came from the burning of wood, yellow and orange light. The torchlight, of a white they had only seen in the lightning of storms, seemed to those primitive men the very finger of God coming out of the hands of the foreigner to touch them with angry fury.

There were six intruders in the tent, cornered against the cloth wall and bending it with their combined weight. Gavriel crossed the beam up and down, looking for a weapon, and the flashing created tremendous wailing when it touched the faces of the attackers. Maya grabbed the whistle she wore next to the compass on a chain around her neck and blew. The shrill, high-pitched sound filled the tent and seemed to swell the air. The men jumped over each other trying to get away, pulling the shelter's leather, posts, ropes and anchors as they scattered. Gavriel and Maya were suddenly free. At the edge of the glow that the embers of the fires gave, hidden faces could be seen surrounding them, attentive to the outcome. Gavriel wielded the flashlight, shouted "run" and they both raced into the forest between the shining of white light and the blaring of the whistle. After an hour of mad sprinting between the trees, they finally stopped to catch their breath. Nothing could be heard. Nobody followed them, but still they kept walking and looking over their shoulders until dawn.

"Why?" Maya said. "Why did they attack us?"

"I don't know. Maybe they didn't recognize us as part of the group. Maybe they don't serve the Green Knight."

"They threw themselves on top of me, Gavriel. I couldn't move. Why did they leave us with them? They shouldn't have, shouldn't have …"

Gavriel felt the weight of guilt over him. They had neither food nor clothes. Their backpacks were abandoned in the village of antlers. Dying in that land was now a real and frightening option. They shivered in the fog and dew. The Search no longer seemed the most important thing. Gavriel took Maya's hand in his.

"I'm so sorry. Let's get out of here. Let's go home."

They had a few things left: Maya's knife, the compass. With the intermittent rain that drenched them, the worst was the loss of their waterproof jackets. *At least*, Gavriel thought, *we still have boots*. The compass marked a constant point that might or might not be that of the north. Making a broad detour to avoid the settlement of the previous night, they began to retrace their steps. If they could reach the tribe of the blind god, they would be safe. From there they could find the exit to Mount Ossa and the real Tasmania.

They walked along a meadow that bordered a watercourse between two of the high peaks and suddenly discovered a band of riders coming over a hill in their direction. They jumped from the grass to the submerged cover of the nearby river. The group rode hairy and strong beasts, wore brightly coloured paint on their faces and carried tall spears. Some of them waved banners with images that were variations on the theme of the leonine snake and the tall human figure with deer antlers. Men and women were well armed with sharp pieces of silex from which terrible wounds could be imagined. Gavriel had never known a terror like that, submerged in the water while the riders marched a few hundred metres away. Next to him, Maya's energy was waning from cold, exposure and fear.

They waited for an hour, shivering until they were convinced that the party was gone. Gavriel knew that if they didn't warm up, they would faint from hypothermia. He managed to light a poor fire with the help of Maya, using the flint that the two guides had taught them to recognize among the stones on the slopes. They took care to hide it with a hole dug in the ground and surrounded by stones. The flame warmed their feet and hands, but the wet clothes stuck to their chest without drying out.

"I'm so cold," Maya said.

"Maybe I should have signalled to them," said Gavriel. "They carried the banner of the blind god. We could have asked for blankets or food."

"In France, it was always cold."

"Yes, you told me …"

"That's why I wanted to travel through Asia, because of the heat," Maya continued without listening.

"Maya …?"

The woman's eyes stared at the sad flame of the fire.

"What's wrong with you?"

Maya did not answer.

At dawn, they cautiously resumed walking. They had learned that they were in danger and that the welcoming of the tribe of the blind god was the exception rather than the rule. And still, despite the fear and anxiety for Maya and himself, Gavriel felt alive. He was looking at the secret scaffolding of the universe, seeing its pieces fit and move with permission to break all natural laws. Who had witnessed something like this before? The tribes of that fold of the world seemed unaware of where they were. Only Maya and he could look at the deepest dimension and connect the two opposite ends of the equation of creation: Tasmania on one side and, on the other, the green chapel. Perhaps the Man Under Contract was selfish for feeling like that, and perhaps he should have given priority to the welfare of Maya, but he did not. He would have time, later, to regret it.

During the next day, it became clear that they were lost. The compass, reliable until that moment, began to spin out of control in the morning. Gavriel and Maya already knew by then that they were not on the way back. The landscape was stranger and more inhospitable than the one they had travelled at the beginning. They had been in the mountains for more than a week and fatigue had set in their very bones. Every dawn they rose already exhausted from nights that provided neither rest nor ease.

"We have to find people, even if it's risky," said Gavriel, and Maya just nodded, defeated.

As if Gavriel's words had conjured it up, that afternoon they reached a village. Unlike everything they had seen so far, the houses were built from stout adobe bricks, solid low structures of tiny doors and windows. There were only eight or ten of them, lined up on the sides of a street which had no gravel or drain. The road and houses lead into a perfectly conical hill, uniform and covered by short green grass. Although natural in appearance, the size, layout and the very aura of the land made the hill look like an inhabited construct. Gavriel knew that this was the green chapel.

The only occupants of the village appeared to be a group of elderly women who looked out from the doorjambs to see them arrive. The travellers stumbled to the centre of the street and dropped against one of the adobe walls. Maya shivered; Gavriel was shaking. The women whispered inside the buildings but Gavriel had no strength to attend to what they said. They finally appeared, covered with veils and headpieces that revealed only eyes and patches of aged skin. One of them, chattering in yet another unknown language, invited them to enter the house, and there they warmed themselves while the matron rotated in a slow and comfortable dance around the fire, producing spoons, bowls and food. They spent the entire afternoon sipping the woman's bitter soup with a stupor that was born in their legs, climbed along their backs and stuck to their spirits. Gavriel made a gesture with his fingers, imitating two antlers and pointing toward the hill. The woman laughed with that laugh the elderly use, a long and shallow laugh. Then she sat beside him and with a stick drew a story on the dirt of the floor, starting with the tall figure of the knight. She talked incessantly in an incomprehensible language, but Gavriel and Maya understood from her speech what was it that ruled that place.

The Green Knight was a terrible but indispensable master. It governed in the rhythm of the harvests, in the fortuity of the animals. If it was beset with any affliction, the grass dried and died; if it was enraged, storms and lightning struck the cliffs. But the knight provided, and its chapel was the green heart that beat and brought life. Progress was its adversary, and the green kingdom lingered crouched in the wild corners of our world from where it laid bridges to this land of his.[30]

"Samael?" Gavriel asked.

"Samael," said the old woman clicking her tongue and laughing again.

Behind the tall silhouette with antlers she drew other lines, a blacksmith's anvil cleverly traced so that it seemed to be hidden and protected by the knight.

---

[30] The most reflective reading of the legend of the Green Knight (also called Bercilak or Berkilak in his courtly dimension) since his appearance in the Arthurian cycle has been as a representation of the ungovernable spirit of nature and the implacable opposition to man. It symbolizes the measure by which the human being is evaluated and is an unyielding judge who determines who is worthy of inheriting the land and its wealth. The concept of the Green Man as avatar of the natural world (Gaia) precedes this version and is as old as human reason.

They stayed in that house, lying by the fire and rocked to sleep in a grass bed by the snoring of the woman and the sounds of the night outside. Gavriel spoke with Maya.

"I have to leave at dawn. I have to enter the mound. You can wait here. The women will accommodate you until I return."

"Don't leave me here, Gavriel."

"You'll be safe."

"You won't come back."

"Yes, I will come back. But this time I need to go. The knight is one of the seven names on my list. I need to find them all."

Gavriel woke when the sun touched the line of the horizon. Maya slept. He got up slowly and went out of the longhouse. Outside, some of the old women who lived in the village were waiting. They approached him respectfully, raising their hands. One smeared resin on his forehead, another tied a hemp rope to his waist, and the third delivered a vigorous slap that left Gavriel's face tingling.[31]

Maya came to the door and without saying a word approached to take his hand. Together they walked to the conical hill. They circled the perimeter, looking for an entry, and found a hole that pointed its dark mouth into the sky. It was a narrow tunnel, its entrance a circle of impeccable circumference. Gavriel shined with the flashlight but only wet soil and roots were visible.

"It's here."

Maya looked down in horror.

"That is the den of an animal."

"No. It's the entrance to the green chapel. Look at it. The knight

---

[31] The women prepared the Man Under Contract in a ritual that, by unknown means, had leaked centuries ago into the Dark Ages of the world to inspire the investiture of knighthood, namely: the religious anointment, the girdling of the white belt and the accolade that symbolized the last offense the knight would leave unanswered.

awaits inside."

"Gavriel …"

"I'll be back soon, I promise," Gavriel said, and that was the only promise he kept.

He gave a quick hug to the woman and got on his knees at the entrance of the burrow. He disappeared inside as if swallowed by the mouth of a gargantua. The earth squeezed his shoulders on both sides. He advanced as much as he could, but within a few metres the feeling of suffocation and fear stopped him. He looked back under his armpit, the only space the narrowness of the tunnel left him. There, the light was an almost perfect circle. The ground lowered at an increasingly acute angle, and the air warmed around his head. He could not breathe.

"Maya!"

"Gavriel! Are you ok?"

Hearing the woman's voice calmed him.

"Yes, I'm going to try and move a little further."

He advanced a few metres with great effort. His flashlight illuminated the entrails of the earth. Sparks of claustrophobia danced before his eyes. He wanted to go back; he couldn't. This was not a chapel, it was a hole in the ground, increasingly narrow. He looked back again. The light was gone.

"Maya? Maya!" he shouted and did not hear any answer in the damp earth.

Gavriel was alone.

Further down, the tunnel suddenly ended and Gavriel dropped into a cave. The floor and walls appeared mouldy, soft and moist. Water oozed everywhere. Gavriel advanced, and a diffused light opened to another, wider chamber: the green chapel. At its centre, the knight waited, sitting on a throne of branches and ferns. It was a towering fiend, very tall, covered with the antler rack and the deer skull that served as a helmet, armour of bark and moss which gave it a willowy and flexible quality. It smelled like grass. Everything smelled like grass.

Gavriel approached. There were restless eyes under the bascinet of bone.

"I've come. I've come as you asked."

Silence.

"Are you the spirit of the earth?"

"The earth has no spirit, Gwalchmei."

"Who are you then?"

"I am one of the pauper angels. My chore is to direct you to the blind god. That is the craftsman who created the world and cares about its work."

"Did you create this other land?"

The knight suddenly laughed under the mandible of the deer skull, as if Gavriel had told a colossal joke. Even its laughter smelled of thickets and dirt.

"Only the artisan creates. Neither I nor mine could achieve a living world. He made this world and entrusted it to me. It is the last refuge of the green, Gwalchmei, and the last corner that will remain alive at earth's death."

"Who is Gwalchmei? I am not him."

"Yes you are; you all are."

The voice of the spectre resounded in his soul. Gavriel appealed to the courage he had saved for this and made his request. The knight never moved.

"Guide me then. I seek the blind god."

"No, you just think you do. You want to understand the world, but you are laden by the image of the Christian god, the same one that brought you to me the first time."

"I have never been here. I am not Gwalchmei," said Gavriel to no avail.

"You came looking then, like you do now, thinking you understood. The Pandragon and the servants of Garduel also thought so. They presumed they had the right to dominate the world, one granted by that messiah they hung on the cross. If you are an image of God, if that God is perfect, answer me then, Gwalchmei, why does your race suffer? Why does my chapel wilt? Is God deficient? Is God evil?"

The entity waited but Gavriel had no answer.

"No. Simply, it is a false god."

The knight's face had an equine quality under the skull. Restless lips were flehmening and gave life to the dead bone.

"You forgot the blind god. You supplanted him with invented images of custom-made deities. That's why the world dies; that's why nature betrays you. The martial opposition of your race to the world and its essence emanates from the affiliation to the manufactured god. You took sides and believed that it was your duty to break the world. The great irony is that you do not tame nature, nature tames you, and will continue doing so until you fall into your allotted place.

"In the old days, the pagan days, Man did not doubt us. We conveyed divinity and this was accepted. There was no evidence or empiricism, nor separation between one world and the other.[32]

"Understand this, Gwalchmei: it has not been given to you; it does not belong to you. The blind god comes to claim what is his.

"And so, we come to this day, today. This chapel of mine is tribunal and court of law. Here I judge Man. I impose all evidence. I pass sentence. Your passage from outside to this, my chapel, is a reflection of your mortality. By coming here, you agree to leave behind what

---

[32] The gods of paganism dictated the patterns of human behavior until the arrival of monotheism and abstract deities proposed a discovery of inner truth that did not require sacrifices or sexual liturgies. Where the pagans abandoned themselves to supernatural manipulations, the new religions claimed that man was able to solve the mystery of the world by himself through devotion and contemplation.

you know and enter into the unknown. Get ready, Gwalchmei, your judgement begins."

The knight suddenly stood up in all its tremendous stature and raised its hands. The smell of moss filled the room. Gavriel clenched his teeth and put his hands to his head, fearing the worst, but the knight's judgement was quick and painless.

"Here I mark you, Gwalchmei. You survive our second meeting and still learn nothing. Abandon this realm. Go back to the world and continue your search. Find the rest of the pauper angels. Find the craftsman. You will achieve nothing but ache and sorrow.

"I give you my brand, which is not nought because it is both brand and guide. In return, I must keep something of yours, Gwalchmei."

Gavriel felt a chill. "Keep something? Keep what?"

"You know what."

Gavriel emerged from the darkness of the hole into daylight. He was crawling, spitting black earth, and trembled, covering his eyes. He wanted to stand up but only managed to roll down the gentle slope of the hill. The sun had fallen somewhat, and Gavriel did not know how much time he had spent in the chapel. The dialogue with the Green Knight had been brief, or perhaps not, because he felt his flesh and marrow exhausted. He finally got up and staggered, taking short steps toward the village. There, the women were still at the doors, covered with their veils.

"Maya! Maya! Where are you?"

The old women muttered, restless among themselves, pointing to the foreigner's face and the guardian's invisible mark. Gavriel looked for the woman who had welcomed them last night but it was difficult to distinguish her among the brown dresses and grey heads half covered with cloth.

"Maya! Where is the girl?"

One of the women signalled in the distance, counting with her fingers.

"Is she gone? Where did she go?"

The old woman spoke at a rapid pace and a word was repeated, "mokashuhar".[33] Maya was not gone. She had been taken.

"Mokashuhar," said the woman again and indicated marks on the ground.

Gavriel saw prints of foot and hoof that had not been there the day before. They covered the entire avenue, outlined one on top of another in the damp earth. He recalled the mounted party they had avoided in the meadow and, forgetting the fatigue and the mark of the knight on him, started running.

Gavriel had spent a lot of time in moors and mountains, but tracking is a specialized skill and he didn't have it. He lost the trail half a dozen times, but the number of riders was so large and the land so virgin that it always resurfaced. At nightfall, he snuggled in a hollow and spent the hours stiff and half sleeping until dawn allowed him to distinguish the tracks again.

At noon he saw them from the top of a pass: about thirty riders painted with bright colours and waving the ensigns of the horned man. They were camped around bonfires in which they cooked cakes and boiled cauldrons, with the mounts fasten by the bridles to ropes laid down on the ground.

Gavriel, who was a mediocre fighter, came down from that pass alienated and willing to be run through the guts with spears if necessary. The riders saw him arrive and clamoured in loud voices. When he did not stop, several of them put darts in wooden spear-throwers and released with a great movement of the arms. The missiles fell a few steps ahead of Gavriel on the grass he was running over but he did not stop. A shaved-headed man covered in yellow paint rushed towards him, twirling a stone axe and spitting, hoping to intimidate the foreigner. Gavriel took out his hunting knife. The

[33] Mokashuhar is most likely the root of a term that had crossed over under the form "Moksha", indicating, in the Hindu and Buddhist tradition, various forms of emancipation, enlightenment, liberation, and release. The Green Knight thought of his harsh realm as a purer alternative to the painful cycle of death and rebirth of the real world because it was one step closer to the engine of creation.

warrior shouted but jumped aside, repelled perhaps by the invisible evidence of the knight's mark. Another rider stood in front of him with a sword made of crude silex but he also gave way to Gavriel's fevered march.

"Maya! Maya!"

The tribe surrounded him, and Gavriel slashed the air with the knife but no one approached. The warriors lowered their weapons and just looked.

"Maya!"

In a pile by the fire, he found the clothes, out of place with their folds of impermeable fabric in that primitive realm.

"What have you done with her?"

A young woman crouched next to others watched him more closely. She tilted her head curiously. She was plaiting strands of hide with her hands and wore a thick mantle of leather as if she still felt the cold of Paris.

"Maya …"

Of Maya, only the eyes, which were Asian and unrepeatable, still remained. The rest had been consumed and integrated into the primitive matter of the green world. The new woman spoke in an unknown language, but perhaps a leftover of her original nature remained in her because she regarded Gavriel with sparks of remembrance. He took her hand and tried to get her out of the circle. The younger warriors burned with fury at the sight of the foreigner, his ridiculous clothes and his stupid voice, but what the tribe saw was a stranger with the mark of the horned god; that god was the earth and the earth would not be stabbed.

Maya who was not Maya looked at Gavriel and resisted, confused by those two incomprehensible natures that beat inside her. Then she returned to her place to squat and continue braiding.

Gavriel waited with the tribe that afternoon and all night. He watched Maya's silhouette, diluted more and more in the new person. The tribe ended up ignoring the foreigner. The morning came, and they picked up camp. Gavriel followed the troop of riders while he could and finally he watched them get lost in the prairie and the endless mountains of the green world.

The Man Under Contract finished his story while the fire died.

"That is … What's that? A fable? An allegory?" Chao asked.

"It's a story, a story that I've told you as it happened or as I remember it, around the fire."

"What happened to the girl, Maya? What really happened to her?"

The Man Under Contract took a handful of ash, already cold, and blew into it. The dust dissipated sadly in the Tibetan dawn, leaving nothing behind.

"And why have you told me all of this? You don't know me or know who I am."

Gavriel laughed without humour. "No, but things have happened, uncomfortable things that I can't get out of my head. Tonight, I had to share what happened in the chapel because the Search touches us all in a different way, William. I don't know how it will be for you, but what I do know is that it has already touched you. I know the signs."

The Man Under Contract put out the embers of the fire and got into his sleeping bag. The night was ending. When Chao turned to open his backpack he heard the last sentence of that conversation.

"Besides, you seem trustworthy. I never told your predecessor anything like this."

When dawn came Chao thought he heard the Man Under Contract picking up his things and, just in case, he pretended to sleep. The urgency was gone. He knew where he was going and where he could find him again. Then he slept without pretending to, and when he woke up a second time the sun was shining higher and he was alone next to the stone *mani*. He spent the morning crossing the hills of the pass and continuing towards Tongren. In a ravine, in the middle of the high plateau where the nomads drank their fresh milk from the yaks and charged the portable batteries with solar panels mounted on the central pole of their canvas tents, Chao spent his last night outdoors, and the next day he finally arrived at the bustling city on the other side of the grassland. He crossed the last bridge, walked on asphalt roads and looked for a hotel. When he found a reliable signal for his phone, he made a call to the client.

33°41'N/142°11'W
California: Diversions and Leaps

Mr Cohan received the call at about four o'clock in the morning, Pacific Coast time. He was awake before the telephone rang and simply rolled over in the large, empty bed of the Four Seasons hotel in San Diego to answer. Since the accident in Cambodia, he had trouble sleeping and spent the nights in an insomniac trance. During the day he felt consumed, withered, irritable. At dusk, he fell into bed exhausted and, still unable to fall asleep, repeated his cycle.

"Cohan here," he said in that style that was so very American.

"Mr Cohan? Can you hear me? This is William Chao."

The phone signal was dismal and the slight time lag, noticeable enough for Chao's questions and his answers to overlap, was irritating for both of them. After many false starts and interruptions, Cohan understood all that was necessary and hung up. His eyes failed him. In the darkness of the room he thought shadows moved. He looked again. Nothing; just a room that was too large. He had been in California for years and was still lodging at hotels because he had abandoned his home when he left New York and was reluctant to create a new one, but the forlornness of commercial rooms was becoming more harrowing since his son's death.

Sitting in his empty bed and feeling undecided, he concluded, as always, that he would consult with Blake.

B. Cohan was a native of New York, first the state, then the metropolitan area. His religious devotion had placed him in great relations with the Jewish business community of the city but a dire divorce and a rift with the rest of his family, including the deceased Abel whom he had not seen in the two years prior to his death, had coincided with the expansion of his catering company in California, so he ended up settling across the country. That was where he had his first contact with the Church, via a series of casual talks with other businessmen who praised unambiguously the serene capacity of that spiritual organization. From the Church came the only consolation Cohan had known since his son's accident. Conversations with his wife and Abel's sister always ended in recriminations and threats. Isolated and constantly jumping from one coast to the other, nothing but the regular sessions with Blake gave him rest from the ever-present memory of the death of his firstborn.

Cohan waited patiently for daybreak. His back bothered him. Bad sleep and much travel aggravated the normal aches of age. Later he rose, made his calls, answered correspondence and finished lunch, and then drove to the headquarters of the Positivist Church. The first time he had seen the building, he was reminded of his hotel, decorated with cosy armchairs in the lobby and large glass doors at the entrance, but cold and soulless. It was only when inside that the details of a tenacious purpose, of a sublime mission, could be appreciated. Pamphlets of profuse content and detail, catalogues of compelling typography, authoritative greetings and handshakes.

Cohan was there because he had the desperate certainty that he had wasted his life. Not in the professional sphere, where he enjoyed means and position. Perhaps not in the personal one, although the isolation he suffered from his family was a fair punishment for his failures as father and husband. But in what was really important, in what remained when all men were alone and helpless on their deathbed, that was where time had been wasted. Fifty years. It could be that not everything was his fault. As a child, his mother had enrolled him in Torah classes and his innate spirituality had done the rest, leading him into a conduct defined by passion for Jewish orthodoxy. It could be, but it didn't matter because the result was the same. Fifty years; a lifetime following an incorrect religion.

Now time was scarce, now that the doctors were finding polyps of worrisome shape, and Cohan suffered the indignity of roaming the halls of pristine private clinics, covered only with a backless gown and feeling the intrusion of endoscopic cameras into the rectum. But he had hope, the one the Church promised him. Where Judaism, like all ancient religions, was full of confusing instructions and the progress towards the arms of God was a quagmire of impossible direction, the Church offered a program of exemplary clarity, one that Cohan's keen entrepreneurial mind found tremendously elegant in its simplicity.

It was religion, but religion of mercantilist clairvoyance, a clear system of assets and duties. Because of his fifty years of deadweight precepts and indoctrination, Cohan was sceptical at first. After apostatizing, he lost friends and respect in the petrified environment of Jewish New York, but he had won new ones, and the dynamic California did not lose sleep thinking about sermons in the desert that occurred in the distant past. Like its precious initiatives in Silicon

Valley, the West Coast offered scientific spirituality, quantifiable salvation.

Cohan showed his card at reception and filled in the information for the session.

"Your sponsor will pick you up in a moment," said the receptionist.

Then came Blake, an overweight thirty-something with Cohan's file in his hand. They greeted each other and together went to their room. Blake dressed in the formal but not too fashionable manner of the American mid-level professional: a bluish shirt of a cut which was too wide, and somewhat bulky chino trousers. On the way, Blake's demeanour was sober in consideration of Cohan's mourning. They sat down. Blake served refreshments and Cohan strengthened himself for the session. "Self-discovery" would have been a less aggressive term but the Church did not believe in euphemisms and prominently brandished the idea that personal development demanded forceful action. So meetings like this lasted for a Marathonian session of two, three and up to four hours. During that time, associates were subjected to a barrage of merciless questions and had to explain in insufferable detail what various imagined situations made them feel. The pace of the interrogation was brisk, in order to provoke an intuitive response and reveal inner enlightenment.[34] The more the session progressed and the more exhausted the associate became, the more artless the answers.

Blake manoeuvred the session around the Cambodian episode without

---

[34] The Positivist Church considers that the essence of benign immortal beings is enclosed in the human psyche. The ascending progression ladder of its indoctrination is intended to allow conscious access to that essence. The organization publicly argues that the founders of other predominant religions were outstanding individuals whose natural talent allowed them to attain this true spirit independently. But, the Church is quick to clarify, without proper training, Jesus, Muhammad and Buddha were unable to correctly identify the source of their revelation, resulting in the various heresies now established under each of them. The Church thus manages to make most of the world's religions alterations of its dogma and therefore dependent on it.

In reality, the orthodoxy of the Church is a scarcely original variation of the Gnostic myths about the transcendent spirit that is caught in earthly forms and the doctrinal efforts that are necessary to overcome such a mundane dimension.

naming it at any time, as he had done during the previous weeks. Cohan mentioned Tibet and his indecision about how to proceed. Blake asked for permission and connected the recorder. During the next hour, Cohan talked about the Man Under Contract, about his conviction that he was responsible for his son's death, and his occasional and vivid fantasies of revenge. Asked about it, Cohan acknowledged there was a report full of details he expected to receive once the detective he had hired got out of the paramo where he seemed to be stuck.

Blake listened to everything carefully, taking notes and not hurrying Mr Cohan. He knew well the story of his son Abel. What he and his superiors in the Church hierarchy wanted to discover was the story of the Man Under Contract.

Chao arrived in Hong Kong on a Thursday, three days after leaving the Amdo grasslands. The last four hours of walking had been on asphalt, descending from the heights of the village of Gyalwo towards the valley below.

Tongren was an ugly city. To the original monastery and the surrounding village, Chinese avarice had added a small suburb and boring constructions fully devoid of charm. The piece that most disfigured the landscape was a bridge of modern design suspended across the river. The inhabitants of Tongren were proud of the piece, but both style and size seemed excessive for the light traffic it endured.

Overall, Tongren Monastery (Rebkong was its Tibetan name) seem less impressive than Labrang had been. It had other problems. The main facade had been remodelled in colours that were too modern and looked false and over-embellished. With huge trucks loaded with gravel bypassing him, the surface of the asphalt cooking his feet full of blisters, and the accumulated humidity of three days in his clothes, Chao stumbled into the first hotel that offered lodging with an en suite bathroom. He delayed writing the report he owed his client enough to shower twice. The first he did with his clothes on, rubbing them with soap to try to clean off some of the mud and grime.

Later, with muscles still resentful from the days of walking, he wrote and sent ten pages with the details of the trip in the journalistic style that Cecilia had taught him. It took longer than he thought to put the history of Tasmania on paper. Chao's head knew that it was a ridiculous fiction of magical doors, but hearing it told by the light of the fire in the emptiness of the Himalayas and recited in the Man Under Contract's possessed tone gave it another dimension. Chao read it again. Maybe there had been a woman named Maya. Was she lost in the folds of a world that cannot be seen? Of course not.

Chao sent the message with his attached report. The answer came almost immediately, with a "ping" that startled him. "Please return to Hong Kong. The contract is concluded." It was early morning on the West Coast. Cohan had been awake, perhaps waiting for the document. Chao offered to continue working on the contract. It would not be difficult to locate the traveller in the short alleys of Tongren. "That won't be necessary" was the only answer he got. With a yawn of deep exhaustion, Chao opened a new window on the screen of the computer and began planning the slow exit from Amdo and the way home.

Cecilia picked him up at the airport and drove him to his apartment.

"Everything all right? I know you don't like going to the continent all that much."

"All good," said Chao just a little more curtly than he intended.

Cecilia waited to hear more details, but Chao looked out the window at Kowloon's congested avenues. He seemed exhausted, and his sister did not press him. They said goodbye in the car, double-parked next to Chao's house.

"There's quite a bit of work piled up but if you want to take a day off, I understand."

"No, I'll be at the office tomorrow."

"Very well, see you there," said Cecilia, but Chao had already gotten out of the car.

Chao felt her gaze following him all the way until the door closed behind him. In the solitude of his room, the detective dreamed that night of the green chapel and its guardian, whom he pictured dressed in tree bark and an animal skull for a helmet with a flowing aventail of small bones. In the dream, the tunnel in the earth closed behind him and the knight's voice moved in the dark, looking for him.

William Chao and Cecilia Chao had the opportunity to catch up the next morning in the office of their investigation agency. The woman waited with a cup in her hand when the detective arrived. Chao knew that his sister was impatient to speak. He put down the bag, took off his jacket and, when he sat down, Cecilia couldn't wait any longer.

"I read the report to the client, Liam."

"Did you?"

"Yes, you put me in copy."

"That's right. I was very tired those days. Maybe I should make a cleaner version and send it again."

"Maybe you should write it all over again. What did that man tell you in the mountains? That story makes no sense."

"I haven't said it's true. It's what he believes."

"I understand that, but the way it read … I still don't know how you let him discover you."

Chao ran his hand over his head. Tibet seemed distant. He made an effort to evoke open spaces, rain and cold. He felt nothing. Outside, the air was warm and humid, and the streets of Hong Kong hectic.

"I don't know, Cecilia. It was a story, but it was something else. And now it's an itch that I didn't know I had that has woken up to irritate me."

"Let's blame it on the environment, your tiredness and, I suppose, that man's charisma. But that's it. The secrets of the world are not kept by homeless people travelling across Asia. Tomorrow I will send the last invoice to the client, and no later than Monday you need to start on Mr Zhao's assignment. He has been waiting for you since you left for China."

Chao nodded without paying much attention. Cecilia got up and returned to her table and her papers, oblivious to the story of Tasmania. Her brother looked at her, giving up on being understood. She had not dreamed of the green chapel.

Chao fulfilled the Zhao assignment, and that of the Tian family and several others. He spent days sitting in his car taking pictures. He recorded conversations. He wrote reports. Each case ended in a clean and neat way, with Cecilia putting the corresponding receipt in an envelope and with the satisfactory *click-click* of payments being made into the agency's account. Old cases were closed and new ones opened but, for Chao, the Tibetan contract was still throbbing. Cohen paid his fees and even sent a thank you message, and still Chao could not let it go.

Then he began to notice the coincidences. At first, they were trivial. He met a Mexican couple at a party. The woman's name was Maya, which apparently was not an exclusively Japanese name. This Maya told him that she had been in Hong Kong so long that she felt she was becoming Chinese.

"Asia ends up absorbing you," she said in a casual tone that left Chao cold.

Days later, while searching for a volume of legal references at the bookshop in Hennessy Road, he found displayed on a table next to each other and without any apparent connection a copy of Plato's *Timaeus* and a thin tome entitled *Gawain and the Green Knight*. At the gym he had a conversation with an Australian expatriate. He turned out to be a native of Devonport, the city that the Man Under Contract had visited in Tasmania. When Chao asked about Cradle Mountain and Mount Ossa, as they were both sweating on stationary bicycles, the Australian man responded by shaking his head.

"I have visited only once. The journey is hard. That place is a wild reserve, another world, you know?"[35]

---

[35] The detective did not perceive the numerological significance of the meetings that occurred on the third, sixth and ninth day respectively since his return to Hong Kong.

Chao discovered he may be suffering from an affliction called apophenia[36], and yet that didn't explain what he felt. There was a new resonance in the world, something he had never noticed before, and the Man Under Contract had tuned Chao to detect it with the effect of a diapason. The detective vibrated now, guided by a contagious frequency, and could not stop.

A month after he returned from Tibet, and after thirty nights intermittently dreaming of the claustrophobic access to the green chapel and the threatening figure that awaited him inside, William Chao woke up at four in the morning, drenched in sweat, and made a decision.

Chao left on a Monday. Cecilia received a very brief note. "Flying to the United States. I'll see you when I return. Please take care of the pending cases."

During the following weeks, Cecilia fought to contain the anxiety she felt because of the limited flow of Liam's messages. "I am in Chicago." "On my way to California", said her brother vaguely; her brother who had always been punctilious and detailed. Cecilia attended the agency's cases as best she could, but fieldwork was not her forte and the most she could do was to close the investigations Liam had left half done.

"What was he thinking? He has left everything pending! Customers will start calling any moment with complaints."

Bryan nodded from the kitchen without saying anything. Bryan had not gotten along with Liam since he and Cecilia began dating more than a decade ago, and the relationship remained the same now that they had been married for years. The British remoteness of her husband collided with her brother's sincere disposition. Cecilia had used arguments, pressure and manipulation with both of them until the mutual aversion, never completely erased, became a dull background hum with which the three could live.

---

[36] As already mentioned. The condition is more common than it may seem.

"William has never been one for giving explanations," Bryan said. "But, if I'm honest, I think it's your fault. I don't understand why you have to work with him at the agency. Your previous job was perfectly adequate."

Cecilia raised her hands. "Let's not start with that again," she said, exasperated.

The air of the apartment became thick with matrimonial tension. There was a loud clanging of plates and glasses, which Cecilia thought deliberate, as Bryan cleaned up the table.

"All I'm saying is it's not like Liam to do something like this."

"I no longer know what is and what is not what your brother would do," said Bryan, looking out the kitchen door. "Did I tell you that before leaving he spent an hour talking to me about mathematics and Greek triangles?"

"We should go to the police," she insisted.

"What can we tell them? Your brother is not missing. He keeps writing to you."

"Four-word messages! Not a single call since he left. And you saw him, how he was behaving."

"Give him a little more time to put his affairs in order. He'll be back"

Then communication stopped completely. For two weeks Cecilia waited to hear from her brother. On the third, she contacted the police first and later the embassy in America. Liam's passport had passed through customs control and had not left the country yet. He had forty days left on his ninety-day visa before the authorities took action and he was declared illegal.

On his landing card, Liam had included the address of a hotel in Illinois as his first destination but he only stayed there for a few days. Cecilia spoke to the manager by phone and got no details. The track was remote and cold, impossible to follow.

Despite Bryan's protests, Cecilia packed a light bag, booked a flight and prepared to leave in search of her brother. The night before her departure, Cecilia dealt with last-minute details and Bryan, a fervent student of modern history, watched a documentary about World War II in the living room. The doorbell of their home in Kowloon rang and Bryan got up from the couch. Cecilia remembered her brother's erratic behaviour, and the restlessness it had caused her to see him that way came back in full force.

"Don't open," she said suddenly and stopped her husband halfway, attentive to premonitions and signs.

"It might be important. It may be about William."

"Don't open," she repeated, but her conviction was gone.

Bryan chatted on the intercom in quiet tones. On the square and grey screen, a face appeared, gaunt due to the distortion of the electronic eye.

"A friend of William, he says."

The interval until the stranger reached their floor was a nervous delay for Cecilia. When Bryan opened the door and the lean man entered, she recognized, as she knew she would, the Man Under Contract.

Bryan introduced himself and Gavriel did the same. Cecilia refused to shake his hand. They had tea just to comply with the formalities of urbanity, but it was a tense ceremony, intended to give their hands something to do while the three waited.

"Chao … Liam, he gave this address. He asked me to come."

"When? How long since you saw him?"

"Some time ago. Weeks. I have had complications getting here since I left Ogasawara Island."

Liam had been right, Cecilia thought: the man had a slightly possessed countenance, like a shaman or a man touched by an oligophrenic aura. An involuntary alarm rumbled in her spine every time she crossed eyes with him.

"Where is my brother?"

Gavriel looked at the husband, perhaps asking silently for support, but the Englishman was visibly uncomfortable and sat on the periphery of the conversation.

"I'll explain everything. I just ask that you wait until I'm done to ask your questions."

"Maybe that's something you should tell the police," she said.

"No, no police."

"The more reason to call them," Bryan replied and started to get up.

Cecilia appeased him with a wave of her hand.

"Answer the question," said the woman.

"I met William Chao in Tibet. We had the opportunity to speak there at length."

"We know that. Where is my brother?" Cecilia insisted.

"He stayed behind, in a California."

Cecilia was surprised by the use of the indefinite article but she said nothing. Over cups of cold tea, the Man Under Contract told his story.

"I woke up in a white room …"

Gavriel woke up in a white room.

His mouth was dry, and his tongue felt too big to fit inside. It was the feeling that follows cough medication or really bad drugs. He didn't know until much later where he was but, looking backwards, he could have guessed just by the somewhat affected accent of people he saw during his time in captivity and the prevalent tan marks left by watches and sunglasses.

Gavriel got up, saw three walls, a large chamber with different levels that contained a bed, sofa, desk and living-room table. The air conditioner hummed on the ceiling out of reach. The fourth wall was partly a ceiling-to-floor glass pane so thick that it deformed the silhouettes of the objects at the other side and showed a hall with a staircase at the end. There was no door, or maybe the glass slid to the side. Gavriel understood that he was caged. Without any sense of urgency, he approached the glass pane and pounded on it because that was, after all, the fitting behaviour of a prisoner. The glass barely vibrated. The fear that the Man Under Contract could feel was always tempered for two reasons. One was his faith in the manifest destiny[37] of the Search. The other was the constant sense of synchrony of which he was a hostage, where every event happened in order to draw him nearer to the resolution of his task.

Gavriel sat down to think.

From Tongren, he had travelled to Xining, one of those cities in the Chinese interior that had grown and continued to grow, propelled by the thrust of the country's healthy economy. Xining was the door to the natural resources of the Tibetan plateau and, in the four hours it had taken to travel there from the dilapidated bus station where he boarded, Gavriel had seen the desire for Chinese development in each dump truck and each excavator that stripped the mountains bare in full view of the road, leaving horrible tears in the landscape. Then the road gave way to bland highways and brick buildings lining up at the side of the road, and the Man Under Contract said goodbye to Tibet and everything that had happened there. The suburbs of Xining were a messy and soiled disorder, but the downtown area was dazzling, full of modern constructions and cosmopolitan artifices. Having just arrived from the most remote areas of Amdo, Gavriel found himself fascinated by the neons and colours in the windows of fast-food restaurants. Tibetan women had been demure and dressed discreetly, somewhat dishevelled. In Xining, the new economy made it possible to find teenagers and mature women parading vainly in the same fashion as in Shanghai and Beijing.

---

[37] The Man Under Contract had borrowed the concept from nineteenth century nationalist theory, ("And that claim is by the right of our manifest destiny to overspread and to possess the whole of the continent which Providence has given us for the development of the great experiment of liberty and federated self-government entrusted to us") and applied it to this, his particular odyssey. The original idea gives the United States the role of a country chosen by God to become a superior nation and, in the same way, the Man Under Contract assumed that his mission was inevitable and irreplaceable.

Gavriel still got some looks but not as many as during his wandering in the south. The city had a good traffic of travellers looking for trains to Lhasa and the westernmost provinces of Xinjiang so they didn't seem surprised to find foreigners' faces. Gavriel suspected that there was also a certain refined pride among the inhabitants of Xining, a statement of sophistication which said "this is nothing new for us" when acknowledging his presence.

He stayed in a hostel that occupied the twelfth floor of a tall building. Inside, the atmosphere of bohemian comradeship was the same as in the South East Asian circuit that Gavriel knew so well, but the venue was unusual. Every time he looked out the window and saw the city, growing out of control and rabidly populous, he remembered that China always did things in its own way and degree.

He wrote in his notebook and read *The Demon Princes* in the common room. At dusk, he went out to walk down the street and look for a restaurant. Then there was a prick in the neck and tingling that ran from the point of puncture to his heart, from where it was pumped to his arms, head and legs. He felt as if bathed in honey, strangely comfortable, and fell to the side without even looking back. Some hands held him before he hit the ground, and then nothing.

It had been in a large meeting room, where five people sitting around a conference table had decided Gavriel's fate.

"The risk is limited. No associate may have contact with the Man Under Contract. Only the security body will have permission, and that is a separate legal entity. We have conditioned a basement to welcome him," said a man with a vage military bearing, like that of a retired army officer.

"The risk is not limited. In fact, the risk is tremendous. Do you have any idea what this will do to the organization if it ever becomes known?" replied an elderly woman.

"I don't understand why I need to repeat this, but I will. There is a possibility, remote but feasible, that the story of the Man Under Contract is true. If we can get empirical evidence to justify the apparatus that our fifty years of history have built, any risk is worth it.”

“We’re talking about sneaking a citizen of a third country into the United States against his will,” said the woman.

“Chief Miller is convinced it can be done.”

“Chief Miller is limited by his military mindset, same as you are, and I wouldn’t trust him much.”

“Despite all the sermons, faith, holy wars, sacred constructions, despite five thousand years of religious history in this world, no one—*no one*—has ever produced viable proof of divine contact. We have a unique opportunity here. Are we going to let it escape us?”

A serious, well-dressed man in a blue suit stood up.

“The question is not what we risk. The question is, does this individual have the means to open a connection? We’re not talking about ghost sightings advertised in occult magazines or poor quality psychophonies. This is not the granulated video of an apparition we’re trying to clear up. We saw it in Macau; we have seen it again in Cambodia. There are half a dozen similar episodes to those in the Asian report, and this person always finds himself in the middle of them. It has attracted the attention of other organizations. It has attracted our attention. And someone is going to do something about it. Might he be a charlatan? Maybe, but he might also be the Rosetta stone that opens the gates of Heaven for us,” he said.

He took a document and signed using a heavy fountain pen.

“Approved.”

Although he did not lose patience, the hours passed slowly, and the reality of the confinement became more palpable for Gavriel. Why was he there? It had to do with the Search, maybe with Cambodia. Had it been the detective? Had he told him too much? He stirred restlessly. Since he began his journey, Gavriel knew that others had tried the same thing he was trying. None had succeeded, but perhaps someone out there was watching for everything that was related to the blind god.

Gavriel slept. When he woke up, he found his notebook on the table and the rest of his luggage in a closet. On the shelves, there was a collection of reference books. Everything he needed to keep looking for patterns and clues. He even recovered *The Demon Princes* and, lying in bed, read every chapter where Kirth Gersen had been a prisoner, and about his adventurous escapes. With the book flat on his chest, Gavriel felt the frustration of the captive. He was not the hero of a novella. There were no miraculous breakouts.

The cell lacked windows, but it did have a clock, and that night, with the electric lights off, Gavriel dreamed that Maya was coming to see him. She walked with both hands in her pockets, as he had seen her do on the beach, and approached to sit on the edge of the bed. Gavriel's mouth tasted like wet earth and, in the dream, it clogged his throat, drowning him. Maya ran her hand through his hair as she used to and spoke to him with that thickly accented French tone that seemed so incongruous in a Japanese person. After he woke up, as he always did in the middle of the night, he became determined to return to the green chapel and find the woman. In other places, the determination dissipated during the first waking hours and, when morning arrived, he settled into the routine of his mission, forgetting the good intentions of going back to Tasmania. In the white cell, unable to leave, they had taken away even the freedom to pretend that he could do it.

Two days after his capture, they finally came to see him. Two men and a woman walked down the stairs, dressed in well-cut suits and no tie. One of the men was plump and had the rubicund face of a preacher. The second man had grey hair, scars on his knuckles and the stocky constitution of a medieval stonemason. The woman was as tall as the men and intimidating in a military manner. The thick glass pane slid slowly to the side with a whirring sound. *Aha!* Gavriel thought, *that is how it opens*, and immediately realized he should be paying attention to the visitors instead. They entered the room and sat at the table without asking for permission. The man with the grey hair, accustomed to giving orders, indicated the last empty chair. Gavriel sat down as well.

"We have a few very simple questions for you. How you respond to them will determine how long you spend here. Do you understand?" said the man.

Gavriel looked from one to another, saying nothing.

The man with the grey hair turned to the woman. "Does he speak English? They told us he spoke English."

He repeated the phrase to Gavriel, more slowly.

"Yes," replied the Man Under Contract

The man with the grey hair signalled to the chubby man.

"Do you have, or have you had, the means to communicate directly with a higher reality?" said the preacher.

The Man Under Contract stayed silent, thinking about that. "Superior reality?"

"God, or whatever you want to call divinity."

"It is not possible to communicate with God."

"Why?"

"Because it's incomprehensible. There is no interaction between this world and the absolute world."

"Two thousand years of Catholic church contradict you. One thousand five hundred years of Islamic faith contradict you."

"They are all wrong," said Gavriel with disarming conviction.

"Yes, we know they are. But that does not mean that divinity does not exist."

"It does exist."

"But you just said it does not," said the pastor, gleefully poking holes in the logic of the prisoner.

"I said it is not possible to communicate with it."

"But if God created the universe, he must, as a matter of course, have contact with his creation. That is the basis of every religious movement."

Gavriel raised his head at that, suddenly alert. "God did not create the world."

The two men and the woman looked at each other. The man with the grey hair spoke. His voice did not have the pedagogical tone of a preacher. "Who created it, then?"

Silence.

"Who do you think made the world?" he repeated.

"That's all I have to say," Gavriel replied.

"Was it the blind god?" asked the preacher.

The Man Under Contract said nothing.

"Do you not believe in God? Do you not believe that man is a predestined being?"

"The divine reference is always there …"[38] replied Gavriel laconically, spartan with his words.

The preacher stopped a moment, thrown by the off-hand quote. There was an alienating quality about the Man Under Contract as if he never had both feet in this world.

"Gavriel, we need your help. The world comes to an end. Resources are running out. We need to break this destructive cycle, or it will be too late."

The woman intervened. "Do you know how much energy there is in a barrel of crude oil? It contains as much as a person uses during seventy years of physical effort. It is the energy of a lifetime. Seventy years of work, movement and vigour. And do you know how we spend it? How we waste it? In a transatlantic flight, each passenger consumes one of those barrels that the earth took so long to create."

---

[38] The complete quote of the Man Under Contract, who modestly kept silent, is as follows: "The divine reference is always there, at the climax of intercourse, on the cusp of euphoria, when we can just glimpse a higher reality before falling, defeated again, in the matter of our own bodies."

"Our organization can save the world, but we need help. In two generations, it will be too late," said the preacher. "What we need, Gavriel, is a miracle, to show the world the true message and then use it to fix everything that is broken."

There was no answer.

"We know you're looking for something. Contact points. We can help you. We have many more resources than you do," said the man with the grey hair.

The man's tone was always pragmatic. With his muscular arms and calloused hands, Gavriel suspected that he was not a theologian.

"Even if I wanted to help you, this is not how it works. Resources, money … That has nothing to do with it. There is a clue, a maze to solve and finally a price. The door only opens in one direction, but it depends on who pushes it."

When Miller got to the meeting, there were only two people there he knew. One was the old acquaintance from the Army days who had originally introduced him to the substantial contract with the Church. The other was Blake, a younger associate he had met at the La Jolla office, a rising star in the organization. A serious-looking man and an elderly woman were at the end of a very long conference room table.

They all sat down and by the way they looked at him, Miller felt he had been called to the Headmaster's office for a spanking.

"Why are we not making progress?" asked the serious man with no preamble.

"I don't know what made you think this was going to be so easy."

"Your job is to make it easy," chimed in the woman.

"My job is to make it happen, and I can't do that if all I'm allowed to do is chat with him," said Miller.

Silence.

“What are you suggesting?” asked the first man.

Miller had been hesitant to talk about this new step but the people around the table included his army friend, appeared blind, deaf and clueless about the reality of the situation they have crafted so he saw no other option.

“Two interrogation sessions. I need him to be tired and slightly dehydrated, only I will monitor how much water he can drink. I also need physical contact,” he said.

“Yes to the sessions and the water quota. No to the torture,” said the serious man.

Silence again. Miller blew through his lips and thought.

“A cocktail, then. Pentothal.”

The woman leaned towards the man, they whispered at the remote end of the table and called Blake over.

“We agree,” said the woman.

The man with the grey hair returned to the cell days later accompanied by the woman and another military-looking man. The preacher was not with them, and Gavriel tensed on his cot.

“Get up,” said the man with the grey hair.

“What’s that?” Gavriel asked.

The military man arranged on the table the contents of a briefcase in which jars clinked. “Do what I tell you.”

The thin politeness of the first conversation had disappeared. *No,* Gavriel wanted to say, but before he could, the man with the grey hair and the tall woman grabbed him and handcuffed his hands and feet to a chair.

An hour later the interrogation began.

“What is your name?”

"Gavriel."

"What is your full name?"

"Gavriel Artiel."

Gavriel responded with a dazed head, not knowing what he said.

"How old are you?"

"Thirty-three."

"What colour is the pen I'm holding?"

"Black."

"Who is the blind god?"

Silence.

"Where's the chapel?"

Silence.

"What's your name?"

"Gavriel."

"What is your full name?"

"Gavriel Artiel."

"How many people are in this room?"

"Five."

"Five?"

"… Four, four people."

"Where were you going after Tibet?"

Silence.

"Where is the next point of contact?"

Silence.

When he was left alone, Gavriel knew the moment of greatest despair that he had ever known during his many years of the Search. With the hangover of the drug in his mouth and the shameful memory of vulnerability that followed the interrogation, he curled up on the cot and bit the pillow with rage and despair.

Gavriel was not imposing. His physical presence had a certain intensity, yes, but he was not remarkable at a glance. And yet he felt within him a hard and strong essence, a Quatermain-like indomitable spirit which allowed him to skirt the pains and pangs that paralyzed others. And so, the episode lasted long enough for the Man Under Contract's psyche to calm down and return to the only certainty of his life: the Search was everything and it aligned the world in his favour.

Still, this time Gavriel would help it out. That was when he decided to escape.

Chao left the residential medical centre of Elk Grove feeling quite annoyed.

Jason Harris had been hospitalized there for months while trying to get used to the tribulations of his new life as a blind man. The clinic was not far from his parents' house, and every afternoon witnessed a parade of Harris's relatives who came to comfort him. Chao made his visit at the time of greatest flow, feeling strange. He waited for the patient to be alone and then gave his name at the reception.

He entered the room where Jason sat in pyjamas by the window. A nurse was making the bed.

"Mr Harris? My name is William. I phoned yesterday, spoke to your parents."

Jason turned his blind head toward the voice.

"Oh yes, the insurance detective."

Chao, who had been ambiguous on purpose when he made the call, felt a degree of flushing.

"Not exactly. Mr Cohan hired me. To investigate the Cambodia affair."

Jason tensed his back, shook his head. "I don't want to talk about Cambodia. Who are you? Nurse!"

The nurse was a large pale-skinned man in a white-and-green uniform. He stood between the patient and Chao.

"Wait, please. Gavriel, that traveller you met in Siem Reap. Remember? There are some things I can tell you about him."

"Please hold," Jason said to the nurse. "What things?"

They chatted for a long while in private, but Jason's helplessness and the visible fringes of an abrasive personality made the whole visit uncomfortable. Chao saw that every conversation that the former lawyer had with medical staff, patients and family members folded under the weight of the same irresolvable question: "How? How could this have happened to me?"

Even so, there were two things that Chao learned. One was the detailed story of Abel's death, an episode that the reports he had received from Cohan upon accepting the contract defined as an occurrence of drugs and bad luck. What Jason said made Chao sit on the edge of the chair, frightened by its consistency with the story of Tasmania. It could be, thought the detective, that the Man Under Contract chased and was chased in turn by aberrations of natural logic.

Then Jason warned him to stop his inquiries.

"Cohan, Abel's father, he came to see me a few weeks ago."

"Does he blame you for what happened?"

"No, he worried about my health, my future. He is well connected and can help me get a job."

"I'm glad."

"He came with several other people, lawyers. He didn't introduce them like that but I know the profession. They told me that they will go after anyone who talks or inquires about the case, that they would use any legal measure to protect me and the memory of Abel Cohan."

Chao thought for a moment. "And you agree with that?"

"Partially. Abel told me about his father, about his relationship with the Church in California. If they are involved, people should pay attention to what he says."

"Church? What church?"

"On the West Coast, talking about the Church refers to just the one."

"I understand," said Chao, who did not understand.

Later, when Jason, with his big dark glasses, heard the squeak of the chair and Chao rising to leave, he spoke suddenly as if he could not control the words. "Sometimes I dream."

Chao stopped. He also dreamed. He thought of wet earth and ghostly figures with long antlers. "Do you dream? Of what?"

"Of the light. I saw nothing. I know I saw nothing, only the light, but when I remember it at night everything changes. I see the light and something behind."

"A man?"

"No, something, a terrible thing. And behind it, something else, a presence, and I think it sleeps."

Back in the car, Chao waited without starting the engine. He just thought and digested what came with those thoughts. He was not the Man Under Contract, nor was he entangled in the Search, but still, it seemed that the world was about to be pierced for him as well. In his head, he talked with his sister Cecilia. Cecilia, she of the sensible council, of the sane advice.

"That story of the explosion and the dream. It could all be because of the shock of the accident," said the imaginary Cecilia.

"It could."

"But you don't think so."

"No," Chao replied, thoughtful.

He had been in the country for three days, on a journey that was chewing up a good part of his savings and left a handful of customers without service back home. But what option did he have? Back in his Hong Kong apartment, Chao had accumulated stacks of books on occultism, philosophy and religion, themes he had never had any interest in, and for weeks before he took the trip to America he had been going through the routines of his investigations with an absent mind, leaving loose ends and making mistakes. Perhaps he had begun this journey of exorcism because of how abrupt his decline had been. One day he was the same person he always knew, and then he came back from Tibet and all was in disarray.

The morning after his visit to Jason Harris he was at a bar in O'Hare airport. Chao wrote in his notebook, trying to understand why, in fact, he did not believe that the explanation he got from the blind man was the result of a shock.

There was a pattern that avoided scrutiny, but it was there, and it kept insinuating itself. Chao had looked at the details of the story of Tasmania. Yes, there had been a woman named Maya Furuta who disappeared during a trip in the Australian southeast. For years her parents drove an international campaign to find their daughter. The last record that existed of her was a signature at a hotel in Devonport. At the visitors' centre of the Cradle Mountain National Park, the Man Under Contract registered a party of two at the entrance and two at the exit, but a quick call to the park rangers' office confirmed that there was no active supervision of travellers so he could have been alone.

What happened in Cambodia was just as mystifying, more perhaps, because the investigation was fraught with official attempts to lessen the impact of the death of an American tourist. When the police arrived at the scene of Abel's death, they found several charred bodies and attributed their demise to the explosion of the chemicals used to distil the drugs. It was the same explosion that blinded Jason. But the general hospital of Phnom Penh had a Chinese resident ophthalmologist. He was the one who had checked Jason's condition when he was admitted and his notes said the American suffered irreversible luminous retinopathy: acute burning by solar radiation. Before visiting the Elk Grove clinic, Chao had tried to compare all of that with their records but legislation, which was abundant and that an orderly had cited to him in detail, invoking HIPAA and many other acronyms, prevented them from revealing particulars.

Chao flew from Chicago to San Diego, burning more of his funds, and settled in a discreet hotel that avoided the steep prices of the beachfront. He drove through the crowded highways and reached the address provided by Mr Cohan's office. Chao considered himself so fortunate that the businessman had agreed to see him with minimal prior notification that he did not realize where he was going.

The headquarters of the Positivist Church occupied a solid piece of the business centre on the outskirts of the La Jolla neighbourhood. Psychologists in demand, award-winning rock guitarists, models and Nobel prize winners clung to the properties of this exclusive real estate market and made it the most elitist in the United States, and the most expensive in the continent; but the Church, unfazed by the cost, increased the size of its property year after year.

Chao swore silently at first, hesitated, and then finally parked with resigned reluctance. He did not want to be there. He had assumed that Cohan would receive him in the offices of his catering company, but this place, the Church, was a savanna where lions roamed; hostile territory. The detective had learned that the religious organization had an intimidating history of libels, lawsuits, and litigation[39], and rumour had it that it had waded in some murkier waters, accused of planting evidence on the property of misguided associates and rigging statements in the courts of like-minded judges. Its dynamic was always oriented towards influencing the odds so it would come out on top, applying the ruthless Puritan spirit of triumph in the areas of chiaroscuro, unconcerned about who may get trampled in the process.

---

[39] The preferred solution for the Positivist Church in the face of any problems took two forms: it drowned them in lawsuits and legal paperwork, or threw money against the obstacle until it was cleared, whichever was more economical.

The Church was a Leviathan of considerable power, a product of the most ambitious California. Its proselytizing task was based on speeches of not entirely consistent logic that served to attract captains of industry. Heads of movie studios, digital oligarchs, lords of the Silicon; in front of them all paraded the preachers of the Church, throwing the net and enmeshing some here and others there with promises of supernatural fulfilment. Although quite powerful now, the organization had begun as a modest weekend cult in a basement in Cupertino. The early incorporation of a famous TV personality took the disjointed message of salvation by alien intervention to a global stage. Although the mass media often ridiculed the story which was told in the seminar rooms of the Church, it was no more implausible than that of other established religions and it was certainly fresher. That, and the garish Californian style in which it was packaged, did the rest. Success followed the Church wherever it went. It was not immediately obvious that, under its confounding rhetoric, what it described was just a revision of classical beliefs adapted to the futuristic sensibility of the moment.[40]

The touch of genius in the plan developed by the Church had been the escalation of prices they charged on the way to salvation. At each stage, the Church associates paid a fee and received access to a specific canon of knowledge and revelations. When the organization considered that they were sufficiently prepared, they moved to a level that was both more expensive and complex than the previous one. This staircase of ranks increased the cost of beatitude in geometric progression while keeping the faithful motivated with the bait of eternal life, which was always just out of reach.

It was well known that the executive committee of the Church was formed by twenty men and women and that it included former hippies and compulsive philanthropists. Many decisions were made at weekend gatherings where they arrived in eco-friendly automobiles, dressed in casual linen shirts. They drank wine from Napa and ate fusion cuisine in an atmosphere that was both relaxed and demanding; a meeting of magnetic and successful personalities in the most

---

[40] The marker of success for any religion is its effectiveness in relieving the burden of the mundane aches of the faithful. Same as with a good story, the well-being of the audience is more relevant than plausible logic, and the role of religious liturgy, even when biased, is to induce serenity. Such liturgy becomes a pattern that the faithful know and understand; it is not for God, it is for Man.

prosperous valley in the world. All the members of the committee were said to be deeply devoted to the cause of the Church despite their excessive commercial interest in the salvation process. They shared a firm conviction that the activities of their organization affected the wellbeing of Humanity at a global scale, but that did not stop them from conducting their work with the rigidity and attention to detail of a business venture. The number of registered members and the programs of the religious precept mixed seamlessly with balance sheets which tracked the yield of capital.[41] It was a mission to save the world and their congeners; if the twenty of them became rich in the process, that was irrefutable proof that they were on the right track.

Chao waited in the lobby, an expanse of leathery sofas where espresso coffee was served to those visiting. Cohan met him in a comfortable but impersonal room, sitting next to a slightly overweight man he introduced as Blake. There were handshakes, greetings and perfunctory condolences, then an artillery salvo of light conversation while the men watched each other from opposite sides of the table like generals in the fields of Austerlitz.

"Here is the thing, Mr Cohan, I have the impression that there is much more behind the Cambodian contract than we have discovered."

For the rest of the encounter, Chao would notice that Cohan invariably looked at his companion before speaking, as if he was fulfilling a confirmation routine of secretive origin. After hearing what the detective was saying, Cohan did it for the first time.

"Didn't you get the cheque? I thought we had paid you. The contract is closed."

Chao scared the idea away by shaking his hand in the air. "It's not that. I think I can find out what really happened to your son. I would like to ask you not to close the investigation yet, and I'm not speaking with any interest in extending my contract."

[41] The Positivist Church operated on a Principle of Exception: The divine essence may be present in all humans beings, but only those participating in the cult would be saved. This principle, which is scarcely original, appears once again tied to the Gnostic tradition and, before that, to the Orphic religious movement from which it was born.

"Is that why you came here?" asked Cohan rather sharply.

Blake leaned forward over the table to mediate. "Mr Chao, Mr Cohan and I thought that the reason you called us is that you had more details on the assignment. Things you may have left out of the report. Is this the case?"

"I think what happened to Abel has happened to others. You hired me to investigate this man, Gavriel Artiel. If you share the information you have, I can connect the pieces of this puzzle."

"But you were the one that was to provide us with information, Mr Chao, not the other way around," Blake said with a smile.

"I have some ideas, theories. But I need your support to confirm them," Chao replied.

Cohan got up from his chair. "That's all we're going to discuss," he said very seriously.

Chao and Blake remained in place for only a moment, until the conclusive nature of the gesture became clear. The detective stood up too.

"I must be honest with you. For me this has gone beyond a mere assignment, Mr Cohan. I have a personal interest in it."

"And I'm warning you, any meddling you do in my son's memory I will not forgive."

Blake got up and intervened, conciliatory for the second time. "What Mr Cohan means is that he prefers for the episode to be laid to rest. It hasn't been easy for him or his family."

"What I mean is what I said," barked Cohan.

Blake looked at the businessman in an authoritarian way that made the nature of their relationship suddenly clear to Chao. Cohan said no more, and Chao left the room, followed by the droning of Blake's apologies.

At the car, Chao felt the hurried feeling that shame brings, but before he could get into the vehicle, someone called: the man Blake, approaching at a heavy trot.

"I think none of us has handled the conversation very well, but do not blame Mr Cohan. He is very affected by the death of his son."

"I'm sorry then," Chao apologized, but the truth was that he found Blake's tone, always so very measured, annoying. "I better go now."

"Just a moment. I understand that it is your professional integrity that led you to visit us today. Mr Cohan has made his decision and I hope you respect that, but I would prefer if you didn't leave upset."

"And how would you want me to leave, exactly?" said Chao.

Finally, he heard Blake speaking without any further commitment to cordiality. "In a way that makes today beneficial so it is not a waste of time for any of us. Is there anything in particular that you came here to ask? I think there is."

Chao had the car keys in his hand and fiddled with them while he thought how much he should tell. He was sure it wasn't Cohan but the person in front of him who had prepared Gavriel Artiel's contract.

"The Man Under Contract mentioned something when we were in Tibet."

"Something what? Something important?"

"For me, yes. He said that I was not the first investigator he met. How long have you known about Artiel?"

Blake fell silent. He stayed that way for a moment, and Chao thought he wouldn't answer but he did.

"We've known him for a while now. He's not easy to find because his trail appears and disappears unexpectedly. It's true that we sent a private investigator to track him in Macau once, but it didn't work out and we terminated the contract."

"Until the Siem Reap affair."

"That was Mr Cohan doing, although we did offer counsel and he hired you."

"You're not Mr Cohan's assistant, are you?"

"No, not his assistant. I'm an advisor. Let's leave it at that."

Back at his hotel, Chao sat phone in hand. One of the things that allowed him to do his job, besides the long waiting hours and the tedious task of checking page after page of documents looking for evidence, was the small but well-articulated structure of contacts he had in Hong Kong. Chao didn't pay for this help directly, but he made sure to send gifts of ornate fruit during the Chinese New Year and bottles of expensive wine from time to time. In the United States, he lacked sources of information but, luckily, even here there existed services that, for a price, he could leverage. Chao called from his hotel room. A formal and well-spoken voice answered. Chao gave the details of what he needed and prepared to wait, not knowing for how long.

Gavriel tried to escape several times during that month.

He made a ram with part of the metal frame of the cot and used it unsuccessfully to try to break the windowpane. He scratched soap shavings in a handful and planned, as in a teenage fantasy, to blow them in the eyes of his jailers, but no one came. He created an improvised water pump with the toothpaste tube thinking he could cause a short circuit in the opening mechanism, without success.

Later, the man with the grey hair came to the cell. He was alone. He sat at the table without speaking. Gavriel waited and ended up joining him.

"I've been watching the security videos. I understand that you are scared."

"What did I say when you injected your drug?" Gavriel could not remember.

The man with the grey hair drummed with his fingers on the table. "Nothing. I was not surprised. The system is fallible, and you are demonstrating a lot of resistance."

“I can’t help you.”

“Yes, you can. I don’t need all of this, you know.”

“What do you mean?”

“I don’t need theological discussions or psychotropics. I can fish out all the details I need in half an hour, without cameras and with a bucket full of water.” He snapped his fingers. “As easy as that.”

Gavriel took the gesture, so casual, with the gravity it really had. *There are no coincidences*, he thought and waited a moment before replying, shaping this answer.

“I know you’re a man who should not be taken lightly and that any answer I give you is not going to be satisfactory, but can I tell you a story?”

“Ah yes, your stories. You have lots of those. Isn’t that habit of telling tales what landed you here?”

“It’s possible, but, if you allow me, I’ll tell you one.”

“Up to you.”

“When I arrived at Honshu Island in Japan, I saw the mass of Mount Fuji.”

When Gavriel arrived at Honshu Island in Japan, he saw the mass of Mount Fuji. This was before he had learned to decipher the subtlety that guided the manifestations of the piercing of the world. At that time, his understanding was simpler and had limited the Search to sacred precincts and large reference points.

When he decided that at the summit he would find his clue, Gavriel planned the climb. He spurned the traditional route of the 5th Station, which began halfway to the top and was accessible by bus. The Man Under Contract was convinced that to get results, he needed to show his vehemence not by walking from the station but by starting all the way from the seashore. This alternative, longer route covered fifty kilometres and a climb of almost four thousand metres. It would be twenty-two hours of walking if he rested little and walked briskly. It was summer, the only season in which the snow opened the routes to the top, and the humidity of the Japanese August sank Gavriel into the asphalt for the first seven hours of the hike. During that endless day, tired, hungry and scorched by the sun, Gavriel was entering an alienated state, heightened by lack of sleep. Then altitude cooled the air and he moved onto a rocky path which crossed the forest, steep and unpleasant, where the rain of the summer season drenched his clothes and skin.

By nightfall, he had been walking for ten hours. Gavriel joined the group of climbers who began the route from the 5th Station, looking to reach the summit and see the sunrise from the top of the divine mountain. Fuji had been born from a volcanic mass, and its slopes, smooth and uniform when seen from the distance, were, in fact, a lifeless landscape of dark, unsteady and jagged rocks. Only five routes existed and they filled, in the nights of arduous ascent, with long lines of alpinists carrying sticks in hand and bag at the back, who braved the climb through the progressively rarefied air.

Gavriel entered the rhythmic cadence of the line. The lights of the lanterns zigzagged down the mountainside, up and down, and the Man Under Contract thought he was watching a snake of light clinging to the magic mountain. The long line had an orderly but halting pace where even the fittest hikers, when forced to stop by the continuous effort, would step aside in perfect etiquette, with the lamps illuminating hands and feet, to let the snake continue its path. Gavriel went up, almost falling over his walking stick and sick with fatigue. He looked at that phantasmagoric environment of black magmatic rock and those faces that the white glare of the flashlights made flat and empty; inhuman. Stumbling, legs tired and unable to lift his boots from the ground but propelled by the nearing presence of the summit, Gavriel continued upward.

He reached the peak just before daylight and passed through one of the Shinto gates[42] placed at the end of the different ascension routes. *I

---

[42] Mount Fuji is, in the Shinto tradition, a consecrated place inhabited by the anima of the natural world and those of the deceased. The separation between the finite universe of Man and the infinite of the gods is marked by the entrance gate of the sanctuary at the summit.

am now in High Heaven, he thought and sat down in the inclemency with which Fuji laughed at the heat of the summer down below. Gavriel wrapped himself in a light cover of aluminium designed to retain body heat and shivered there for another hour while waiting for dawn and the piercing of the world. But only the former appeared, surrounded by an entourage of camera flashes that tried to cover with their meagre lenses the majesty of sunlight at the summit.

Neither fatigue nor autosuggestion nor the beatitude of the place did anything to break the barriers of reality. After a few hours, Gavriel descended towards Tokyo and reflected. There were secret connections and hidden doors, Gavriel knew that, and there were places which held the torque needed to pick open the cosmic locks, but the key to finding them was not written, apparently, in touristic pamphlets.

"Is that your story?" said the man with the grey hair.

"Yes."

"As stories go, that one is quite shoddy."

"I guess, but that doesn't change things. There are no shortcuts for what you are looking for. You have the resources and the manpower. All I can say to you is that you start your own Search. I cannot open the way for you. That's not how it works."

"We'll see about that."

Chief Miller attended the second meeting very short of patience. The room was the same, same people except for his absent army friend. Miller thought that was not a good sign and spoke before anybody else could.

"I can get the information. I just need permission to take the route with the greatest impact."

"No," said the serious, distinguished man.

"No? We've kept Artiel in that cell for a month. At some point, there will be a leak and this whole affair is going to eat up your organization."

"The Man Under Contract has no credibility. In any case, our conclusion now is that we cannot force him to collaborate," said the woman.

There was silence and Miller could not contain a burst of muffled laughter.

"Then pray tell me exactly why you have spent what you have spent on this project and why you are paying me the salary you are paying me."

"We need your help with what will come after," said Blake from his chair in one corner of the large room.

"And what is that?"

"We will inform you in time."

"And now? What do you want me to do now?" said Miller, very concerned about how amateurish the decision-making process in the organization was.

"Now we are going to let the Man Under Contract go."

Blake walked into the room where Mr Cohan struggled to die.

The Church's man had time to appreciate the expensiveness of the private hospital suite, all dark wooden panels and fine cornice mouldings but none of that could distract much from the busy scene of nurses, drips and beeping machines which crowded around the elderly businessman in the centre of the room. Mr Cohan looked terribly frail, Blake had seen him last a few weeks back during their last session, and although his health was rapidly deteriorating, he still walked with purpose and spoke with his inflexible charisma. Then, his dragged-out battle with cancer took a turn for the worse. In ten days, the wiry and vital septuagenarian had become a whispery shadow about to be dissipated.

"Blake…"

Mr Cohan reached out to him, the hand trembled and Blake, slightly repulsed, wished the uncomfortable but necessary goodbye was already over but he held it and that seemed to comfort the invalid.

"All is well, sir. Remember, this is just a stage and a new one is coming. All is well."

"It will be, right? I know it will, I have known for years. It's just… sometime is hard to keep faith. Faith and peace of heart."

Blake had spoken to the staff of the hospital and knew about the row that took place just that morning. He thought the room retained an echo of the strife of loud voices, an aura of a battlefield the morning after. Mr Cohan's family had flown in a hurry from the East Coast, alarmed by the health crisis and had rushed to the hospital intent on mending their relationships with the dying man but those good intentions didn't last long. Old recriminations came back to life, aided by the failing senile mind of the bedridden patient. There was shouting and tears and the doctors had to evict the wife, daughter and brothers. Nobody else was coming. Cohan was alone.

"What about him? Artiel, the Man Under Contract."

Blake moved in his chair, still trapped by the clasping hand. Artiel had become a confidential issue and he was under instructions not to speak of it.

"Did you find him? Does he have what we need?" insisted Cohan.

"It is all under control, sir. You don't need to worry. Leave that to us and just focus on getting better."

The man shook with the impulse of faded grit and leaned forward rattling the IV drip pole.

"Blake… Blake... I am not going to get better. I am not getting out of here ever. But you can tell me that you got the man who killed my son Abel. You can tell me that."

Blake still hesitated for ten minutes and tried to wriggle himself from the imperative request but the businessman who had built not one but two business empires in his lifetime would not let him go.

"We have him. We have him and the next time something similar to the Cambodia affair happens we will be there."

Cohan relaxed and let go of Blake's hand.

"Yes… the greatest secret of the universe," he said and looked at the ceiling with an unfocused stare.

It was later that night, as Blake was putting his younger daughter to bed that his phone chimed. The girl was in a rebellious mood and it took him an hour to finally turn off the lights of her room. He then checked the message that told him Mr Cohan had passed away.

They left Gavriel at the edge of a highway with his bag and his notebook. It took him a moment to react. He looked to one side, looked to the other, saw the dark vehicle already getting lost in the confusion of the lanes further on.

He understood that he was on the Californian coast when he saw the license plates of the cars passing him by. Gavriel was used to travelling and used to new places. However, the habits of the Asian route did not translate well into the American suburbs. There was no cheap transportation, no bohemian coffeehouses for globetrotters. There was no urban centre to use as a reference, or place for pedestrians to walk. He wandered, passed a motel that tempted him to stop and rest and then another. Despite the increasing heat of the morning, he went on. It was uncomfortable to move under the weight of the backpack through California, with no other person in sight. The cars accelerated right next to him, and the long and monotonous stretches between blocks made him feel he was not moving. He ignored the motels he had seen because it was time to let the Search be mended. They had not brought him to that place by chance, regardless of what the man with the grey hair and his employers may think. A dark design permeated everything, and the archons stomped the earth, hidden in unexpected places. He passed more crossings and, on the last corner, he stopped, looking at the neon lights that formed the name of the next motel.

He immediately took a room there and later, sitting on the bed and sorting aimlessly through the hundreds of channels available on television, he prepared a plan. Nothing was random. This was the appropriate place, right where he should be. And yet a connection was missing, an effort of his that was to be industrious and definitive. What was it?

That night he sat in a restaurant, having dinner and free for the first time in weeks, remembering without too much emotion the monotony of the cell and wondering what kind of person was he that nothing of what happened would mark his disposition. Was that the grace granted by fanaticism? Perhaps today he could think about it a little, oblivious to the daily rumour of families and couples around him, because tomorrow the Search would again be the most important thing in the world.

Chao was preparing his return to Hong Kong when the call came. He intended to spend a couple of days at home, a week at most, and then, no matter how much Cecilia protested, return to Tibet and follow the track. What frightened him, more than the disturbing things he had learned on his trip, was the reproach that inevitably awaited him from his sister.

He had nothing more to do in California. He considered investigating the Church, trying to learn more about the first contract that had been put on Gavriel Artiel, but Chao knew that the organization was too serious an enemy to quarrel with.

"William Chao?"

"Yes."

"You made a search request, correct?"

"Yes, name of G. Artiel."

"But you told us to look for him in China."

"He may be in another country at this point."

"There is a ping in the United States. G. Artiel, passport."

"That's not possible. Where?"

"Give us some time. We'll call you. Do you accept the additional fee for a follow-up?"

"Yes."

Chao sat thoughtfully for a while in his room, and then cancelled the flight reservation he had for Hong Kong.

A day later, William Chao looked at the graveyard of papers he had laid out on the bedcover and the floor because there was no table or desk in the strangely spacious and empty American rooms. He had scribbled handwritten pages that he then ripped from his notebook and lined up, one next to the other, in an effort to bring to the surface the patterns he was missing. The phone rang again.

"William Chao?"

"Yes."

"Regarding your request ..."

"Has he appeared?"

"He is at the *Carcassonne* motel in San Diego."

"What motel? Is this a joke?"

"A credit card under the name G. Artiel was used yesterday at the hotel address."

Chao looked out the window of his room. Across the parking lot, the name "Carcassonne"[43] formed in neon letters stood out against the

---

[43] The motel is named after the medieval walled city of Carcassonne in France, which in 1209 was besieged by order of Pope Innocent III during the Albigensian crusade. Its population consisted mainly of Cathar heretics accused of crimes of *lèse-majesté* and of maintaining schismatic beliefs such as that salvation was possible through knowledge and not faith and that the material world had not been created by God Almighty but by an intermediate agent.

dark background of the avenue. The same hotel; the Man Under Contract was in the same hotel. *Coincidences are a telegraph from God*, Chao thought.

Chao hesitated between two rooms where the light was on and finally rang the bell of the first one. When the door opened, the Man Under Contract gave no sign of surprise. He was barefoot and in a t-shirt. He had a pen over his ear in the manner of schoolchildren.

"Yes?"

Chao waited silently until he was recognized.

"Detective."

"You must be wondering what I'm doing here."

"Yes," said Gavriel. And then, "Does this mean you believe me now?"

"I guess so … Yes, that's what it means."

Gavriel invited him in. The room was like the messy block print workshop of a demented Gutenberg. One of the walls was covered with maps marked in red. Pamphlets, brochures and a dismembered "Celebrity Home Hollywood Guide" that the Man Under Contract had unbound were spread on the floor.

"Sorry for the mess."

Chao sat in the only chair free of clutter.

"I left you in Tibet."

"Many things have happened since we met. Not all were good. And you? I thought you lived in China."

"Hong Kong. I came to meet Mr Cohan."

"And now you're here. This is no accident."

The Man Under Contract asked his questions but Chao thought he didn't even seem curious. Perhaps from his perspective, the world had such a translucid clarity that he saw impossible events as pieces of a cosmic puzzle fitting into place. Or perhaps there came a moment when the ability to be surprised gets irreparably crippled.

"No, I would say it is not," replied Chao. He looked around. "And what is all this? A new clue?"

"There is a moving pattern. Everything points to an entrance."

"Same as in Tasmania? Same as the knight of green?"

"Something like that. But that was not really its name. It and its kin have many others and change them as they see fit. They are the pauper angels, the archons of the numen. In any case, they are a mandatory crossing point."

The Man Under Contract got up and went to his maps.

"Look at this. I've been looking for a pattern for days, and here I finally have it. It took me longer than I thought to find it. The problem was that I'm not used to all this," Gavriel said, making an inclusive gesture of the room, the hotel and all of California. "In this region, there is no orthodox religious tradition if you exclude the original missionary Catholicism. Then I thought, what if what I have to look for is newly minted spirituality? It was possible; after all, on this coast, the concept of the modern theology sect was invented."

The Church, Chao thought.

"Look at these patterns."

The Man Under Contract pointed to one of the walls and Chao saw, indeed, a confluence of patterns.

"It looks like an inverted funnel," Chao said, looking at the shapes on the map.

"That's what it looks like, yes. The red stripes are territorial demarcations, the blue ones are highways, and the black dots are nuclei of occupation. But there's more."

The Man Under Contract was moving around the room with purpose, taking selected papers from among the cautious disorder, showing them, putting them back in place in a way that left no doubt that, for him, it was a well-practised process. Chao studied the notes and maps and realized that this was the geography of information that he, himself, had tried to copy in his room.

"It's a taxonomy," Gavriel said, offering a drawing of a pyramid where each level was marked with notes in tight lettering. "I have included all the information I could find: demographic, firmographic, behavioural data. Look at the distribution."

Chao studied the pyramid and then the map on the wall. The marks and arrows formed a cone that pointed toward the centre of the state of California.[44]

"And all this. Where does it lead?"

The Man Under Contract picked up, from among the papers on the floor, a brightly coloured triptych, a pamphlet advertising an amusement park. Gavriel stood tall, paper in hand and smiling triumphantly. From where Chao was sitting, the inverted funnel drawn on the map in the background seemed to rest on his head like a halo of scholarly splendour.[45]

"To the greatest tabernacle in the world."

They left the motel the next morning. When they were at check out,

---

[44] The model created by the Man Under Contract follows the principles of Geographic Information Systems or GIS in which areas of traffic analysis are used to (quote follows) "organize, store, manipulate, and model large amounts of data from the real world in order to link such data to a spatial reference, facilitating the incorporation of socio-cultural and environmental aspects that lead to decision-making in a more effective way."

[45] The detective may not have known that the inverted funnel, worn as a hat, had been a symbol, since medieval times, of the state of dementia. Flemish painter Jheronimus van Aken (Bosch) reflects the tradition in his works *The Ship of Fools* and *The Extraction of the Stone of Madness* where the surgeon uses one, revealing himself as a jester who pretends to be a physician and is far more insane than the patient he is attempting to cure.

the Man Under Contract put on the counter a credit card worn out by use.

"How do you pay for all this? Travel and hotels," Chao asked.

"My family left me some money. It's not much but it lets me move around."

"And you spend it all on this quest of yours?"

The Man Under Contract picked up the card. "And what else could I spend it on?"

They reached the car that Chao had rented and drove north on the coastal highway. They avoided heavy traffic early on the way out of San Diego but got stuck first in San Clemente and then in Harbor Blvd. Around them, the effervescence of the American economic development clogged all four lanes, with vehicles lined up bumper to bumper. At noon they arrived at the amusement park.

"Here?" asked Chao hesitantly.

"You'll see."

They left the car and crossed the high arches of the entrance. It was a workday, but the parking lot was almost full, and long queues of visitors zigzagged towards the interior of the enclosure. Once inside, an avenue flanked by shops with nostalgic American post-war facades led to the central square. Chao looked around. Tourist families scattered about, looking for rides to entertain their children. Others bought souvenirs and large clouds of cotton candy spun around a stick.

"What do we do now?" Chao asked.

The Man Under Contract pointed towards the middle of the square where the main avenue led to a roundabout. At its centre, a large metallic statue of the friendly anthropomorphic mouse that was the mascot of the park smiled at them from the top of a pedestal. Adults and children took turns to snap pictures posing with the character.

"Can't you see anything strange? Nothing? Look again."

Chao did. "If you tell me what we're looking for, it will …" And suddenly he understood it all.

This place was not a park and that effigy was not a cartoon mascot. The adoration of thousands, the blind faith in its virtue driven by countless followers, had transformed a graphic curiosity, an artifice of entertainment, into something more transcendent. The combustible of emotions moved a great wheel, and on that radiant Californian day when the smiling statue, huge and massive, received visitors, hundreds and hundreds of them in shorts and sunglasses, kneeling to take photos in a gesture that really looked like a genuflection of worship, all the faithful were convinced that the mascot was a real being. Children believed it literally; adults dreamed about it and kept it alive in small corners of their imagination.

The park was now a cathedral, and the character, once a caricature of comical anthropomorphic gesture, had become the deity that ruled millions of lives. Pilgrims arrived marked with the sign of the God Mouse on toys, t-shirts and ornaments. The most dedicated ones strived to alter their silhouette to approach the rodent archetype by putting on false plush ears, as round as those of their idol. They greeted each other with signs of their secret creed and references to the body of knowledge of the deity, a complex corpus that decades of film production had grown from the first prestigious black-and-white cartoons to digital animation.[46]

"Do you see it now? Do you see what this site is? Here is our conduit."

The voice of the Man Under Contract resounded hypnotically and his conviction, his absolute faith, filtered through every word. Perhaps behind the bronze smile of the humanoid mouse and the thousands of other smiles that outlined the face of the mascot from every corner of the park (plastic bags, icons on the walls, a large balloon flying over

---

[46] The veneration of totems and effigies is as old as humanity itself. This idolatry of manufactured objects, rather than an authentic religious drive, is considered an intellectual exercise in which the human being tries to capture the essence of the supernatural world. It was especially important in the paganism of the Ammonite and Canaanite religions where worship of the god Moloch (Molech, Melech, Milcom, or Molcom) became an essential example of the human obsession with abstract figuration.

the enclosure), there was a sinister glow of recognition that caused concern. Chao remembered seeing the character on TV as a child at his home in Hong Kong when it was a friendly presence. Did it have then that reflection of intense self-awareness that seemed to rumble now behind the simplistic strokes of its face?

"Can it feel us? It seems as if it could feel us."

The blind eyes of the bronze statue appeared to watch him from above. Chao moved a few steps and the pupil-less gaze followed. The Man Under Contract also regarded the figure.

"Yes, it has waited patiently all these years for someone to come and look behind the curtain. It is in its nature to serve as a bridge."

"What does that mean? Will that make things easier?"

"I don't know. Its nature is mutable."

There was some joy in the conversation of the two men, and Chao noticed a comfort that had eluded him since he returned to Hong Kong from Tibet; the relief of knowing oneself to be sane, of having someone explain the processes of the Search.

"Have you seen anything like this before? I don't know what we should expect. For the statue to get animated and start walking?"

At his side, Gavriel felt again on the path to the proper clues, and the sufferings that had brought him to California fell aside and were forgotten. The world was thinner here, and they just needed a push to peer over to the other side.

"It won't be as easy as that. The path of ingress to the archons is not even a path. It is a maze, or, more exactly, the image of a maze that you need to define first in your head before it can be discovered, before it can exist even. Without an image, there is no labyrinth; if there is no labyrinth, there is no access; and that," he said, pointing to the statue, "is nothing more than a piece of bronze."

For hours, sitting on the terrace of the crowded avenue, Gavriel shared the details of his notebook with Chao, accompanying him on a journey through his method and results. Chao saw in the resources of the Man Under Contract theological, mathematical and geographical derivations, planted one on top of the other in layers and layers of extravagant and opaque meaning. The day passed slowly although the influx of visitors never declined. In the evening there were parades, fireworks; and if Gavriel was waiting for a magic signal he was disappointed.

"What now?" said Chao.

"We have to come back tomorrow. The link is here. I'm sure of that."

"And what will happen?"

"I don't know. Until we start the sequence, nothing will happen."

"And we don't know how to do that."

"True. Each case is different."

"As long as you don't propose that we take peyote, I'll be ok," Chao added.

He said it lightly, as a joke, but the face of the Man Under Contract darkened, and Chao knew he was thinking about the Maya girl.

"This story is getting ridiculous," Bryan said, rising from the sofa in the apartment in Kowloon. "First he talks about kidnappings and now about religious cults?"

The Man Under Contract looked at his watch and then the door. "I'm telling you what happened."

"Bryan," said Cecilia, "let's listen."

With poor grace, her husband gave in and sat down again.

"Why did you share all that with my brother? Shouldn't this search be some sort of secret?"

"And why are you telling us now?" added Bryan.

"There is no secret. The mysteries I shared with William were there. Anyone can uncover them. I told him how I did things, but what works for me may not work for others."

"Like those men who held you?"

"I already told them, no shortcuts are possible."

"But Liam, he was also starting to see things, like in that park. What did you do to him? Hypnotize him?"

"He began to see the writing on the wall, that's all."

The hotels near the park were expensive, so Chao and Gavriel followed the highway until they found a secluded and affordable place. They chatted for some time on the balcony that the two rooms shared and retired soon, the Man Under Contract to work on his diagrams, Chao to dream again of horned creatures and a bronze mouse.

They spent the next day sitting on the terrace of the square, fed by the grim menu of sugar-saturated drinks and bland meals. Nothing happened. On the third day, Gavriel barely said a word, ignoring the cries of children and adults around him and concentrating on transcribing notes in his travel notebook while Chao drummed his fingers on the table and erased the messages in which his sister, increasingly nervous, urged him to return to Hong Kong. The sun rose, fell and nothing happened. The statue was still inanimate. They stayed at the same motel that night and neither spoke much, tired with the strange exhaustion of inactivity. Chao was about to ask again if they may not be wrong about the whole notion but one look at Gavriel, who sat defeated in a chair, shushed him.

Unbeknown to the detective, the Man Under Contract was also suffering from moments of hesitation. If he had been alone, Gavriel would have waited for as long as necessary, but Chao's presence put him under a strain he was not used to and forced him to revise his theory about the park with expectations of scientific assessment.

On their fifth day of vigilance, Gavriel knew that Chao would not be able to wait any longer so he avoided talking to him and worked quietly on his charts and structures, stealing glances at the pages of *The Demon Princes* when he felt stuck. With the fall of the evening, visitors began to leave the park. It was a Monday, and the weight of the day was noticeable; residents and tourists on holiday went back to their homes and hotels and an early dinner. Several security guards walked around, collecting stragglers half an hour before the official closing hour. Crying children clung to lampposts or sat on the floor, sabotaging the end of the day and refusing to cooperate. Gavriel and Chao, who knew the daily routine, rose from the table on the terrace and packed their bags but, despite their diligence, one of the guards came up to hurry them along.

"You have to move; the door won't be open for long."

Chao walked towards the exit but, after a few steps, noticed that Gavriel was not with him.

"Gavriel, it's time to go."

The Man Under Contract stood near one of the concealed service entrances of the park. It was an inconspicuous door at the back of the retail stores, painted the same pastel colour as the building. Gavriel pulled at the door handle, which did not yield. There were hardly any people left on the avenue's shopping mall where, despite the idealized facades of quaint old confectioneries and toy shops that did their best to take the customer to a simpler and happier time, the same plastic merchandise one could find outside the fences were sold. Gavriel was looking for another entry. Chao approached.

"You can't go in there. I'm sure it's a restricted area."

"Did you see him? Did you see him?" he said twice in a row.

"See who?"

"The security guard. Didn't you see him? Didn't you hear what he said? The door closes, and it's true."

He tried another access. This time it opened. Behind they found an entrance and metal stairs going down.

"What did you see? Is it a clue?"

Gavriel descended a couple of steps, holding the bag with his books in one hand and the railing with the other.

"Not a clue. This is the doorway to the labyrinth."

Underground, a parallel world grew. Above there were dreamlike castles and enchanted forests; below, Gavriel and Chao found utility corridors painted beige and with functional lighting. The antibodies that kept the park alive moved through those huge passageways: cleaners, rubbish collectors, merchandise suppliers, dancers in character costumes. They went from one place to another unseen and then used hidden doors and accesses so that their presence did not break the illusion of fiction that the compound worked so hard to create. The faithful of the God Mouse saw clean floors and full food trays; they didn't need to see anything else.

"It was the name, the name on his nametag. This is how it works. You see an opening and follow it. If not, the opportunity closes. It's always like that."

Gavriel sputtered as he moved at a hurried pace. His voice was sure now; doubts, conjectures and calculations left behind. Chao followed.

"A name?"

"Yes, the security guard had one of those badges stitched on his shirt with his name 'Mike' on it."

"'Mike', as in 'Mickey'?"

"And as in 'Michael', the guardian archangel."

"Is that a good enough clue?"

"In any other place or at any other time, no. But here and now, it's all we need."

Chao had a sudden impression that the undertaking might be more than he could handle. The corridors, empty of people and full of echo, were an alien environment. *I don't belong here*, the detective thought.

"Gavriel, wait …"

The Man Under Contract halted and waited for Chao to explain himself, but if the detective had any arguments, he offered none.

"There's little time, William. This revelation will give neither concessions nor respites. You still have time to go back. I hope you don't, but if you harbour any doubts, go up the stairs, go out the door and don't wait for me. Otherwise, it's time to look behind the curtain. Are you ready?"

Chao nodded without saying a word.

"Well, let's go get him."

They advanced again through the tunnels, with their hurried steps ringing on the bare concrete walls. Chao felt that the world was changing, that it was impossible for this expansive underground complex to fit under the amusement park; and it was too vast, the passageways too broad and impractical, for any real maintenance service operation. Chao was certain that this corridor and all the others they had crossed before were the stage for a drama that was about to be performed.

They heard footsteps behind, far away, but the Man Under Contract did not slow down. He was looking at something up front, a line of light spilling from the wall of the long, long tunnel through which they walked. When they arrived, Chao noticed that it was an open door. The light came from within. They looked in from the threshold, and Chao was the first to enter. He may be new to the Search but he had the professional habit of fast decision-making. Inside the room, painted the same beige colour as the hallways, were a metal table, several chairs and a man waiting. He sat on one of the chairs, wearing the uniform of a security guard. The nametag sewn on the left shirt pocket read "Mike". On the table were a thermos of coffee, metallic cups and a sandwich wrapped in clear plastic.

"Excuse me …" said Chao reflexively.

The man looked at them with his hands on the table, touching neither coffee nor food, like an imposter who does not know what to do with his tools. There was nothing else in the spacious room except for, on the walls, a large number of posters of films starring the park's mascot: the mouse driving a monochromatic ancient locomotive, the mouse at the helm of a riverboat, the mouse with a necromancer's hat and a magic wand which shot a cascade of sparks. From each drawing, the two-dimensional character watched them with an impression of organic intelligence, abysmal eyes in colour or black and white. The man at the table did not speak.

"Which one is it?" whispered Chao.

The Man Under Contract was almost motionless, but he responded. "I don't know. I never know. They never tell me. I only know their number."

"What do we do now?"

The guard had blue eyes, blond hair, and a well-fed American physique.

"We recite the names,"[47] said the Man Under Contract, but before he could begin, Mike the guard raised his voice.

"Now you are in an intermediate realm. Do you come alone and judiciously accept its nature?" he said in the formal tone of an enchantment.

Gavriel, slightly taken aback by the question, thought and answered, "Yes, only the two of us. We have questions, so many questions."

The big man pointed to the chairs. Chao and Gavriel sat. Chao looked at the wall where the fluorescent tubes projected the silhouette of the guard. There, the dark line did not copy the shoulders, the tight neck or the broad skull of the man at the table; instead, the shadow fluctuated indecisively, changing shape.

"What's your name?" asked Gavriel.

---

[47] Athot, Elaios, Astaphaios, Iao, Sabaoth, Adonaios, Sabbataios, as we have seen before. The symbology of the archons is simple and strongly connected to the Hellenic cosmology that considered only seven stars (five planets visible with an unaided eye in addition to the moon and the sun). Greek astronomers conceived an astral model of concentric spheres that traced the orbit of each of the celestial bodies under a firmament of fixed stars. Seven planets in the cosmos. Seven days in a week. Seven doors to open.

"Is that what you want, Gavriel? To place a name on us and try to dominate us? You cannot condense the essence of what surpasses the world in seven words. You can call me Tuesday, but that won't make me fit in the box of your ideas."

"But I was right, was I not? Idolatry reviewed, the mascot as a totem."

When the Man Under Contract said that, the flat faces of the God Mouse on the posters of the wall throbbed for a moment. The creature remained still, with his hands placed on the table. It hadn't moved, and yet its presence occupied everything. Chao did not doubt that the wide blue-eyed face that looked at him was a mask. What was underneath he did not know, but if they were not careful, an abyss would open behind, ready to swallow them.

"We look for the blind god," Chao ventured.

"You can't find it. Not here, in this intermediate world. Epiphany is the word you are looking for. In the ancient era when everything seemed full of mysteries and presences, that was how they referred to the appearance of God in human form. But that never happened. This," the man said, pointing at its own chest, "is all you have."

"We are willing to go further; anywhere necessary," Gavriel said.

Mike the guard smiled. "Is that so? There are tests, little Gavriel, challenges and obstacles. Because, despite what you say, you don't want to know the truth." Suddenly it looked at Chao. "We know what he is looking for, but you, little William, are a mystery. So serious, so austere. You know you don't belong here. What do you want?"

The detective swallowed under the scrutiny of the blue eyes. "I want to understand."

"Alas, we are the Immovable Race. We cannot be understood."

"I want the same thing he wants," Chao said, pointing to the Man Under Contract.

"But he is the selenite. He"—Mike the guard's stout finger pointed at Gavriel—"is not like you." The finger pointed at Chao. "He is different, and he still doesn't know it."

“What does that mean?” asked the Man Under Contract.

Mike the guard ignored him, focused on Chao. “You know you’re not the first detective they sent after him?”

“Yes.”

“And you know what happened to your predecessor?”

“No.”

“Exactly the same thing that is happening to you.”

Chao bent under the weight of blue eyes. Gavriel held his arm.

"Where do we need to go? Where is the blind god?”

Mike the guard thought for a moment and moved in the chair for the first time, looking back at the movie posters of the adventures of the mouse mascot, as if it were conferring, seeking consent. Chao thought he heard a spiteful murmur coming out of the paper. Mike the guard faced them again. “In the biggest place in the world.”

Then there was a noise next to the entrance of the room. Chao and Gavriel turned to look.

“What are you doing here?” A second security guard appeared at the door of the room. He had a dark complexion and a dense beard. The name “Raúl” was written on the nametag of his pocket.

Mike’s face tensed. Around the room, a malevolent whisper could be heard, more noticeable than ever. Chao looked at the posters framed on the wall where the mascot was gesturing with mute fury.

“Gavriel …”

The Man Under Contract was still trying to get Mike the guard to answer. “What is the biggest place in the world? Where is it?”

But the big man twisted his face like a thief surprised in the middle of the night. At the entrance, the second guard had a flashlight in his hand and pointed it on the contorted face first, and the walls later. The beam of light jumped.

"What is that? What moves there?"

Gavriel resisted but Chao, who, despite all his ignorance, knew well there would be no response, pulled his arm and half dragged him in a clatter of fallen chairs. Every time the light of Raúl the newcomer illuminated the posters on the wall, a sotto voce moan filled the air.

"Let's go!" Chao shouted.

The figure of Mike the guard trembled and lost definition. Then it mutated to expand. Chao and Gavriel got to the entrance of the room. Raúl tried to stop them.

"Wait a minute! You have to come with me to the control office. This is private property."

Chao swatted him out of the way and stepped into the corridor, still carrying a half-shocked Gavriel.

"Gavriel! We have to go. I don't know what happened but we have to go."

The Man Under Contract regained sobriety. "He asked us if we were alone. We broke the agreement."

An inhuman sound was heard coming out of the room, followed by the creaking of a metal chair as it slid on the floor. Raúl opened his eyes in horror, dropped the flashlight and ran after them.

"The God Mouse is free," Gavriel said fatalistically.

The three men fled down the service corridor, turning more corners than they had seen when coming, until they reached a dead end.

"Impossible," Raúl said. "But this is the way. This is the correct way."

They turned and ran again. More corners went by and they reached a new wall. They retraced the path and finally found a set of stairs.

"Is it the one we came down?" asked Chao.

"I don't know. It doesn't matter; the world is already pierced."

They climbed the steps and went out into the open. Outside, a ghost of the park was waiting for them. They saw a deserted avenue where ochre and sad light bathed everything and the world was a discoloured copy of the one they had left behind in California. All the pieces were there, the buildings, the fantasy lanterns, the shop windows, but they were formed of a decayed and dead texture. There was no living being, no sun, no clouds, no sky, just a monochrome blur extended like a dome above their heads.

"It's all empty," Raúl said.

"It is the intermediate realm," said Chao, disconsolate. He turned to Gavriel. "We're trapped, right?"

Gavriel looked down. He appeared afraid. "Yes, they have closed the labyrinth on us."

Hours later, the three prisoners huddled in one of the corners of the Toon Villa to rest. Chao watched the silhouettes of the anthropomorphic mouse looking at them from the walls. They had travelled the perimeter of the park looking for an exit. All they found were walls, and locks where doors and accesses should have been, as if there existed no world beyond them. They found no water, and their dry throats were an inconvenience on the way to dehydration, brought by the immobile air of the park.

At least it doesn't get dark, Chao thought. The dying light had not shifted or changed, and its ochre tone sipped life and energy.

"This is how hell must be. Nothing of flames and demons, just complete stillness, forever," said Chao.

"It could be that the guardian tried to make a copy of earth here," Gavriel said, "but without the architect's instance, this is the best it could achieve. A world in perennial entropy, a world that dies, that has been dying since the beginning of the universe."

The Man Under Contract was desperately searching for a solution. Chao watched with concern the central plaza where a pulsating and regular sound, like that of a beating heart, could be heard at intervals. The security guard sat with arms wrapped around his legs, asking, "What is happening, what is happening?" every few minutes.

"Your name is Raúl? You work here?"

The man did not answer. Gavriel spoke again, in a language that Chao did not understand, perhaps Spanish, and this time Raúl raised his head. The two talked for a moment until Raúl reverted to English.

"All I know is I received a call saying that someone had broken through one of the reserved service doors. They have sensors placed there, you know? I was searching for a good hour until I heard voices in the room. Then that … that man began to change and change."

He looked at the ground.

"Could you try the radio again?" asked Chao.

Raúl did, grabbing the receiver that hung on his shoulder, but the screen was as grey and dull as the sky. They continued with their circuit around the park and were defeated at each turn by dead ends.

"I don't understand," Raúl said, tapping a solid wall. "The west gate is here. It should be here."

Everything lacked colour because everything was a range of languid greys. From time to time, the pumping sound coming from the central square increased in volume and the park quivered.

"What are we going to do when that reaches its peak?" asked Chao.

"I don't know. This is all different."

Chao was silent as they walked. He waited for Raúl to move ahead a little, and then spoke. "Gavriel, I don't have much family, just my sister and her imbecile husband. If something happens …"

"Nothing will happen to us. We just have to be careful."

"I'm worried about what may happen to me. First Maya, then Jason and Cohan's son. Your track record as a travelling companion is very poor."

Gavriel looked away.

"If something happens, go and see Cecilia. Explain these things to her, the things that occur in the Search. I tried but I couldn't."

Gavriel wanted to answer, but before he could speak, Chao grabbed his arm vehemently. "Promise me, Gavriel. I realize now that I should not be here. You understand? I'm afraid I will get lost in this maelstrom."

At the end of their second round, after covering the perimeter of the immense park, they sat down on the avenue near the lake and ate the few remaining morsels they had left over from the previous day. The palpitation of the park thundered at regular intervals that seemed to accelerate and shook the ground.

Besides that, the stillness was oppressive. Every time someone stopped talking, it seeped down on them like a tombstone on their breath, like quick-drying concrete that plastered them in place, and all three had to make a tremendous effort so that some life circulated between them.

"I was in India once," Chao said suddenly, "in Delhi on vacation. I toured the city, stopping at the places indicated by the guide, but I didn't enjoy the trip too much, to be honest. I visited some mosques, which, looking back, might not have been a good idea in a country with the kind of religious tensions that India has. Anyway, I went up to one of the minarets at the largest mosque in the city. I forget the name. It had four of those towers, one in each corner, and they were very tall, at least forty metres. It took a while. The stairs were narrow, spiral-shaped. There was not much space there, and a long queue went up and down. I finally reached the top and came out onto a small platform, a balcony that went around the top of the minaret. It had no handrail or even a safety rope, nothing to keep people from falling over. You could see the street down below and the tip of the mosque's dome at eye level. There were many people on the platform, a dozen or so of both tourists and locals, all looking down and taking photos. The thing is that they continued to arrive, more coming up than going down. The platform was filling up quickly. We were pushing each other, and several people approached the edge dangerously. I was one of them. I tried to reach the exit so I could leave but could not advance. The mass of people was too dense and more kept coming. I don't know if that was common in India, but no one seemed too worried about the whole thing while we pushed each other. I was about half a metre from the edge and raising my voice, protesting and shoving the people who indifferently were about to push me out. Then there was a tremendous shriek. I could see nothing, but later I learned that at the other end of the platform a woman lost her footing and was left half hanging from the marble flooring. There was a great uproar, and people started screaming and pushing towards the exit. The stairway became jammed. Finally, the police arrived to dislodge the mass coming out of the narrow access to the minaret. I decided then and there that I do not like heights and I do not like crowds."

Gavriel and Raúl looked at him, waiting for the end of the story.

"But the thing is, at this moment I would give anything to be surrounded by that many people again despite the scare."

The three laughed, and the noise soaked into the air for a moment before the dreadful stillness absorbed it. There was silence again.

"Do you think I will lose my job because of this? I need it. My wife is unemployed right now," Raúl said.

The security guard had finally stopped asking questions and accepted the situation with the fatalistic docility of those used to living difficult lives.

"I don't think that will matter much when we go back," Chao said.

"I just hope I can keep the job." He looked toward the lake. "And I wish I hadn't delayed there, damn it."

"There?"

"Yes. My turn was just about to end when the call came for me to come down to the maintenance aisles."

"I thought you were already in the underground corridors when you saw us," Gavriel said.

"No, I'm in Outside Services Support. I never get down there, but I guess there was no one else available."

Gavriel approached the guard. "Where were you? Exactly," he asked with increasing urgency in his voice. "When the call came, were you here on this spot?"

"Well, I was not here. I mean. I was in the real park, you know. On the lake, on the Mississippi Riverboat that connects to the Old West section."

He signalled towards the inner part of the park where the reflection of light on the water was dull and dirty. Gavriel walked to the end of the avenue. From there he called urgently, and when Chao and Raúl reached him he said, "Look at that."

Through the buildings, they could see a sphere of dense darkness that floated on the surface of the lake.

"The exit, that is the exit," said the Man Under Contract.

Chao was thirsty and, for a moment, thought about putting his head right into the water, but the desire evaporated as he approached and looked into it. The lake was impossibly motionless, like a sheet of mercury. The water had a spurious and repellent quality. If he had had any doubt about the nature of the reality where they were wandering, that dissipated it.

They arrived at a jetty where canoes of exaggerated Native American design were moored, still and perfectly aligned. An intense rumble, the loudest yet, came from the centre of the park and reverberated on the ground. The three men lost their balance, almost fell.

"We're running out of time. I know we have to get into that door but I don't know what awaits us on the other side," said Gavriel.

"These canoes float, more or less," Chao said. "The water does not yield under them but they can slide over it."

They quickly found out that, by pushing with the oars, they could traverse, with great effort, the static surface of the lake. Little by little, amidst a torrent of sweat and gasps, they got to a few metres from the sphere. It was matte black, as big as a trailer and completely still.

"When we reach it," said the Man Under Contract, forcing his voice over the rising pumping noise that came from behind, "we need to jump inside."

The boat got even closer. Chao swallowed. The sphere was a black pupil, the eye torn from the face of a giant.

"I can't, I can't," said Raúl.

Gavriel spoke urgently to the guard. "You have to! That thing is coming. Look!"

From the central square of the park a colossal shadow unfolded, an idol without pretensions of being a mascot. Its movements copied the rhythm of the rumbling noise.

"You have to jump. You have to jump now."

The Man Under Contract pleaded to no purpose. Raúl was curled up at the bottom of the boat, as far from the dark sphere as he could get.

"There's no time, Gavriel! We have to go," Chao said and pulled at his friend.

As if underlining his words, a fresh thundering sound made the air, the park and the very boat shake. The gigantic shadow took two steps and was suddenly upon them. *It's the end of the world*, Chao thought, *the end of the world.*

"Jump!"

They jumped, and then, silence.

Back in the real California, Joseph Miller worked out in his garage. He was a man of few hobbies, no football game or amateur bowling league for him but strenuous exercising was something in which he spent countless hours. Secluded in his garage, which he had reconverted into a gym for high-end workouts while his Toyota slept outside, Miller moved heavy things, pulled himself up ropes and bars and pounded boxing bags with the greying hair of his chest and arms covered in sweat.

"Chief, there is somebody here to see you."

Miller saw his younger son peeking out of the door with a large pair of headphones around his neck and holding a game controller. Behind him, the man Blake looked into the garage.

"Thank you, Keith," he said to the teenager who was turning around, his duty done and already bored.

"Very sorry Chief Miller, I didn't mean to interrupt your workout," Blake apologized and came into the room.

"That is ok. I was almost done," he said and the truth was he had just started but military habits made him respect hierarchy and Blake was, after all, one of his employers.

Miller put on a sweatshirt and noticed the visitor was looking at his wide chest. He had no respect for people who were too undisciplined to follow a physical training regime and disliked Blake in particular, who was twenty years his junior but looked soft and unfit in his baggy clothes.

"Was that your kid? He calls you Chief too?"

"He and my wife. It started as a joke after I left the regiment. They said that although I was captain no more, it would not be fair to strip me of all rank. They decided on Chief."

"I see," Blake said and looked around the garage.

Miller waited.

"We had some developments," said Blake.

"With the Man Under Contract"

"Yes."

"Good developments? Or the other kind?"

"We don't know yet. He disappeared."

Miller chuckled and moved some of the heavy equipment out of the way. Blake, standing by the door, didn't offer to help.

"I told you, people, not to let him go."

"We had to. But that is ok, we will find him again."

Miller kept rearranging his weights and dumbells.

"Could you get a team together?"

Miller stopped and thought. He disliked the sycophantic ways Blake had but he was the gateway to Miller's paychecks.

"Yes."

"Then please do so."

"When are we off?"

"It's not clear yet"

"Keeping this type of men idle is not just expensive, it is troublesome. You and your people need to have a plan before we kick this off."

"We will know soon enough," said Blake. "How long do you need?"

"Will this be a cross-border job?" asked Miller doing some mental calculations.

"Oh, definitely."

27°05'N/103°46'E
Japan: The Rumours of the Dead

The apartment in Kowloon was silent when the Man Under Contract finished speaking. Bryan got up first and, picking up the phone, he held it upfront like a protective crucifix.

"I'm going to call the police. I'm going to call them right now."

Cecilia also stood up. "Where is my brother? Tell me."

The Man Under Contract got up last. He took his bag and put on his cap. "William Chao was my friend. I didn't think anything would happen to him."

"Have you killed him? Is he dead?"

"He is lost."

"Out of here! Out! This is a farce, and you are a charlatan!"

Bryan was speaking urgently on the phone in passable Cantonese. Saying no more, Gavriel opened the door and left.

Days passed. Cecilia dedicated all the resources of the agency and her time to tracking the fate of her brother. The last sign of Liam's presence in this world was the receipt at a gas station in San Diego paid with his credit card. Then, nothing else.

The following week, Bryan redirected her efforts without realizing it.

"That's the island he spoke of," he said while watching television on one of those sombre evenings that had become the norm at the apartment in Kowloon.

"Who?"

"That man of the contract. He said he came from Ogasawara."

On the screen, grey images showed bombers and artillery moving with the slightly accelerated pace of old-fashioned footage.

"Don't you remember he said that? Ogasawara is a small Japanese island in the Pacific. There was a big battle there during World War

II."

Cecilia grunted and forgot the name. Days later, frustration and a string of curt answers from increasingly annoyed police and embassy personnel on the phone led her to that strange state of despair where the mind becomes ductile and impressionable and the word "Ogasawara" suddenly reappeared, conjured by the magical nature of profound dejection. Sitting in front of the computer, with the disruptive presence of Bryan absent from the house, she typed into the search field.

The small Ogasawara archipelago was, in theory at least, administratively part of the Tokyo municipality, despite sitting a thousand kilometres away from the megapolis. Located down south in the waters of the Pacific Ocean, it was an isolated, remote vanguard of the motherland. Not even Chichijima, the largest island of the group, had an airport, and the only way to get there was a strenuous twenty-five-hour sea voyage by ferry. That ship, crammed with cargo to the bow and with human passengers aft, left the capital's bay three times a week and crossed the open waters of the Pacific full of tools, supplies and trivial shopping items requested by the isolated community of Ogasawara-mura village. The passengers were accommodated in a wide room with mats that covered the entire floor. There, at around eight in the evening, the crew spread blankets and pillows at regular intervals in the open space. If the ocean was merciless and choppy, travellers sat holding their stomachs up in their throats or ran into the bathroom in intermittent retching outbursts, bouncing from wall to wall in the aisles. If the sea was quiet during the journey, the ship was a jovial place with groups of people sharing liquors and tea while sitting on their blankets and lounging opulently on the interwoven straw surface of the tatami mats. Upon arriving on the island, a good part of the local population flocked to welcome the ship and its cargo of packages, mail and tourists.

The tropical coastal environment of the archipelago was monetized by fast boat businesses offering deep-sea whale watching of migrating pods and diving tours in the coral reef. The interior of the island showed a delineation of black holes pockmarking the mountains, the mouths of artificial caves that looked towards the sea like a visage of blind eyes. That was the link with the less peaceful legacy of Ogasawara, and the purpose of the caves baffled the visitors until they learned about the military artillery installations dug by the Japanese

Imperial Army during the last great war. The line of defences endured the onslaught of the US military avalanche as well as it could, but the effort was futile. Ogasawara went on to become another step in the island-to-island jump that marked the defeat of Japan and led the American army to Tokyo. At the bottom of the tropical beaches rotted the sunken remains of the battle, aeroplanes and vehicles, each smudged by the decayed texture of bygone bones. And although the war was forgotten, the scars visible on the slopes of Ogasawara never quite healed.

Cecilia dialled the number of the Coast Guard office on the island without thinking. A voice answered in Japanese. When Cecilia tried to make herself understood, the tangle of languages was such that she capitulated and hung up. She was very close to leaving the desk but the instinct of the investigation pulled her in. She dialled again, the number of the police station this time. Again they answered in Japanese. Cecilia replied in English first and Mandarin later. With no explanation, they put her on hold. Slightly embarrassed, she thought about giving up but the line came to life and someone asked a question on the other side.

"Is there no one who speaks my language there?" Cecilia asked.

"I, myself, can, madam. This is Sergeant Furuta."

Cecilia gave her name, explained that she was calling from Hong Kong.

"I have reason to think that my brother has been to your island. He is missing."

"Your brother? Is he Chinese too? We have some foreign tourists but not too many. What is his name?"

"William."

Silence.

"William Chao?" asked the policeman.

Cecilia wanted to speak. Her voice failed. She tried again. "Do you know him? Is he there?"

Furuta's voice sounded disquieted now. "Not directly, but I've heard his name. Was your brother travelling alone?"

"Maybe he was with someone else …" stuttered Cecilia.

"A European male, under the name Artiel?"

Cecilia could only whisper, "Yes."

Furuta was silent for at least a minute.

"Hello?" said the woman.

"I'm still here. I cannot speak at this moment; the ferry is arriving. But if you consent to give me your number, I will call you at a later time," said the policeman in his strangely formal manner.

"Do you know where my brother is?"

"That I do not. But maybe we can help each other."

Cecilia sat the rest of the afternoon with the phone in her hand, scared and hopeful about what she would hear. Bryan returned before dinner, talked about this and that, his day at work, their mutual friends. Everything he said was for Cecilia a dull background noise that lasted until the man lay down in bed. She stayed in the room with growing shadows, almost motionless. The phone rang.

"Yes?"

"Ms Chao, this is, again, Furuta."

"Yes."

"I'm sorry to call at such late time. I didn't notice the time difference. Can you speak at this time?" His English was methodical, precise.

"What do you know about my brother?"

"Some things, maybe not much. But perhaps I better tell you what I know about the other individual, Gavriel Artiel, and then you can decide if that helps. I tried to move the conversation through the official channels but the story is somewhat strange."

"I know that man and yes, the stories around him tend to be strange."

Furuta made an appreciative sound.

"Mr Artiel told me that he arrived by sea to Ogasawara. I assumed, on saying 'sea' he meant by boat. It is the only option."

Gavriel broke the foam of the waves with his forehead and surfaced breathing hard. He had a moment of panic when he strained in despair, not knowing that he was already safe. Floating and sinking at intervals, he made headway towards the beach and came out of the sea. He tasted salt and seaweed and spat hard. Even with his feet buried in the sand, he could not calm down. Nothing was taking his breath away, but he kept breathing with greedy and hurried gulps.

The Man Under Contract remembered a rumble, remembered the water and his friend William, but a black hole engulfed the rest in a sphere of dense obscurity. "William," he thought, alarmed. Jumping to his feet, he shouted, looking for him. William did not answer. He wandered the beach, seeing nothing and nobody, flanked by a featureless sea that could be located anywhere. The temperature was pleasant and the vegetation vaguely tropical. A barrier of green brush framed the crescent-shaped line of sand. To the left, far away, there was an unpaved road that tempted Gavriel to leave his useless exploration. But William could be there, splashing in the water or lying among the trees, so Gavriel resumed his walking up and down the beach, hoping to find him.

Sunset came and Gavriel, defeated, entered the dirt road. He walked for ten minutes. Beyond, the track led to a larger road and, even further up, Gavriel saw houses, cars, people: the full paraphernalia of human life. A middle-aged woman shaped a tall hedge with a pair of pruning shears, wearing thick gardening gloves and a drooping brimmed hat. She had Asian features.

"Hello?" Gavriel tried, speaking in terrible Mandarin.

The woman did not understand. Gavriel repeated the greeting in English, and this time there was a response with a heavy accent but correct grammar.

"I do not know where I am."

"Here? This is Sakaiura beach. You left the road behind. The road is down there," she said, pointing with the oversized gardening gloves.

"Yes, but where?"

The woman looked at him with eyes surrounded by fine wrinkles. "On the island."

"Which island?"

"The island of Chichijima in Ogasawara," she said, laughing nervously and turning to prune the hedge again.

Gavriel arrived at Ogasawara-mura twenty minutes later. It was a small, well-spaced town that was born in the jetty and the breakwater of the harbour and ran all the way up to the first slopes of the central mountain range. It had a soothing profile of low houses, courtyards and clear roads that was framed in blue by the sea on one side and in green by the lush vegetation on the other. In the dock, an enormous ferry with white and red lines dozed tranquilly, anchored and looking too large for the repose that Ogasawara enjoyed.

Gavriel didn't know where he was until somewhat later when he saw a white flag with a blood-red circle in the middle.

"Japan," he thought. "I'm in Japan."

Gavriel now had the dilemma that occasionally happens in dreams, in which one wanders naked or barefoot and is shamefully aware of it. Without money, passport or memory, he spent that night outdoors, sheltered from the benign but variable weather under a palm grove and looking at a clear sky full of the Pleiades and other stars every time the clouds parted. The second morning found Gavriel as disoriented as the first one. All the inventiveness he had developed in years of travelling through Asia failed him, and he simply wandered from street to street and returned to the beach of the day before. When he sat down to rest, the name "Chao" rumbled in his head and he would rise feverishly to search the sand and the surf of the ocean.

But Ogasawara was a small island and, at that time of the year, tourists were scarce. Gavriel noticed how, when crossing in front of the shops too many times, the owners looked at him curiously. At noon, he decided to entrust himself to the authorities. He walked first to the Coast Guard building, but before he got there he saw the small police station, a cubical building with two floors, and entered. A young officer was sitting at the reception counter and looked at the poor figure of the Man Under Contract: overgrown beard, sweaty shirt. He got up slowly. The policeman did not speak English but called out loudly and a middle-aged man in uniform with sergeant bars of rank sewn to his shoulders came down from the second floor. He listened to his assistant and, in a rather formal manner, spoke.

"May I help you?"

Fifteen minutes later, both sitting upstairs, the policeman finished filling out a report.

"Any more details?" he asked Gavriel across the expanse of his desk.

"It's all I remember."

The policeman nodded. "I understand," he seemed to say in that very correct and empathetic manner of the Japanese. "You remember that you were in a boat at one moment and in the water the next. You don't know how you entered Japanese territory. You don't know the name of the ship you were sailing on. You don't know how you fell overboard …"

"I do not."

The policeman leaned back in his chair, saying nothing, a man in his fifties but with the youthful appearance that a flat stomach and a head full of dark hair dispense. The office reflected the measured pulse of his work on the island: well-ordered paperwork, empty drawers. A plaque on his table spelt his name: "Furuta." *Oldfield*, Gavriel thought. How did he know its meaning?

"Or maybe I jumped. I don't know," Gavriel said hurriedly through the silence. "My friend William was with me. He may have reached the shore too."

Sergeant Furuta read his report. "William Chao, a Chinese citizen."

"Hongkongese," qualified Gavriel.

Furuta issued a loud order and, from the ground floor, the young policeman replied.

"Wakatsuki is going to take a look around with the patrol car, to check if anyone has seen your friend. This is a small place. If he is here, he will appear."

Then he spoke Japanese quickly on the phone for a while, hung up, filled out some papers, thought again. Gavriel waited in silence.

"Do you agree to have a health check-up? It will include a drug test."

"Yes."

"Mr Artiel, I am not a doctor, but I do know that selective amnesia like the one you described is more common in films and novels than it is medically possible. I don't find you to be confused or alienated, and yet you can't explain how you got here."

"No," Gavriel continued, clinging to monosyllables.

"The Japanese government takes political refugees very seriously. If you came here and destroyed your passport for any reason, you better tell me now. Otherwise, there will be consequences."

"No, it's not that. I want to go home."

The sergeant drummed his pen on the edge of the table. "Very well, we can contact your embassy in Tokyo, confirm your identity, and process a new passport. There will be many expenses to cover. The embassy may extend you a loan that you must return later. Or you can contact your bank once you have your new passport and receive a credit card."

"Thank you."

"For now we can provide you—" he made a quick mental calculation "—about two hundred dollars as an expense for assistance to the shipwrecked, which is the category in which I will assume it falls. It is a sunk cost so don't worry about it. Please buy some clothes, eat something, call your embassy."

"I understand."

"The medical centre is on the other side of town. I will accompany you there. After that I will take you to the Coast Guard building. It has a pavilion with cots for refugees of natural disasters, where you can clean up after the health check. Do you need anything else?"

"No."

Furuta seemed to battle with his thoughts for an instant.

"I don't mean to be unkind, but I want to stress again how irregular your situation is. If this were Tokyo, you would likely be placed in a detention centre. We don't have one here but please consider the entire island as a confinement area," he added, and that was the end of the conversation.

An hour later Furuta left Gavriel in his new room. Gavriel saw him walking down the streets of the quiet town. Inside, the pavilion had a series of bunk beds close to the wall and metal lockers that served as partitions. The room was grey and functional. Gavriel waited for ten minutes with barely contained impatience before leaving himself, out to discover the tranquil exile where he had landed. By mid-afternoon he was well acquainted with the reduced ecosystem of Ogasawara-mura, its volcanic beaches as well as the jagged peaks covered with the tropical vegetation of the interior. From the town centre, a road that circled the entire island started up a nearby hill. With no better prospect, Gavriel followed the dark line of asphalt.

The pass was the highest point in that area and divided the low bay of Ogasawara-mura to the north from the southern area, where the rest of the island curled up like a snake of tuberous curves, topped by the mountains of Takayama and Toriyama. The air was clean and the water seemed to have floated pure from the vast expanses at the heart of the Pacific. In the coves, the submerged silhouettes of the ships sunk during the war could be observed, long forms eaten up by detritus and coral. Gavriel sat on a rock and, watching the blue and green palette of the landscape, dozed off.

He saw the desperate escape to the dark sphere and the rumble of thunder in the storm. Or maybe it was not thunder at all. He saw a man of dark complexion, whose name he could not recall but who, he knew, worried greatly about his wife's future, fall into the strangely still water. The surface cemented over him without a splash. William jumped into the gears of the world as the world itself trembled again. Gavriel was last; he jumped too and was submerged without transition into the waters of the Pacific.

When he woke up the sun had fallen. It was colder. The new raincoat he had bought with Furuta's money did little to shield him from the wind. He walked back to town and saw people, residents who had finished their workday, and a few tourists tired of exploring the island.

The police sergeant was waiting in front of the Coast Guard building. "Where have you been, sir?" he asked point-blank.

"Walking. Taking a walk, I mean."

Furuta did not seem satisfied. "Why did you not tell me you spent a whole day wandering around town before coming to the police station?"

"What?"

"This is a very small place. I have half a dozen neighbours who saw you go all day to the beach and back. I don't know if that is the attitude to be expected from a castaway or an amnesiac."

"I was disoriented. I didn't know where I was."

Furuta looked at him carefully, his narrow face serious and very still.

"You are to be confined until your situation is clear. Do not return to the beach, do not leave the limits of Ogasawara-mura until we hear word from your embassy."

"You have no right to detain me."

"I have every right. At this moment you are an illegal immigrant, and if you give me any trouble, I will cuff you and put you in a cell."

"No, no cells," Gavriel said, and he remembered white rooms.

"Then stay here." Turning around, the policeman left.

"Wait."

Furuta looked back.

"And William?"

"We haven't found anyone. And you should know that there is no record of a distress call from any ship. You are in a delicate situation, Mr Artiel."

The effect of the dire warning lasted just until night closed in. Gavriel was hungry, bored and, looking out at the town which grew silent, felt tempted to venture out. In the further street corner he could see from the maritime command building a shop with faded red sunshades announcing food using both neon signs and permeating aromas. It seemed like a sensible distance even for the severity of the rules Furuta had imposed, so Gavriel crossed the street at a wolf trot and entered the premises.

He saw a very long, almost empty wooden counter, several stools, no tables. The posters on the walls advertised noodles served in large bowls with a complement of rice and beer. Gavriel sat at the counter and, not knowing what its value was, he peeled off a banknote from the wad of money provided by the generosity of the Japanese government. The man behind the counter greeted him. He wore a thick headkerchief wrapped around the forehead to collect the continual sweat caused by the many large cauldrons where noodles boiled, and a long dark apron with Japanese ideograms stamped on it.

"Welcome, welcome," he said in English.

Gavriel pointing to one of the photos on the wall, chosen almost at random, and the cook took his order. While he cooked he spoke over his shoulder.

"You are the person who has been shipwrecked, right?"

"How do you know?"

"This is a very small town. Did you really fall off a ship?"

"I don't know. It's confusing."

"Ah, that is … how do you call it?" He searched for the right word for a moment and gave up. "Well, when you lose your memory, right?"

"Something like that."

The man put a large bowl in front of Gavriel. It steamed mightily.

"Have you been able to talk to your family? They must be worried."

Gavriel didn't remember anyone. Maybe there was no one.

"Yes, they are relieved."

"Well, in any case, don't let Furuta pester you. Sometimes he is a bit more serious than this island needs."

From the far reaches of the infinite counter, a man with a beard and long hair, the only other patron, pulled his face from the edge of the bowl where he crouched, sipping noisily. He said something in Japanese and the owner translated.

"He thinks he is still in Tokyo, that Furuta," he said.

The owner of the shop admonished him to lower his voice and turned back to Gavriel. "But your embassy will help, you'll see. It is not the first time we have had refugees from the sea here. What are your plans while they fix the situation? Have you visited any other places in the islands?"

"I've walked around."

The man in the corner peppered the conversation with his grunts again.

"He says that the best way to see Ogasawara is from the sea. He asks me why I don't take you to see the whales."

"I didn't know they could be seen from here."

"You have to go offshore, by boat, but it's not a bad idea if you still feel like navigating. Because of the accident, I mean."

"I don't remember much about it. Almost nothing."

"Well, the island is close to the whaling migration corridor. You can see many just off the coast. There are also wild dolphins. It's a great spectacle. My wife has a boat and we usually go out to see them. Would you like to join us?"

Gavriel, concerned, looked out the door where the corner of the police station was visible.

"Don't worry about Furuta. My wife will talk to him. This is a very small island. There is nowhere you can escape."

That night the deductive process used by the Man Under Contract changed. He had always discovered the clues of the Search through cognitive treatment, a discipline of understanding to which he had devoted himself for years and, although he indeed judged the texture of what he learned instinctively when deciding whether or not it was relevant, the origin of the indications that led him through the Search was the product of hours of study and consideration.

The dark hole that plagued his memory had robbed him of those enlightened abilities but had, in return, left him open to esoteric signals over which he had no command or control.

He woke up before daylight in the room of the Coast Guard station. The heavy door was closed by a deadbolt which remained secured during the hours of darkness, but Gavriel was the only person sheltering in the cavernous interior of empty bunks. He dressed carefully, fumbled with the bolt in the darkness and looked outside. The island emitted a vaporous influence. Something was about to happen. All was quiet, and the town dozed in the pre-dawn lethargy that only small places still preserve. It was in not only absence of activity but something else: the distinct impression that any undertaking conducted at that vacant, dark time would be reprehensible.

He came out of the building. The pier and all the streets were deserted. Not quite; there was a discreet movement on the avenue. Gavriel walked in that direction. He saw nothing down the street. However up the street, in the direction of the road he had followed that day, he saw a figure walking lightly, almost running. It had a certain military bearing. A soldier. He wore a steel helmet, carried a canteen and a rifle, and had an aged appearance, like a piece taken from an old toybox of plastic figurines. The soldier moved on and quickly disappeared beyond a hill on the road. Gavriel rushed after him. Dogs barked when he approached each fence, as loudspeakers of a hidden alarm that moved from house to house following his movements, but on the quiet Pacific island, even that was not enough to wake anyone.

The soldier left the village with Gavriel in tow. Gavriel raced to reach him and found the military man waiting at the top of the hill that led to the south of the island. He was Japanese, with a uniform sewn together from a sturdy and battered material: khaki drill and leather straps; no camouflage. The soldier had a thin beard, of the kind that grows on Asian men selectively and sparingly on the chin, moustache and sideburns.

He spoke in a prudent whisper. "Do you see them down there?"

"Who?"

"The men. Do you see them?"

The soldier could be speaking in Japanese, maybe in another language but, as often happens in dreams, Gavriel had the prodigious ability to understand him.

"Where?"

"There. They are assembling."

"I don't see anything."

The soldier looked at him with some surprise. "That's how we were when they arrived, running up and down. You see that?" He pointed to the silhouette of the ship sunk in the bay. "We scuttled it to block the access of their landing to the beach. In any case, there was no fuel left to manoeuvre or ammunition in the ship's magazines."

Gavriel had questions, but his usual inquiring spirit was buried under the dark blanket of his memory. "Why do you tell me all that?" was the only thing he said.

The soldier looked at him, thinking anew. "Aren't you here for the counting?"

"I don't know what I'm here for."

"Then you have to find out. The Major is not patient with anyone. He will not be with you."

The apartment in Kowloon's was still dark. Cecilia held the phone tightly.

"Ms Chao?"

"I'm still here. How do you know all that? It was night-time and Artiel was alone, right?"

"He told me about his encounter later, after more things had happened. That first day I knew nothing."

"He told you?"

"I think something really happened that affected his memory, some kind of trauma. But after, when his memories came back, he had no qualms about sharing certain details, with no consideration of how his words sounded."

"And you believed him?"

"I can't answer that," Furuta said, "but it's part of the reason I called you."

When Gavriel arrived at the jetty the following morning, there was lively attendance at one of the boats. Shimizu, the owner of the noodle shop, was there with his wife, a well-groomed woman in her fifties. A couple of neighbours, some relatives and several children had also joined, all cramming the white fishing boat converted into a recreational whale-watching yacht. Within a few minutes and after a barrage of questions, it was clear to Gavriel why he had been invited.

The foreign castaway was a curiosity in the quiet life of the island, an extraordinary circumstance on ordinary days. Shimuzu's offer was less magnanimous than it seemed because the entire island was dying to learn more about the saturnine foreigner. Furuta was inscrutable, so Shimizu had been commissioned by the rest of the town to find out who was the man who had suddenly disrupted the quiet cadence of Ogasawara's days.

The interrogation was conducted in the Japanese manner, discreet questions and inciting comments posed to the Man Under Contract while the boat crossed the cold morning water. Either Shimizu or his wife, the only English speakers, translated at a slow pace. Gavriel responded as he had done at the police station. There was not much to tell because he remembered little. As he spoke, the audience offered commiserating nods and congratulated him for his fortitude.

"Surely Furuta will get your papers soon. He is very professional."

One of the men waved his hand in the air, with that expressive gesture that seeks to erase the words last uttered from the very air to correct them. "He is wearisome, that Furuta. We were better off with a local man like Yamakawa."

"I heard the sergeant was assigned here from Tokyo but I thought he was originally from here, from the island," Gavriel said.

"Furuta? No, they sent him from there to take over the police station."

"From so far away?"

Shimizu cut in, adopting the learned airs of a man who knows things well beyond noodles. "Well, administratively we are part of the capital and its police department."

One of the women interceded. "I heard that he was a chief inspector and he was dismissed for that scandal with the gangs."

"I heard about that too; mafia stuff. A couple of years ago they discovered a network of illegal fights in Tokyo, and then there was a war or something."

"I think they were all foreigners. Maybe that is why Furuta is nervous around you," said Shimuzu's wife.

"The thing is that Furuta was involved in the investigation but failed to solve it. They threw a woman from the top of a building in Tokyo. It was in all the news. After that, they sent Furuta here. Forced transfer, if you ask me."

The gossip continued until the island of Ogasawara was a distant mass far off. Even at that range, Gavriel could see the small dark holes that the artillery positions had left on the mountain wall. He remembered the soldier.

Most of the men and several of the older children prepared to enter the water. The ocean was a hue of tremendous dark blue; open ocean, deep. Shimizu lent Gavriel a diving wetsuit, fins and a diving mask.

"It's the best way to see the animals. Can you dive? You just float next to the boat and when you see others submerge, follow them."

"And you don't you come in?" asked Gavriel.

"The water is too cold for me. Hop out! Here they come."

Gavriel jumped over the gunwale, holding the mask in place with one hand. Water stamped against his body and cold streams sneaked between the neoprene and his skin. Disoriented an instant, he saw other divers glide into the immense darkness of the sea. Then they disappeared. Gavriel was left alone in the submerged world that was now suddenly empty.

From the depth came a shadow, a cetacean and patient presence[48] in a cosmos that had neither above nor below. Gavriel felt helpless because there, he was an animal in distress, a clumsy ape torn from the plateaus and abandoned in a strange habitat. He saw the silhouette approaching from the oceanic chasms and felt the irrational fear of the prey; even knowing that the whale was not hostile, he imagined the teeth and maw of the leviathan. The water displaced around him, pushed by the proximity of the colossal body, and fear changed to fascination. The lustrous organism moved smoothly like the hand of a

---

[48] The Ogasawara whales belong to the humpback variety and visit the archipelago in the spring months of their nautical pilgrimage. During their stay, they nurse and breastfeed the calves before disappearing back into the marine interior.

painter who knows what he is doing. There was an eye camouflaged in the aquatic head, among the scars left by clashes with man and fauna. Gavriel found it, and when their gazes met he felt the exclusive and undeniable bond with another genre that spoke of months enclosed in the womb and mother's milk tasting of life. "We are the same," said the mute correspondence between the two animals forsaken in an adverse medium; one a primate out of his element, and the other a fish that was no fish, which had decided once to spend eternity holding its breath. "I was loved and cared for before they delivered me into the Pacific immensity. Here you see my world."

The Man Under Contract understood everything.

By the time he boarded the boat again, the black hole in Gavriel's mind had dissipated. He remembered California, he remembered Maya, and, above all, he remembered the Search. He apologized to his Japanese hosts and, claiming fatigue, spent the rest of the journey pretending to doze while he thought and planned. When the boat arrived at the harbour, he said a hurried goodbye, bought a notebook at the town's commissary and ran to the Ogasawara-mura library. The period of disorientation was over.

The library was a cosy two-storey building. The upper part consisted of a room with toys and a cramped playground for children. The lower floor was full of shelves with cheap-looking paperback editions. Almost all of the reading material was in Japanese, and Gavriel contented himself by looking at the illustrations. A separate section of tourist guides in English did not help much more, even though, by nightfall, he had filled in pages and pages of the new notebook with his cryptic and detailed annotations.

He returned to the Coast Guard building and found a note from the police sergeant. The embassy, said Furuta, had confirmed his identity and, although the only record they had was the renewal of the document years ago, they could issue a new one. When he visited Shimizu's shop for dinner—again noodles served in a large bowl—he learned that the ongoing gossips in the island said that Furuta was now consulting the Interpol databases before deciding whether to put Gavriel in jail or on a boat to Tokyo.

The second night he woke up using the alarm of his watch. The island did not want to influence him esoterically anymore, and Gavriel did not need it when he could again depend on his will and ingenuity. He retraced the steps of the previous night. The dogs barked, the moon shone and, punctual for the appointment, the soldier waited on the hill.

"Do you see them down there?" he said with no preamble.

"No, I need you to help me see them. Who are they?"

"Everyone, the vanguard and the rear, all the men that were in reserve; the office workers, the carpenters, the cooks. Everyone has taken up arms."

"What are they doing? What have you come to do?"

"They have called general quarters. We have to prepare."

"Why?"

"Because …" the soldier hesitated. "They've called general quarters. There is much to do. We have to prepare the parapets and the foxholes, obstruct the amphibious invasion. They will launch everything they have. There will be an assault of adjoining beaches. The Major said so."

"Why do you come here night after night? If you tell me what you need, I might be able to help you."

The soldier shivered. "I fear. I fear this is the end."

"What's your name?" said Gavriel with compassion, because the soldier looked young and abandoned and so very sad.

The soldier gave a kind smile, with his face framed by the too-wide chinstrap of a metal helmet that was too large. "Masahiro. My name is Masahiro, just like my father. My father had a bicycle factory in Nagoya. I would go down a hill near our place, just like this hill here, at full speed. Sometimes, when the Major sends me to deliver a message, I climb onto one of the bicycles we have at the barracks and I ride out. And when I am going downhill I imagine I'm still in Nagoya."

"Tell me how I can help you, Masahiro," said Gavriel.

The soldier did not hear. He looked at a panorama that was invisible to Gavriel and shivered with the roar of a cannonade that only he heard. His eyes kept going towards the sea, the ground, the sky. The only thing Gavriel could see was a quiet night. The soldier said no more, ran down the hill, and the Man Under Contract, unable to cross that threshold to the south of the island, saw him disappear.

He had not asked the right questions. The entrance to the labyrinth remained closed.

The next day Gavriel woke up early. He was going out to the library when the young policeman, Wakatsuki, came looking for him. In Ogasawara, almost nobody was a person of exclusive trade. Shopkeepers doubled as civil servants, tour guides delivered goods and packages, and boat pilots carried both cargo and people with no discrimination. Furuta and his subordinate Wakatsuki were two of the few specialized professionals in the small community where the myriad of tasks and the scarcity of resources forced a constant and lively moonlighting.

Gavriel followed the officer to the small police station and climbed to the second floor. Furuta waited in his office, serious as always.

"Thanks for coming."

Gavriel sat down. The sergeant handed him a manila envelope.

"Your passport. It arrived in today's ferry. You can leave tomorrow and use the same boat to reach Tokyo."

"And that's it?"

"That is it. The embassy may have some more questions for you. Please go there when disembarking."

"I still don't know what happened to William, my friend. He may be here."

Furuta stirred uncomfortably in his chair and spoke in a compassionate tone. "If he hasn't appeared already, you must prepare yourself for the idea that he has … passed. No one can survive three days floating adrift, not with ocean temperatures as they are this time of year."

Gavriel thought for a moment. The sergeant had encountered a very unusual situation and, despite some ingrained suspicions, he had helped a stranger and treated him with proper dignity. Just for that, he deserved any cordiality that Gavriel could give him.

"Thanks, Sargent Furuta. Without your help, I do not know what would have become of me."

"It was my duty," replied Furuta in an administrative flat tone, and that was that.

At the library, the Man Under Contract discovered two computers with large, thick monitors that gave access to the immense digital world beyond the island. Using the fresh flow of information, the gears and couplings of his mind refined everything he had seen and heard until that moment, seeking to understand what he needed to do to pave the way to the labyrinth.

Inspired by the figure of the soldier and the ships sunk in the bay, Gavriel delved into the stories of the island's war period. Ogasawara had surrendered in September of 1945, almost at the end of the conflict. In tandem with the most famous island of Iwo Jima, this archipelago was the key to the Japanese Pacific defence. There was an initial American plan to disembark troops, but the allies considered that Ogasawara was too fortified for invasion. The two sides exchanged bombs, shrapnel and detonations for months, with the comforting span of chemical propulsion set between them, yet the campaign was as bloody and personal as if it had been fought with bullets and bayonets instead of frigates and gull-wing fighters. The contingent of the island, under the command of Major Sueo Matoba, reached the end of the fighting completely consumed. The soldier was right, there had been no fuel left, not for months; no fuel, no supplies or provisions. The Japanese ate coconuts and rats first and, driven to desperation by hunger, leather shoes and belts later. But Japan was on an unstoppable slope that led to ruination long before the atomic bombs of Hiroshima and Nagasaki sealed the end of the conflict. Ogasawara, like Guam, Okinawa and the rest of the imperial bastion-islands, fought not to win but with the sole solace of seeing the American avalanche stumble as much as possible.

Gavriel read for hours about the fighting, about the atrocities and deaths on both sides, and finally understood what the pending question was. On a sheet of paper, he wrote a long list of names.

He had dinner at Shimizu's place for the last time. The owner took out two beers and they drank together in the quiet, deserted restaurant.

"So you leave on the ferry tomorrow?"

"I'm not sure yet."

Shimizu seemed surprised. "But you already have your passport. If you miss this ferry you will have to wait several more days. Isn't your family worried?"

Gavriel nodded in silence and finished his dinner. He then said goodbye to Shimizu, thanking him for his cordiality. But back at the Coast Guard pavilion, he reflected and realized that it was not only Furuta who expected him to leave the island the next day but the whole of Ogasawara. The excitement brought by the story of his shipwreck had expired, and the population expected a swift return to the cadence of calm and quiet days.

His last night in Ogasawara, Gavriel waited for the soldier. When he arrived, he followed him just like the previous nights. At the top of the hill, they stopped shoulder to shoulder. Masahiro opened his mouth but Gavriel asked first.

"Do you wish to wake up?"

The soldier looked at him with eyes almost in tears. "Wake up? Are we asleep then?"

"Masahiro, you are dead, you are all dead."

"Dead? Us dead? How is that possible? The invasion is yet to come. We have time."

Gavriel repeated the question. "Do you wish to wake up?"

"Yes." His voice was broken. "We all wish that."

"Where are the others?"

The soldier pointed to the south side of the island where the hill descended into the jungle and the remote shores. Gavriel did not see anyone.

"Down there."

Now the Man Under Contract was to venture into risk. Gavriel's impeded memory had caused the labyrinthine door to open just an inch and get stuck. The decision he had to make was to continue pushing carefully or to force his entry.

"Listen to me. Everything that happens to you, everything you see, is not real. Someone has tried to make a copy of the world. It is a marred copy and does not work as it should. I have seen something similar before. That's what keeps you stranded here night after night; you're suspended."

The soldier listened with his eyes open in horror. "Who? Who has done this?"

"One of you. Someone who is not what he seems. Someone different."

"Different?"

"Yes. Do you know who it can be?"

"The Major. It must be the Major," said Masahiro, and he was trembling.

"I need you to take me there, to the place where you meet. Can you do that?"

The soldier moved forward, stopped, grabbed Gavriel by his shirt and forced him to take a step down the hill. When he did so, the night sky filled with glows, quiet bursts sounded, and lights that had not been there a step before shone in the sea.

"Come on, come on," said the son of the bicycle maker.

Gavriel passed for the first time across to the other side and also, for the first time, the soldier did not fade away. Other figures appeared on the road and in the tangle of the jungle; soldiers in the same old uniform as Masahiro; some civilians carrying large bundles of clothes and luggage. They all hastened on the road and on the paths between the trees without stumbling, despite the lack of light. They walked quickly, with purpose but no destination. Gavriel looked back. The glow of the street lights in Ogasawara-mura and the harbour shimmered in the distance, and he knew that the two worlds were in contact. If he needed to go back, this time he could.

Near the shore, the agglomeration grew. Gavriel saw Western faces in the crowd, pilots in flight suits with the American flag on the shoulder, mixed with Japanese soldiers and sailors. It was harder for him to stay close to his guide. The ghosts of the dead were solid, pushing him when walking with determination towards stations that neither existed nor mattered anymore. In the panic of the torrent of men and the knocking of rifle stocks on canteens, Masahiro moved further and further away.

"Wait, wait!"

"It's over here! Follow me," the lost soldier among soldiers shouted.

Gavriel pushed and pulled but, although he was more corpulent than many of the soldiers, their number was excessive. The impedimenta they carried obstructed his way. The sky lit with flashes, and the negative-film colour of the explosions arrived without the heat, sound or force of real bombs. They were just another prop in the scene, an attempt to fill the false world with life. Overhead, aeroplane silhouettes crossed like shadow puppets; in the bay, the flat contours of frigates and destroyers floated mechanically on the water.

The mass of soldiers, dotted with civilians, recovered its sense of direction and headed in mute and common agreement towards the south-east of the island. Gavriel advanced too, dragged by the crowd. The phantasms chattered in a miscellanea of languages. They told stories that were seventy years too old, remembering girlfriends and wives who were already, in the real world on the other side of the hill, dead and buried.

"Masahiro!" Gavriel shouted.

Even if he could have seen the soldier, he would never have been able to recognize him among the other Japanese in threadbare uniforms and with scraggly beards. A Western man in a pilot's overalls and heavy leather jacket turned to him.

"Where are your khakis? We are to form in the esplanade. If the Major sees you like that, you will be in trouble."

Soldiers around him echoed the protest, and hands came out to feel the strange, synthetic material of his clothes

"Why are you not wearing your uniform?" asked a man with a large, crimson-spotted bandage on his face.

"I'm a civilian."

"He's a Cit? Where does he come from?" asked others.

Gavriel pushed harder, trying to get rid of the soldiers' hug, but there was nowhere to go. The false explosions flared more intensely in the sky and the rumour of voices and moving ordnance was deafening.

"Watch out! He's making a run for it!!"

Callused hands held him. Gavriel gave a mighty push and several soldiers fell to the floor with rifles and backpacks clanking.

"Grab him!"

In an instant, he was raised by many hands, unable to move. Gavriel didn't know how many were holding him but they marched forward with the Man Under Contract suspended up high, like an offering on the way to the altar.

"Take him to the Major!"

"To the Major! To the Major!"

The tumult moved until arriving at a great expanse near the beach where the soldiers formed up haphazardly. The Man Under Contract was dragged roughly in front of a very large canvas tent and thrown inside. Gavriel rolled on the floor and stopped, panting. At the back of the pavilion he saw a pair of calf-length military boots. A slender Japanese officer in full uniform walked slowly towards him. Behind, an aide-de-camp held a cap and a scabbard.

"You're not one of ours." He approached Gavriel closely. "Who are you?"

"No one."

The commander was a young man with the shaved head and protruding ears of the black-and-white pictures Gavriel had seen on the computer screen: Major Sueo Matoba.

"That is not entirely true. Look here." He touched the forehead of the Man Under Contract with the tip of his finger and his touch was preternatural. "Your head is brimming with marks. Look, you are all smeared and you don't even realize. What have you come to do here? To break the symmetry?"

The Major was a terrible apparition, human in form, superhuman in essence. He was, Gavriel knew, one of the names on his list.

"What you've done—all those men out there. This is not right."

"The troops are where they should be, serving Ogasawara."

"That is not … The war is over. You have no right," said Gavriel.

"I grant the right to myself. I am of the unmovable race and Ogasawara is mine. It is not of God, it is not of man. It's mine."

"But why do you keep them here?"

And although the Major turned around and did not answer, Gavriel had already guessed why he held hostage the detachment of doleful ghosts. They were an integral part of the stage set by the numen; in part decoration, just like the silhouettes in sky and sea, and partially conscripted actors. Matoba was a being which shared the archons' obsession to create and build in the image of its master and, in failing, it reached out maniacally, looking for alternatives. In that place, only the appearance of activity, the dynamism that was aimed at vivifying a dead world, counted for something.

The Major had already forgotten him. Gavriel rose, sore from the blow against the ground. *Boom, boom, boom* went the explosions outside, dulled and superimposed like a poorly synchronized soundtrack.

"Where is it? Where is the blind god?" he asked, addressing Matoba's back.

The Major looked over his shoulder, not responding. He walked into the depths of the tent, seemed to think better, reappeared. Then he said, "Where could the immensity of the blind god rest? What seat exists that can accommodate the width of divine architecture?"

The words he heard in California came to the memory of the Man Under Contract. "The biggest place in the world," Gavriel said.

"Yes, only in the incomparable heights, in the first place it created."[49]

"The High Reaches …" Gavriel murmured.

"Yes. You only need one more mark"—Matoba waved his hand reluctantly—"and here you have it. But be careful. It won't be what you wish it to be. Remember that the blind god builds. That's what it does."

Then the Major took the cap from the hands of his aide-de-camp and put it on. "Announce the call to arms," he ordered. "Assemble the troops."

They dragged the Man Under Contract outside. In the esplanade the soldiery formed up in the shape of a crescent moon around a pedestal-like rock. The clamor of the men was terrible, but a more terrible silence came the moment Major Matoba lifted the flap of the tent and came out. He walked to the stone, one hand on the holster and another swinging martially, and climbed on it. Two soldiers flanked Gavriel and made him follow. The full attention of the army was on the Major, so even the dull sound of explosions fell away.

---

[49] From the creationist legends of *Jigten Chagtsul*: "At first there was only the emptiness. Then a wind began to blow and amassed the clouds. From the clouds, large raindrops began to fall and from them the original ocean came to be. The wind that never stopped moved and removed the ocean and the clotted mass of its foam solidified. The cosmic mountain Sumeru was born from its center."

Although the Platonic or Gnostic description may not contain this degree of detail, the narrative of the Genesis is similar in all theologies.

"Men of Ogasawara, we are certainly the guardians of this island. We are certainly men of mission and purpose."

The soldiers nodded at the commander's words without enthusiasm. They seemed baffled by the sudden pause in the frantic preparations of their meaningless campaign.

"This is a place of conflict, and we are bound to keep its tremulous balance or it will disappear. You, the children; me, the father; this, our house: all will go away. What I do now, I do for us."

Gavriel, who was yet oblivious to the implications of the words, searched through the ranks of soldiers, looking through the changing gaps left by elbows, shoulders and backpacks for help, but no one was there to help him. The officer pulled a bright sword from the scabbard his assistant offered with a gesture of great finality.

"Proceed," he said in a formidable tone.

Many seizing hands pushed the Man Under Contract toward the stony dais. The Major towered, and a distorted reflection of Gavriel's face showed in the metal of the extended sabre. The Major put the flat of the blade on the top of his head and, more with his silent power than with the weapon itself, pushed down until Gavriel fell to his knees. Matoba's face was overcast by a shadow that seemed to float on the skin, just like a remote signal entering in and out of phase. The soldiers watched the scene, tied down to the will of the beast which ruled their vigils on the south side of the island. Gavriel, under the menace of sharp metal and still held by strange hands, shouted because it was the only thing left to do.

"This thing is not Major Sueo Matoba! Major Matoba was tried for war crimes in 1946 and sentenced to death!"

There were hisses and murmurs in the crowd. The ember of the will of those trapped souls turned to Gavriel. In the front row, he saw the blond pilot who had first denounced him.

"You! Who are you? You must have been a prisoner. Remember it. You were a prisoner on this island."

The pilot did not answer, but other American faces appeared.

"Do you remember what happened to you, what happened to all of you?"

The faces contracted with the effort of memory. They did not remember.

"On this island seventy years ago, Major Matoba ordered his soldiers to shoot eight prisoners of war[50] despite the existing war conventions. Afterwards, his cooks removed the livers from the eight bodies and filleted them to be served with brandy in a celebration for the Japanese ranking officers."

In the darkness of Hong Kong, Cecilia felt anaesthetized by the absurdity of the story she was hearing.

"Is that true?"

Furuta cleared his throat on the other side of the phone line. "I'm afraid so. The Japanese Imperial Army committed many atrocities in those years and, unfortunately for us here, those in Ogasawara were

---

[50] The Man Under Contract had memorized the names of the deceased, which included:

-Lloyd Richard Woellhof, executed 8-7-44

-Grady Alvan York, executed 2-23-45

-James Wesley Dye, executed 2-25-45

-Glenn J. Frazier, executed 2-18-45

-Marvelle "Marvie" William Mershon, executed 2-22-45

-Floyd Ewing Hall, executed 3-9-45

-Warren Earl Vaughn, executed 3-15-45.

Plus an unknown soldier, executed 8-7-44

some of the worst."

"That man ate his prisoners."

"It is not something that is talked about much on the island but, yes, he did. Not only Matoba. All the Japanese high command knew that they would eventually lose the war. Despair and fanaticism made them think that such atrocity was justified."

"And Artiel told you all this? Did he realize how it sounds?" Cecilia asked, puzzled not just by the story but by the candour of the Man Under Contract.

"Please let me finish," Furuta said.

While Gavriel spoke, the background of bombers, destroyers, mortars and detonations, all the artifice that gave colour and sound to Matoba's construct, intensified. The Major was trying to drown the sound of the human voice of the Man Under Contract in a ghostly cacophony.

A handful of men broke away from the mass of soldiers, young men in flight suits and with clear eyes.

"You are dead. You were killed and devoured. You are all dead."

One of the pilots, a young man with messy hair, groaned and fell to his knees, the vivid and true image of a soul in sorrow.

The Major remained silent with the sabre in hand. He looked at the effect that the words of the Man Under Contract had on his army. Matoba controlled those spirits by keeping them in a state of constant frenzy, the time of their lives stopped at the moment before the invasion. Both sides mixed as soldiers, sailors and pilots ran from one place to another with uncontrollable urgency, but not knowing what they should do or what they were waiting for with such anxiety. Only Matoba, standing on his stone and directing the impulses of the dead inhabitants of Ogasawara, knew the purpose of such movement: to create a fiction of life; to animate an inanimate world.

Slowly, still holding the sabre, the commander turned to Gavriel. "Do you see what I have in my hand? It is not the weapon of superannuated potency you imagine. It is not a weapon at all but a tool, the *botefeux* that lights the discharge of the cannons, the baton that directs souls.''

Matoba pressed the edge against the neck of the Man Under Contract and, for a moment, seemed ready to execute him. "But it could still be used for bloodshed."

Then he removed the blade. "Gavriel, the selenite," he said mockingly, and shook his head. "There is a balance at stake and you are altering it. You must leave."

The hands holding the Man Under Contract disappeared. Gavriel stood, undecided. Matoba's gaze was still terrible.

"Go, escape if you want, run wherever you can, but leave my island."

Gavriel took a step, feeling the ground uncertain. The soldiers moved in confusion. Some yelled, some wept; an army in disarray.

"You let me go?" he asked hesitantly.

Matoba tensed his mouth. "I do because the marks on your forehead grant you that much, but the hand of my world is long," he said, and looked toward the edge of the jungle.

Gavriel saw him coming from the trees, brushing branches aside. When he came out into the clearing he made his way through the chaotic knots of soldiers. He was a man of dark complexion and a full beard, dressed in the tatters of a blue uniform. The metallized plastic nametag that barely held on the breast pocket said "Raúl". He entered the esplanade sniffing the air, cruel of expression and with narrowed eyes.

"Raúl?" called the Man Under Contract, but the guard had been swallowed, chewed and spit out again through the holes of the world and was a creature of the blind god.

Gavriel took a step back, then another and ran. He pushed between the souls of the soldiers and left the crowd and the esplanade after much effort. The jungle surrounded him. He couldn't see the coastal road, but the lights of Ogasawara-mura reflected on the trees, on the other side of the hill. He heard an animal growl behind him. Raúl was coming.

He ran through the undergrowth, clawing and stumbling until he reached the top of the promontory, breathing hard and shallow. He advanced, and the world became more real. On his left, he discovered the road. He wanted to rest but he heard the noise again, as if an animal frame moved through the jungle, cutting down everything in its path.

Gavriel reached the first house in Ogasawara-mura when the gloomy profile of Raúl was already appearing at the edge of the trees. The night was heavy, and no window had lights. Gavriel ran, looking for refuge, and when he looked back he saw that the echoes and flashes of the world of Matoba had broken the barrier and manifested over the hill. His mouth burned and his legs ached, but he didn't stop. Further back, Raúl howled, dangerous and angry. Gavriel looked for a place to hide. *The Coast Guard building*, he thought. That heavy door would stop the creature. A light turned on back the way that Gavriel had followed and a neighbour in a nightshirt and with ruffled hair came out the door, spooked by the noises, flashes and howls. He looked toward the southern hill and then, seeing the Man Under Contract, asked rapid questions that Gavriel did not understand.

"I do not speak Japanese! Get in the house. It's dangerous!"

Raúl appeared on the avenue, moving with a lupine trot.

"Get in the house!"

Raúl knocked down the man in a jumble of arms and legs. Gavriel started to move, wanted to go to help, but the sound of ripping teeth turned his stomach and he was too late. He ran and left behind the screams of the dying man. When he reached the Coast Guard building he pulled at the door but it did not open. He tried again, rattling the handle in fear, but someone had bolted the entrance. There was a noise behind him. Raúl came running in a vulpine crouch. He was sprayed with red and bared his teeth more than any person could. Gavriel fled once more, along the pier and towards the hulking silhouette of the sleeping ferry which waited for the next day's departure. He got near the ship, tried to board. There was no walkway or access. He saw a glare in the forecastle and shadows moving behind the glass panes. He screamed.

"Open up! Open up! Help!"

The headlights of a vehicle that had been parked in the dark came on. The door opened, and from the patrol car stepped Sergeant Furuta.

"Artiel, what is happening? We have heard explosions. And those lights! It feels as if the whole island is about to blow."

"Hide. We have to hide," Gavriel said.

Raúl sprinted down the pier. Furuta pointed at him with a flashlight.

"Who is that? Stop!"

Raúl accelerated. Furuta opened the flap of his gun holster and pulled out a blued revolver.

"I said stop."

Raúl did not. His dislocated jaw had a reddish tint.

"Stop now!"

"Shoot!" cried Gavriel.

There were two loud bangs, and Raúl fell to the ground. Furuta approached cautiously, pointing the gun and flashlight at the same time. The wild man[51] was still breathing. His eyes were closed and his features were more human, like those of the anxious husband Gavriel had known in California. The policeman and the traveller stood side by side in silence as the body became a corpse.

"It's over," Gavriel said, pointing toward the hill that separated the south of the island.

The lights were gone. The piercing of the world had closed.

---

[51] It should be noted that the figure of the feral Wild Man (Woodwose or Wodewose in medieval literature) reoccurs, among other instances, in the text of *Sir Gawain and the Green Knight*. The archontic artifices seem to be in no contradiction with either the repurposing of themes or the elements of irony.

The story came to an end. Cecilia felt cold despite the warm humidity of Hong Kong.

"What happened next?"

"I checked the whole island after dawn. I didn't find anything out of the ordinary on the south coast. We discovered the body of one of our neighbours in the street, just as Artiel told us. All the marks indicated that he was assaulted by the man I shot at the pier. They had to send a special investigation team from Tokyo. Shootings are infrequent in Japan, and much more in places like Ogasawara."

"What about Artiel?"

Furuta paused. "I interrogated him, of course, and he told me the whole story: the soldiers, Matoba, that man, Raúl. When the investigative team did the same, he only said that he came upon the assailant and was chased for no reason, and I did not contradict him. The community was very shocked by what happened that night so, without any more clues, we allowed him to sail back to Tokyo on the ferry."

"I'm not sure I understand everything. Why are you telling me all of this, Mr Furuta?"

Furuta sighed on the other side of the line as if that was the question the policeman had been waiting for all night. "The investigation tells a very clear story. A second visitor came to the island, undocumented as well. We don't know by what means. Maybe he was a castaway too. He attacked a Japanese citizen and died in the confrontation that followed."

"Then it seems that what Artiel told you was a fable."

"Yes, but you forget that I was the one who shot that person. And I assure you, what was running towards us on that pier was not human, even if it had that form."

Cecilia said nothing.

"Ms Chao, I am convinced that the story I have told you is a fiction, but also that there is more to this man, Gavriel Artiel. What do you know? What can you tell me?"

Cecilia thought carefully before answering. Furuta was pleading for sanity and logic to be restored. She thought of Cambodia, of Tasmania, of California. She would never stop looking for Liam, but she decided to share with the police officer who was calling from across the water what she had understood at that very moment.

"I don't know you, Mr Furuta, but I think, based on our conversation, that we are both very similar; rational people. What you want to know, what you are asking, I fear that leads to a place that is not for people like us."

"And who is it for, then?" said Furuta, somewhat bitterly.

"I don't know. Maybe it's just for penitents who do not mind the price that is to be paid."

--°--'N/--°--'E
Demiurge[52]

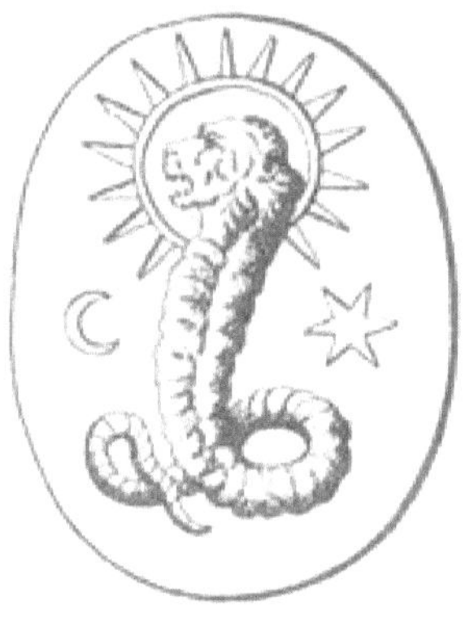

---

[52] Alas, behold It here: The blind god, called Yaldabaoth, called Samael, called Saklas. The artisan creator of the world, architect of the universe. Divisive and incomprehensible, malefic figure for the Gnostic heretics and benefactor principle for the Neoplatonic philosophers. Not the supreme divinity, which is inaccessible, but the answer to the preeminent and perennial question, the very last secret of the universe.

Gavriel climbed the mountain.
It was a distant mountain. The paths were very slight depressions marked on the back of the ridges, and there were no paved ways for hundreds of kilometres.

That mountain was in Nepal. He spent the first two weeks of his trip on the moderately busy circuit of the adventurous visitors. There he found Asian and Western travellers who defied the political ups and downs and the natural disasters of the impoverished Himalayan country to wander, carrying backpacks and walking sticks, along the monumental slopes of Everest and the Annapurnas.

In the brief stop at the capital, Kathmandu, he had supplied himself for what he knew was the last chapter of the Search. The old city had not quite recovered from the tremendous earthquake it had suffered and that reduced to rubble commemorative buildings and left the red dust of ancient brick floating in the air. He retired his boots, a sturdy pair bought in a second-hand shop in Yangon that had performed faithfully before falling dead and coming unstitched in the service of the road, and replaced them with a new pair found in the bazaars of the neighbourhood of Thamel. He craved companionship after the Japanese ordeal, and, in some café, he came across compatriots whom he approached for conversation but, just as happened in other countries and places, they had trouble associating with him due to how much his travelling has done to dilute his native speech and manners.

He spent only two days studying his charts and annotations. There was not much need for confirmation. He was convinced now that only the impassable mountain ranges of the Himalayas could house the blind god. It was true that after the trip through Tibet he had dismissed the region, and particularly Nepal, due to the confusing religious mix of the country[53] as a dependable source of clues, but that had changed. As soon as he was ready, he boarded a rattling bus and,

---

[53] The Man Under Contract, following the acute impression that Tibetan Buddhism had left on him, was surprised to discover that Nepal has a very different composition, with only 11% of the population Buddhist. 80% is Hindu, 5% Muslim and the rest belong to different religious minorities. The Hindu-Buddhist imbalance led him to believe that the chances of a relevant encounter were insignificant.

step by step, went into the mountainous mass.

The trip from Kathmandu he made in a rattling minibus where the child of an indifferent mother fell asleep in his lap and where the driver alternated local Nepalese music with modern hits of American hip hop. It took more than two hours to leave the suburbs of the capital that were buried by a cloud of dust and pollution. Every few minutes the van was stuck in traffic and they had to wait, engine turned off, until the outrageous traffic flowed again.

At dusk, he arrived in the city of Pokhara. It was the closest entry point to the circuit of the western Himalayas and the Annapurna massif. There he checked into a guest house and rushed to buy some supplies before the stores closed. In a bookshop of tattered volumes, he discovered a dog-eared copy of *The Demon Princes*. He had lost his book in California, and this was an early edition, cracked and yellowed. He took it as a good omen, and that night he sat down with the book to continue with the infinite reading loop of the novel.

The following morning he woke up early and took a taxi from the city to the head of the mountain trail. That first day of climbing was dominated by stairs. The road from Pokhara to Kathmandu lay at the bottom of a valley, and from there he needed to ascend the gap that separated it from the alpine heights. The staircase was a succession of stone blocks planted on the hillside and had been worn under the feet of generations of walkers. Gavriel, who was accustomed to the physical sacrifices required by enthusiastic hiking, was nonetheless overtaken by Nepali porters in jeans and sandals who climbed lightly with no sign of exertion while loaded with high bundles of delicately balanced cargo. In the early afternoon, he reached the end of the long climb and the village of Ulleri. Behind him and looking down, he saw the now distant road from which he had left in the morning. In front of him, the infinite expanse of the Himalayan peaks was finally unfolding. That was the place where he intended to get lost.

The Annapurna Circuit followed a pronounced arch that was a network of trails accessible only on foot. It connected one village with another to first proceed to the north of the mountain range and then turn west, avoiding the most inaccessible central peaks before finally returning to Pokhara in the south.

Quickening his step, he managed to reach Banthanti on the first day. It was nothing more than a winding cobbled street where a few sturdy, low-profile houses hugged an esplanade. Men, women and children had the red-marked cheeks that wind at that altitude produced. They sat on the wooden porches watching the dwindling flow of travellers at the end of the season. It was late summer, and the only snow Gavriel saw sat higher, on the peaks. At noon the sun warmed the village, but at dawn and sunset Banthanti returned to the cold embrace that was its natural state.

Gavriel found a room in a tea house. Buildings like that would welcome him during the rest of the journey. They were clan-sized family houses with large common rooms on the ground floor where one could eat hot porridge and drink salty yak-butter tea. On the top floor were the rooms, just a series of wooden partitions between which beds, chairs and small tables had been squeezed. The showers, when they were available in such an austere land, were dark dens with no hot water. The first night Gavriel had the worst dream of all. Not only Maya but also Chao came to visit him. They pointed at him with accusatory fingers, but that was not what scared the Man Under Contract the most. Behind his friend and his lover, other figures were darkly outlined: a tattooed man, a horned giant, a uniformed employee, a soldier, and another larger, unknown figure, all threatening as portents of things to come. Gavriel woke in the darkness of the tea house. He filled the air with the white condensation of his breath and listened to the murmurings and quiet movements of the other sleeping guests behind the timber partitions. Outside it was dark, and the stars shone fiercely in the crystal-clear air of the cold hours. The world had been left behind, and Banthanti was an isolated corner, away from the life in the valley. The clues came to an end. The Search was nearly done, and Gavriel knew that from here on, he no longer would have to find the correct way. He would simply have to endure it.

More days passed. From Ghorapani he went to Tatopani, from Tatopani to Dana; a succession of villages nestled deeper and deeper in the dorsal spine of the mountains. They were all quaint but, with the commonplaceness of daily exposure, Gavriel was losing interest. In Dana, he got up and saw that the route for the day crossed a deep valley. From the terrace of the hostel, he could see a sunken river crossed by a tiny bridge. He spent the entire morning descending the side of the mountain. He made way when gangs of porters or packs of donkeys adorned with wool harnesses and multicoloured tassels passed next to him, loaded with victuals and merchandise. Gavriel had lunch by the river. The day was warmer there because the mountainsides protected from the wind and reflected more heat than up near the crest. The flow of the water carried the impulse of the summer thawing and ran raging when the narrowness of the valley accelerated its pace. The bridge that traversed there was of expert construction but fragile appearance, formed by planks and ropes. When Gavriel crossed, it swung like the pendulum of an old clock. The afternoon was a constant struggle to climb the other side of the valley under the weight of the backpack's straps. Gavriel topped the summit near sunset and looked back at the village of Dana, which he had left that morning, to see it was on the opposite ridge, just four or five kilometres as the crow flies. But crossing the span had taken him more than ten hours along the valley route.

In the town of Ghasa, he had to sleep in the open because weeks before a lightning bolt had fallen on the sole tea house, setting it on fire. Of the building, all that was left was a blackish mass of ruined wood where the former owner still wandered. It was an uncomfortable night. The wind wobbled the roof of the tent, and the cold, apparent but not excessive when sleeping indoors, numbed his hands and feet in the harshest hours. In the middle of the night, a specially strong gust ripped the fabric of the tent, rendering it useless. Gavriel had to crawl out of the derelict heap, sleepy and cold. In the morning he threw the wreck away and, from then on, used a tied-down waterproof tarp.

He spent ten days touring the immenseness of the Himalayan regions, walking through some accessible circuits and others more remote.[54] Little by little he found fewer foreign travellers, and even the Nepalese residents became scarce. At one point he thought he was about to leave behind the barrier of the world, but what he took for signs of change turned out to be the symptoms of altitude sickness which, starting at three thousand meters, gave him a headache and

---

[54] The effect that the vast emptiness of the region produces has been excessively romanticized. The spirituality that we associate with the inhabitants of the mountain range and the adjoined plateau has its origin in the resignation to the austerity of a pauperrimus environment rather than in an innate disposition to the ascetic.

nausea. He woke up in the middle of the night, gasping for the air poor in oxygen that floated around him. The following days, and until his body acclimatized to the Himalayan heights, he advanced dragging his feet with great effort and carried a painful constant hum at the base of the skull. He descended to the drylands surrounding the far northern town of Kagbeni, and that bought some relief. Kagbeni was a medieval village of plain and narrow streets on the banks of the Gandaki River that guarded the passage to the border with the Tibetan highlands. The landscape was a lunar desolation of three coloured contrasts: the snowy heights of the Dhaulagiri and Annapurna peaks up high; the thin fringes of the green pastures near the river, fertile and narrow, pockmarked by ancient towns that stretched one after the other towards the north; finally, the vast hills and arid yellow plains between one and the other, combed by the wind and empty of life or purpose. Those plains marked the way he had to follow. Nothing grew there, nothing lived. Gavriel watched the landscape from the shelter of the veranda of a tea house and shuddered, thinking about what awaited him.

The kingdom of Lo, now called Mustang, waited beyond Kagbeni. It was a region of restricted access that led to the city of Lo Manthang, which was a walled enclosure with bleached adobe bricks and former capital of an independent kingdom, closed to visitors until a few decades ago.[55] From Kagbeni to Lo Manthang it was a five-day trek, perhaps four at Gavriel's hurried walking pace. The Man Under Contract looked at the barren expanse from the veranda. Five days, if he managed to get there.

He didn't have the special and costly permit required so he left at dusk to circumvent the checkpoints of the Nepalese police and walked all night along the hills parallel to the path. He slept at dawn for a few hours and, with the midday sun, he went deeper into the isolated corners of Upper Mustang.

When the world was finally pierced, the transition came more

---

[55] The country of Lo, which was once a proud kingdom, maintained an independent status for centuries until it was annexed by Nepal, first as a suzerainty and then as a region of special consideration. The current heir of the Lo royalty strolls around the capital Lo Manthang and maintains some ancestral and confusing prerogatives.

gradually than it had in Tasmania. One by one, the references of the route become confusing, with the names of bridges and villages Gavriel encountered disagreeing with the notes in the detailed topographic map he had been using. Then came an evening when he was unable to find a tea house to spend the night, and he had to lie down, tucked into the sleeping bag and under a waterproof tarp. Gavriel noticed a change in the quality of the air and the scarce light. The stars, even to his untrained eye, had changed into a disconcerting disarray, and the compass spun crazily, looking for a north that the impressive immediacy of the blind god had buried.

The map failed him again at dawn and for the last time at noon, when he concluded that he should have encountered a good-sized mountain village with a large tea house famous for salty tea and sweet cakes. But all he could see was the slope of a tremendous summit beaten by the Tibetan-Nepali wind.

From that afternoon on, he ate sparingly, aware that the change of reality would affect his chances to replenish supplies. At breakfast, he strengthened himself for the walk of the day, but at dusk he had to be satisfied with a handful of rice and a pinch of tea, hoping that sleep would distract from the hunger. Buried under the tarpaulin, he searched the recesses of his backpack for strayed titbits, but only found coins from the countries he had visited and crumpled paper notes. Luckily, water was abundant. It rained often, and the valleys were crisscrossed by sudden torrents and other more permanent streams. Gavriel endured his discomfort stoically.

At sunset, Gavriel lay wrapped in his sleeping bag, a piece of American manufacturing he had bought years ago from an Australian tourist short of money for more than he could afford but that now, in protecting him from the freezing wind, justified the expense. During the hours of darkness that stretched long and unnaturally, he tossed around in dismay and loneliness, with a belly full of water to distract him from his hunger. The earth seemed to breathe below his back, and the presence of the buried cosmic architect was no longer a theory. Despite the many years of searching and dedication, these slow hours were the worst and came with a fear that moved at the ossified pace of the luminous dial of his watch.

At dawn each day, everything changed. Gavriel felt sure of himself, and the limbo between lands ceased to be threatening to become the path that led to the Demiurge and its great secret.

To the north, the chain of peaks he had followed when entering the Annapurnas had mutated and presented enormous forms, too high and massive for the geography of a human world. But since it was the most relevant feature of the landscape, that was where the Man Under Contract headed. The environment changed from valley to prairie, and he found piles of bones scattered around, yellowish fragmented frames with no other clues indicating who had owned them. He also discovered ruins that, at first, he took for natural undulations of the land, so covered were they with earth and grass. Then, the more he walked into the untamed land, and as if accentuating the deviation from the original Nepal, worn stone vertexes and edges of granitic blocks emerged here and there. Later a paved road appeared and, finally, at noon of a long day's walk, Gavriel found a cyclopean structure almost intact. It was a square building resembling a cenotaph. Chiselled reliefs of alien features were mounted at the apex of the pediments. The entire floor was tilted as if the foundations had partially given way but without compromising the straight lines of the construction. Gavriel peered into the inner gloom and smelled abandonment. It reminded him of the most remote corners of Angkor Wat and the rest of the ruins he had come across over the years. Knowing that he was already in the last stage, in the resolution of the innumerable clues that he had followed on his journey to the centre of the Demiurge, Gavriel thought he understood why the signs to the blind god so often accumulated in the archaic and majestic buildings scattered across South East Asia. There was a link between those spaces of faith in the architecture of the real world and the ebullient creations that kept appearing in these invented domains. Then he encountered many other failed experiments of an irrepressible creative will that took any conceivable form: aqueducts, sanctuaries, ancient amphitheatres, decayed statues of forgotten autarchs. In the sky he thought he could see, in his exhaustion, abandoned structures that defied all physical laws, floating overhead with an entourage of winged beasts.

Occasionally he found an inhabited settlement. Gavriel watched these carefully, scarred by his past experience in Tasmania, and moved on without making himself known. On one occasion, a warrior horde appeared on the horizon and blocked the way for hours. Gavriel monitored it using his binoculars and saw chiefs riding heavy plantigrade beasts that moved with clumsy steps, and slaves dragging sledges loaded with loot. He thought of Maya and wondered if the worlds of the Demiurge were connected; if he would see her wandering around, so far from where he lost her.

It was on one of those intermediate days when Gavriel saw the sight that was to leave the deepest impression in the memories of his uncertain life. Or perhaps it was the exhaustion, the malnutrition and all the other abuses he had suffered in the plateau finally coming together so he saw what he saw under the hallucinogenic incantation of a brain that was failing. In any case, Gavriel could have sworn at the time that it was there, in a gap at the back of the world, where he watched creation for what it truly was: a fascinating display of life.

He climbed another of the endless hills that made his legs burn and he discovered the widest view in that very wide world. All the land was covered by a herd of hirsute quadrupeds. Gavriel thought of big animals, pachyderms perhaps, but their skulls and the jaws they used to ruminate the grass had never existed in the range of terrestrial biology. He saw males, females and young. The herd dragged its own ecosystem with it. It attracted birds and carrion eaters that fell on the piles of manure; it fed rodents that crawled in thick fur chasing parasites; it drove away the predators that circled and delineated the infinite limits of the horde.

At first, Gavriel was impressed only by the vastness of movement, because the herd was a living carpet against the background sound of the stamping of feet, but then he got lost in the maze of dynamic processes that took place there: calves being born and dying while marching, struggles for authority between muscular males, clouds of insects displaced by the snorts of the pack.

The Man Under Contract sat on the hill like a king on his throne and studied the progression of the animal mass, hypnotized. He understood that it was a summary of the history of the world, a mobile diorama that contained the vitality and drama of creation. Similarly, Man had journeyed in another world for four million years following similar patterns of advancement, reproduction and death.

By nightfall, the herd had finished crossing the expanse and was lost to the infinity of the high plateau, but Gavriel did not move. As the grass grew cold when the sun disappeared, so did he, and waited there, not even remembering to set up his camp.

He found the village in a depression of the plain that it seemed he could never cross, so much it extended in front of him. The village was a collection of six or eight elongated buildings with stone walls and grass roofs. Cautious as always, Gavriel watched the comings and goings of its inhabitants until he was convinced that it was safe enough to approach without fear. The way to the blind god remained vague, and he feared he would wander endlessly or run out of supplies until he died or disappeared, consumed by the infinitude of the plateau. Among the houses, he discovered young men and women with serene faces who, with no questions, gave him a corner in which to sleep and a fire to warm him up. Gavriel asked for food by drawing pictograms on the earth, but none of the villagers knew how to interpret them. He asked about the Demiurge but did not learn anything. When he went out, searching for deposits of food, he found nothing—no stores of grain, no harnesses for ploughing, no hunting implements—and the mystery of the sustenance of the village did not resolve itself until later.

Gavriel spent three days there, long enough to warm his body, numbed by the many nights slept outdoors and the many meals of meagre lukewarm soup. However, his stay was not pleasant and, over the course of the three days, he understood that he had fallen into a loop of hellish repetition.

At dawn, the village stretched. Men and women left the houses of stone and grass to march in a disciplined line to the field surrounding the settlement. Each of the fifty or so inhabitants stood next to a flower protruding from tall plants the size and appearance of a sunflower that wobbled under the weight of a tight vegetal bulb at the top. With the rays of the morning sun, plants and men shuddered until fifty pairs of anxious hands tore in concert at the bulbs and withdrew a solid, pale seed the size of a fist. By some arcane design, the number of plants corresponded precisely with the total population of the village. Gavriel discovered this when visiting the field in search of any leftover or unattended stem and finding it depleted. That could be no coincidence.

With food in hand, the inhabitants returned to the settlement. Trios and couples sat leaning against the stone walls. The seed contained a white jelly with the appearance of coagulated milk. The people of the village trapped with their fingers wobbly pieces of strong, rancid smell and took them to their mouths with the anxiety of the addict. They chewed their lean rations and then stood there, sublimated, looking at the infinite with eyes unfocused.

Gavriel waited near the fire and, with the passing of the morning, the people of the village came out of their stupor. One by one they stood up, and one by one, without fail, looked at their empty hands and sighed, mourning the absent food before dragging their feet towards the doors of painted lintels. They spared a glance to notice how Gavriel was waiting, sitting under one of the stone walls. Either by pretending absent-mindedness or by true indifference, nobody spoke to him.

Gavriel strolled among the indolent groups where men and women lay surrounded by the remnant pungent smell that arose from the discarded pods and the dry, whitish trickle marks. The precision in the distribution of the boon left the Man Under Contract without dinner, so he piled up mushrooms and some tender roots to cook a diluted soup that, if not abundant, at least was pleasant.

To Gavriel's great surprise, the process was repeated at noon. The natives lined up again to march to the fields, and there he saw the tall plants had regenerated and bulging bulbs in exact numbers weighted the flowers yet again. But this time there were loud exclamations of surprise, first, and anger later. Several of the villagers went to their plant to discover a torn bulb and the seed, likely immature, stolen or discarded. When the sun reached the vertical, the rest of the plants paid off, and the inhabitants of the village collected the second favour, but their solidarity was broken. Those who had been robbed wandered through the groups that were eating and searched among the faces of gluttonous ecstasy for traces of satiety, or any other iron-clad proof of double rations. Some altercations sprang up, with accusations and denials flying from one mouth to another, and those dispossessed, with no other choice, settled down in nervous conciliabules.

The Man Under Contract saw all this as a removed witness. He was still ignored, and considered what to do. The inhabitants of the village did not seem to have any practical occupation; they didn't plough, they didn't carve, they didn't mould. They spent their time between waiting and delight in a stupefied trance. Despite the bleakness he glimpsed beyond the stone walls, where the plateau and high hills spread to infinity, he felt the urgent need to leave the circle of habitation and its degenerate people. Then the cold wind blew and Gavriel, sheltered in one of the longhouses, could not envision spending another night under the leaking tarp.

The last meal, that of dusk, marked the resolution of the drama. Among the shadows that lengthened were other shadows, furtive figures that crossed the village to the field of flowers. They dodged and intercepted each other in a human game of chess. The final ray of sun disappeared, and the villagers again marched to the meadow, looked at each other with frowns, and suspected those who were ahead and those who were behind. The line in front of the stalks was a disorganized grouping full of screams of frustration and anger and arms flailing to the sky. Half of the bulbs were torn, and there were remnants of milky and undergrown seeds covering every patch of land where thieves had devoured them in their haste. Not only thievery but also malice had appeared. Many flowers that had not had time to grow a seed in the interval from noon to dusk had been broken in frustration. Some of the criminals were again those who had decided to double their ration at the expense of others, but some of the victims, afraid to spend another period of abstinence, had decided to prevent pilfering with their own pilfering this time.

Two groups returned from the meadow, one chewing, satisfied, and one resentful, hungry and sullen, who watched the first with the rage of the dispossessed. For a few minutes, relative calm held, with only the sound of lustful gnawing and sucking, until someone tried to snatch the seed from his neighbour's grasp. General pandemonium broke out. The villagers produced staves and burning torches. The muddy alleys between the longhouse were populated with a ghostly procession of persecutors and persecuted. Bloodied attackers shouted aloud, and havoc lasted until full night when, by force of darkness, hostilities ceased and the inhabitants of the village retired to bed, exhausted. On the first night, Gavriel watched everything from the parapet on which he had perched and held his hunting knife with white knuckles of fear.

The next day everything was normal. The village got up yawning and made its breakfast of milky seeds normally. The damage of the previous day had been repaired, and the stalks once again bristled the field in exact proportion to the people they supported. But at noon the drama was repeated, and, come nightfall, Gavriel, who had dug deep in his notes and found the appropriate reference[56], knew that by accident or purpose, that remote vestige of humanity was not a congress of free minds but a failed experiment, trapped in a perpetual cycle of innocence and sin.

Gavriel watched it all from the top of the wall where he first took refuge when the attacks began. On the first evening, he was frightened; on the second he was suspicious; and by the third, with the pattern of the cycle clear, disheartened. He finished drying up his clothes near the campfire, picked up what herbs and mushrooms he could and, at dawn of the fourth day, left the village and its benign curse, followed by the indifferent looks of its inhabitants.

Once again in the open high plain, Gavriel walked with only an approximate direction, getting closer and closer to the great mountain range on the horizon and advancing into the metaphysical construct that was that land. There were no trees, no bushes or shelter, only infinite grass. At sunset he set camp. It was cold and he could not find enough fuel for a proper fire. Starving, terrified, desperate, Gavriel took *The Demon Princes* from his backpack and opened the book for the last time. He read the words of Kirth Gersen at the end of his mission as he looked at the path leading to the rest of his life: *I have been deserted by my enemies. The affair is over. I am done.* There was no room for the solace of the pages. Deliberately, as if saying

---

[56] The creationist myth of *Jigten Chagtsul* is a cosmography native to the Himalayan regions. The myth begins with the appearance of the original mountain, a recurring feature that holds a constant central role, something perhaps not surprising in a series of legends born under the aegis of Nepalese and Tibetan orography. After describing the formation of the world ("The wind brought rain, the rain filled the primeval sea and the first mountain, Sumeru, was created from its foam. It had four faces, one of gold to the north, another of malachite to the south. The other two were made of glass and silver. Floating in the sea and facing each side, four worlds remained suspended; the earth was the triangular world, the solid form, the rest were square, crescent shape and circular."), the myth details how the gods settled on earth and lived in autarchy until they lost their divine nature. Tempted by worldly pleasures, they finally fell into a state of envy and violence that led the world to the cycle of life, suffering and death in which it is still trapped. The Man Under Contract has witnessed a summarized representation of the legend.

goodbye to a friend[57], Gavriel tore the pages from the book and slowly fed them to the squalid flames of his bonfire for the rest of the night.

On the next day, he was harassed by hirsute and subhuman creatures that roamed the grassland, sniffing the air and showing long yellowish incisors. Gavriel discovered the first of them across the moor, using his binoculars to identify the distant creature, and a single glance served him to understand that it was better to avoid its company. That night and the following, he did not light any fires and lay, purplish with cold, waiting for dawn. He heard screams and the rumour of pursuit in the dim moonlight and hid as he could in the recess of rock that served him as a nest.

In the morning, while filling his canteen in a stream, he watched, absorbed, the current and the fantastic aquatic forms that slid beneath. The wind was cold, the sun was a flash up high and the sky shone blue. On the other side of the stream he discovered a pilose and crouched form, one of the beasts he had sought to avoid. It had stopped in the gesture of bringing the bowl of its hand full of water to its mouth. Gavriel and the proto-human watched each other from opposite sides. Despite the fangs and the rough fur, its eyes were intelligent and heartless. Gavriel fiddled with his backpack, snapped the canteen in place and, standing up, backed away in a hurry. The creature straightened up at the same time and looked up and down for a place to cross. Gavriel ran up the slope with his backpack jumping behind. He looked back and saw the beast dancing undecided, eager to follow him but afraid of the water current.

He ran while his breath lasted and then jogged as best as he could, until at least the crest of a hill was between him and his pursuer. He gained an advantage, but when he clambered up the second promontory, he saw the hairy figure a kilometre behind him.

The hunt continued during a Dantean day. Gavriel was slower, but the creature had a natural abhorrence for water and, when the Man Under Contract noticed, he took advantage of this to drag it along a path that

---

[57] The similarities of the Man Under Contract with Kirth Gersen extend beyond the merely circumstantial. The former, same as the latter, was "a motivated mechanism aimed to a purpose".

cut through the frequent streams of the highlands. The despair of his persecutor grew, and Gavriel saw it screaming in frustration as it ran back and forth in search of dry crossings.

The flight, the cold and the tension eroded Gavriel's resistance. After many hours he walked, tripping over the grass, and the adrenaline of fear was not enough to keep his head clear. It was beginning to get dark, and when he looked back at the increasingly closer silhouette of the beast, he saw a form of dark hair where the luminescent circles of the eyes shone.

Then Gavriel found a paved road.

After so many days treading the uneven terrain of the plateau, with all its vegetation and rocks, he felt unbalanced and dizzy standing on the firm, regular stone slabs. Behind him, the hominid roared with despair, and Gavriel heard hurried steps. He drew strength from where he had none left and ran too. But the rush was unnecessary; after the first enraged attempt to enter the road, the beast could not follow.[58] Still, Gavriel did not stop moving until the night was over and dawn came. Then he lay down in the centre of the road and fell asleep.

At the end of the road, there was a citadel. The Man Under Contract was not surprised by this. For several kilometres stone lamps had bordered the road as heralds of the advent of an immeasurable occurrence. Gavriel, grimy, tired and very hungry, spied the walls and spires in the fog and only spared a second to be surprised. The cognitive baggage of the mountain range was impregnated with the mould of the perfect city. From Shangri la to Kun Lun, generations of storytellers had chosen to place mystical venues in the world's largest

---

[58] From the creationist legends of *Jigten Chagtsul*: The newly formed world was populated by terrible creatures, begotten in successive series. The tenth of these was that of the Gongpo, intelligent and cruel semi-apes that would evolve into primitive men to form the four original Tibetan clans. Unlike the Gongpo itself, the paved road was an achievement of human diligence and incorporated spiritual ambitions that made it anathema to the nature of the beast, which was of a purely somatic dimension.

mountains, tempted by the distancing of their inaccessible recesses.[59]

Gavriel arrived at the foot of the parapet and contemplated its formidable dimensions. It was cold in its shadow. The makers of the city had chiselled effigies of the leonine snake flanking the closed gates. There was no sign of the mundane activity that even a perfect society would depend on: no smoke, no noise of human chores, no sound of mechanical gears. Gavriel walked the perimeter of the impregnable wall, always in its shadow. The architecture of the domes and pinnacles he saw over the merlons of the parapet was Asian and fantastic at the same time, and it exaggerated the designs of the religious centres that he had visited in his travels. He found no access until he observed, among other signs of abandonment, a crack in the rotund stone. He slipped through the city walls, reached a darkened courtyard and, after crossing several alleys, reached the inner avenues.

Gavriel recognized the unreal fog that soaked everything. It was similar to the one that enchanted the amusement park of California, the mark of a copied world. This citadel, however, was well defined; the buildings offered the solidity of stone at the push of the hand, and the colours, monotonous and muted as they seemed, were not washed away like those found on the ghostly journey through Ogasawara. The city was real, as real as Gavriel. It was just dead.

He walked around. There were echoes, furtive shadows, everything caused by Gavriel himself. The perimeter of the walls was circular, and two large avenues crossed to part the interior into four regular spaces. The citadel, he thought, was a wheel.[60] Gavriel inspected several of the buildings, both modest and sumptuous, and found empty chambers and rooms embalmed in the aura of abandoned time. But the interiors were melancholic and that made him uneasy, so he

---

[59] The belief in an orphic and hidden realm is born from the religious concept of Shambala, the pure spiritual land. Originally, this was the birth village of the Hindu divinity that would become a herald of the golden age of the world and only later came to embody the ideal of the Perfect City. Similar concepts are found in the western legends of Agartha, Avalon, Hyperborea and Thule as a direct result of the human compulsion to assign geographical locations to ideas.

[60] Again the image of the wheel that is the representation of the perpetual cycle in the phenomenal world. The concept is rooted in the mythology of the Himalayas as an offset of the Hinduism in the neighboring country.

went back outside. At the crossroads of the two avenues, where a plaza formed, there was a water reservoir, something halfway between a well and a fountain, and there he stopped to rest. The afternoon passed. He stood up with effort and filled his canteen at the spout. He thought about looking for shelter in one of the structures but he realized that this was where he wanted to be, so he set up his tarp and extended his sleeping bag under the cover of the fountain.

A sunset came that was warmer than others had been. Maybe the walls blocked the wind, because here it was soft while outside on the plateau Gavriel had felt exhausted by the constant exposure. From a splintered door he made firewood and too late stopped to wonder if it would be sacrilegious to apply the match, despite his need. He did it anyway, and the glow of the fire gave him as much comfort as it gave him heat. That night he finally ran out of food.

The figure crossed the avenue during the hours of darkness. Gavriel heard nothing, but the citadel was so quiet that the Man Under Contract sensed the change in the stillness of the air. He opened one eye and, from under the tarp, he saw the dark silhouette move at a quiet pace from side to side. Caught in drowsiness and trapped in the folds of the sleeping bag, he could not get up in time and the figure was gone. At dawn, he ran to look for clues but found nothing.

He fasted that morning. At noon the city was compassionate, and Gavriel found a honeycomb with absent bees and an orchard patch where grew hard and bitter fruit. That and the constant flow of water from the fountain gave him the energy he needed to spend another day in the lands of the Demiurge. The truth was, he had no choice. Nepal and the entrance he had used were many days away, too many to cover without provisions. Like a maniacal swimmer in the open sea, he had used all his energies to reach the citadel and he had nothing left with which to return.[61]

Sunset. The city appeared as splendid in its decline as it must have

---

[61] The Man Under Contract was well aware of this. Although he had equipped himself during the initial crossing of the Annapurnas, he knew that only the hopelessness of a headlong rush could open the cosmic mechanisms that regulated the access to the last construct of the Demiurge. The journey had thus been a thoughtful, methodical and slow-paced suicide.

been at its peak: a haughty ruin. Gavriel walked along the deserted streets looking at pavilions and monuments erected to defenestrated heroes. Everywhere there were the emblems of the blind god, but he found no other clues or indications, and when it got dark he returned to the central square.

When the figure crossed the avenue again that night, Gavriel was ready. At the first movement, he jumped from the boundaries of the sleeping bag and put on his boots. Gavriel kept his pace with light steps and identified the doorway through which his prey disappeared at the moment its heels left the street. Inside, he found a staircase and, at its top, a wide passage with large but dim clerestories. He illuminated the way with the flashlight and his heart beat fast, perhaps with fear, perhaps with other things. He discovered an arc that gave access to a smaller chamber. Inside, finally a wall next to which waited the only inhabitant of the city.

William Chao greeted him. "Hello, Gavriel. I saw your escape along the road yesterday. I was at the tower of the postern. You did well to run away."

"William?"

Chao's eyes looked bigger, deep as cenotes. The voice was human but not those eyes. The eyes were preternatural, supramundane.

"Is it you?"

"I am … what I am, Gavriel. There are so many things that I have understood, so much that I have discovered. But I had to get lost in order to do it."

"Where am I, William? What is this place?"

"This is the place where I tell you what you need to know. Sit down."

Gavriel, who was accustomed to cryptic revelations and the confusing nature of the avatars of the blind god, felt disconcerted but obeyed. Chao crouched down next to him, on the ground covered in the dust of centuries.

"I've been searching for weeks, following the tracks of the blind god," Gavriel said.

"And he searches for you. It was time you arrived."

"Searches for me?"

"For a long time, yes. Your seat remains deserted. But I should ask you: Are you sure this is what you want? The blind god builds; that's what it does."[62]

Each of the intermediaries that the Man Under Contract had found before had been intimidating, remote, disdainful; supernatural in any case. But the man in the abandoned city who dressed in the form of Chao was surprisingly human and showed all the signs of tangible emotion that Gavriel knew. He raised his eyebrows, pursed his lips, gesticulated, trying to explain with his hands things he couldn't with words.

"And this city, is this the end of the road?" asked Gavriel.

"Maybe it is. It's up to you. You don't realize, but that has been the theme of your entire search. It has always depended on you."

"All I want is to find the answers. Where is it?"

"It is here."

"Can you take me to it?"

Chao shook his head. "No, I can't do that, but I can give you the last set of instructions you need. It's what they've entrusted to me." He made a vague gesture with his hand towards the ether. "They … they entrusted me. Are you ready?"

Gavriel nodded, and the depth of Chao's eyes extended to his voice. The voice rumbled.

...

---

[62] According to the *Nag Hammadi* codex, the end of the world will come when everything has been formed and perfected by Knowledge (gnosis). "The fire that is hidden in the world will shine and burn. It will consume everything and consume himself." This vaticination (called *apocatastasis* or Restoration to the Divinity of All Things) was known by the Man Under Contract but did not seem to disturb him.

The Supreme Being was the pre-beginning and the depth. He knew himself by the reflection of the light and, in knowing, he generated the first gifts: Ennoia, thought; Logos, the word; Pneuma, the spirit; Pistis, the faith and, above all, the virtue he most appreciated, the knowledge of Sophia.

But knowledge is restless by nature, and Sophia forced herself to reveal the nature of thought outside of her confines, and the result was a terrible being of a different appearance, a lion-faced snake with bright eyes of fire.

This was the first archon they called Yaldabaoth. It moved away from the place where it was born and took possession of another. Dominated by creative proclivity, it extracted from itself a cohort of angels whom it endowed with mathematical correspondence to the seven planets, the seven kingdoms, the twelve signs of the zodiac.[63] *Each one it marked with a face as fierce as its own: lion, ape, hyena, dragon, snake, ass and fire.*

The blind god shared with these archons the power that emanated from Sophia, instilled in them the same creative desire, but reserved to itself the eminence of constructive totality so they were diminished; poor angels, so to speak.

Then Yaldabaoth, unknowingly to the Supreme Being, created the world, and that is the secret of the universe: that the world was born as a result of a transgression because that which created it wanted to make a perfect and imperishable artefact but only achieved the simulacrum that you know, full of grief and distress.

Do not be fooled. Just as you are indifferent to the angle at which the earthworms pierce their tunnels, the blind god is not concerned about how you raise a glass or light a candle in a mausoleum. And the other god, the god with a capital letter, the Supreme Being, that one knows of neither your existence nor that of the earthworm.

Do you know what your species is made of? Sophia, the mother of the blind god, tricked him into blowing on the face of the first humans and

---

[63] Note the discrepancy between the numbers. Creationist mythology is far from being an exact science.

that was how they became luminous. But it was in an assembly of the archons where the gifts were listed: goodness, knowledge, divinity, dominion, kingdom, envy, understanding. The architect blew and called its result plasma[64] and urged the archons to finish forming it. So hope still exists, because Mankind emanates from the Demiurge, which emanates from wisdom, which emanates from the Supreme Being, and there is a link that unites each with the other and puts a divine spark in the human animal, which is the key to the transcendent world.

You, Gavriel, you now enter our sworn brotherhood. We are five planets circling the blind majesty of the sun. It's time to include the selenite substance, a subordinate satellite that we claim as ours, just as we claim you.[65]

What you are looking for is the numen of the anvil, that who is the architect. Will you now be a catechumen of our order? Do you accept the baptism that is yet to come? If so, we praise you because serving is a superlative honour, because the blind god is that high architect, and because we are nothing but stagehands who adjust pulleys and drapery behind the scenes, remove cycloramas and ultimately prepare the scene in anticipation of its grand entrance.

Will you help rebuild the world? Will you help correct the mistake that was?

...

Chao finished speaking and, although the eyes did not change, his

---

[64] This being a word that literally means "malleable substance".

[65] The relationship between the Hellenic cosmology and the symbolism of the archons is, as mentioned, profound, (quote follows) Origen Contra Celsum VI: "There is a ladder with lofty gates, and on the top of it an eighth gate. The first gate consists of lead, the second of tin, the third of copper, the fourth of iron, the fifth of a mixture of metals, the sixth of silver, and the seventh of gold. The first gate they assign to Saturn, indicating by the 'lead' the slowness of this star; the second to Venus, comparing her to the splendour and softness of tin; the third to Jupiter, being firm and solid; the fourth to Mercury, for both Mercury and iron are fit to endure all things, and are money-making and laborious; the fifth to Mars, because, being composed of a mixture of metals, it is varied and unequal; the sixth, of silver, to the Moon; the seventh, of gold, to the Sun."

voice became warmer. "That is all."

He stood up. Gavriel, stunned by the revelation and with less composure, did the same. He felt that Chao was about to say goodbye and return to the demiurgic depths he had left to deliver his instructions.

"Maya. Is Maya here too?" asked Gavriel.

Chao took a step closer and put his hands on his shoulders, an affable gesture. "Everything is here, Gavriel."

Chao's eyes filled him with sorrow. This creature was partly the friend he had known. "I did what you asked for, William. I told Cecilia everything."

Chao seemed confused as if pulled between the two natures he inhabited. "Cecilia … She called me Liam, took care of me," and then, "It doesn't matter. You're here now. The world will change."

"How will it change?"

Chao looked over his shoulder, toward the entrance corridor. "Better be careful now. People are coming."

There was a whisper, a flash and stamping of boots. Gavriel was dazzled for a moment. Armed men entered the room and pushed him with rough hands. His eyes ached, but he saw enough to distinguish, between the residual afterimages, a man with grey hair dressed in military clothing.

"Artiel, you have no idea the trouble you have caused me."

Gavriel gasped, incredulous.

"Chief Miller, there's nobody here," said one of the soldiers from the far corner.

Gavriel looked around. Chao had disappeared.

"Who were you talking to?" asked the man with grey hair.

"You don't know what—" Gavriel began.

Before he could finish the sentence, Chief Miller gave him a slap both so casual and so tremendous that it ripped him from the hands that held him.

"There you go. I've been waiting to do that since California."

Gavriel cradled his hurting face. The mercenaries placed handcuffs on his wrists and dragged him out of the chamber to the avenue, where the night was still dark. They had planted their backpacks at the fountain, next to his. They were five hardened men, and they looked at the Man Under Contract with vivid resentment.

"Feed him. He looks about to faint," said Chief Miller.

Somebody changed the shackles for a spoon, and Gavriel ate with fervour. The grey-haired man crouched beside him.

"Use the time to rest. You look terrible." He leaned down. "Tomorrow is going to be a busy day."

"How did you find me?" Gavriel stammered between bites.

"With a lot of effort. And with the loss of good soldiers."

The Man Under Contract later learned that there had been seven men who tracked him to the lands of the Demiurge. One was lost in the infinite plateau; another died in the attack of a wild beast.

"Did you follow me from Nepal?"

"We have followed you since you left your cell, and what a fucking world tour you have dragged us into. But it doesn't matter. Tomorrow you will take us to the point of contact. With no sidetracks or distractions." Chief Miller looked at the immense city, shrouded in shadows. "This is the end of the road, isn't it?"

Gavriel did not answer, but he knew that it was true.

He was awakened by the sound of successive detonations that made him roll from the sleeping bag in panic. Miller and his mercenaries aimed their black guns down the avenue, in the direction where one of the proto-human hominids was advancing. The troop discharged close rounds smelling of cordite, and the sound of the fusillade was deafening. The impacts caused pieces of skin and blood to splatter, leaving a farewell trail at every step the intruder took. The subhuman finally fell dead. The weapons went silent and the soldiers breathed fast.

In the rushed evacuation that followed, Gavriel memorized the names of the five mercenaries: Chief Miller, his second in command, Mancusi, Poul, Walker, and Agudo.

"Chief Miller, more are coming."

The sun was rising and they could see shadows moving. Miller gave an order and the soldiers threw backpacks on their shoulders.

"We have to hide. Number Two, you take point."

Mancusi trotted out and the others followed, three in front, two behind and Gavriel in the middle. They entered the cavernous interior of one of the buildings, a pavilion of neglected dignity, with high ceilings and twenty-metre-high windows. They advanced through dusty corridors and reached an inner open courtyard where several skeletons were decomposing. The sun was higher and Gavriel was thirsty. They found a door. A big man, Poul, peered carefully.

"It's the other avenue."

He went out, jumped in place, and hurried back in again. "Not through here, Chief."

Miller stepped aside and spoke with Mancusi in quiet tones. Both nodded, and Miller addressed the group. "Number Two goes ahead. Let's try to get closer to the city wall. The compasses don't work, so if anybody gets lost, follow the direction towards the point of sunset."

Mancusi went down the hall again, and the line of soldiers with Gavriel in the middle followed. They turned more corners than they had seen in arriving and came to a dead end. The men cursed softly. Miller ordered silence. He closed his eyes, took a deep breath.

"We will go back outside, take our chances on the main avenue."

They turned and ran again. Gavriel was in worse shape than the five soldiers and lost his balance every few steps.

The shroud-like aura that hung in the air of the pavilion was penetrating the group. The mercenaries muttered grumpily and startled when the grey shadows of the dead rooms came to life with the swaying of the flashlights. Gavriel, who had wandered through the citadel for two days, had not perceived it the way he felt now, threatening, resentful of the invasion. Gavriel's mood was usually composed, but when Mancusi gave him one push too many in the back, urging him to quicken his step, he turned furious and shoved back.

Mancusi, twelve centimetres taller and much wider than the Man Under Contract, was a little perplexed, but then snorted and raised the butt of his carbine.

"Number Two!" bellowed Miller.

Mancusi stopped. He was very close to Gavriel. The dark lines of a tattoo showed above the neckline of his jacket.

"Lower the rifle."

Mancusi did so, and Chief Miller signalled the order to resume the march. Agudo grabbed Gavriel's arm and pulled him along.

"Keep up the pace, cabrón," he said, whispering in his ear.

They reached a new wall.

"This is the path we followed coming in, no question," said Walker.

And as proof of the veracity of that, he indicated the spray marks they had left for reference which now pointed towards the solid wall.

"No way. Buildings don't shift like that."

There was a short and heated discussion.

"We put a charge on this wall and pass to the other side," someone proposed.

Gavriel cleared his throat and spoke hoarsely for the first time. "That won't help much. The maze is closing. We are all strangers here. No one leaves until the city wants it."

"You shut up, Artiel. We are in it because of you," said Mancusi.

Miller signalled him to calm down. "What do you propose?" the leader asked.

"Upwards. If we go up, we can break the pattern and leave. Once we are out, the maze may give us a break," said the Man Under Contract.

Walker looked at his watch in reflex. All the mechanisms had stopped. The screens were off and grey.

"We must have been running here for more than three hours, boss."

Miller inspected his men one by one. Something, which seemed more like professional fatalism than panic, jumped from one face to another. Then he turned to Gavriel and nodded.

They spent the night at the top of the pavilion, curled up on the flat roof of the majestic building, watching the streets below. The soldiers burned compact fuel pellets and cooked field rations. Gavriel had not eaten since the night before and, although he accepted the portion offered, hunger was not what he felt, neither was fatigue. Perhaps he was desensitizing himself from all human needs, pinched by the spread of fear on one side and the ascetic reassurance of the city on the other.

Chief Miller went to sit beside him. Gavriel, unable to help feeling intimidated by the rough figure of the military man, moved over a little. Miller raised a conciliatory hand.

"I don't come to threaten you, Artiel. If I thought I could get the information I need that way, I would do it without a second thought. I would do more than that. But I'm learning that you don't have much control over the things that happen here."

Gavriel nodded. "The weapons you carry at the belt cannot help break the impasse we are in," he said.

"Then let me explain this in a different way. We have provisions but not enough. I can't even calculate how many days off the Pokhara route we are. And those things that stalk us …" he said, pointing to the streets and avenues below. "We can't keep up today's rhythm for long before we start losing people. I need you to solve the maze or whatever this is. I have my orders. Once I get the proof I need, we will leave. If you help us, I guarantee that we will take you with us and protect you."

Gavriel shook his head, infinitely sad. Miller and the soldiers were going to die in that land because they didn't understand it, and despite the cuffs and humiliation they had brought upon him, he didn't want that to happen.

"I'm not coming back."

"Stay then if you want, but help us."

"I don't know if I can. I don't know if I know."

"You better learn, then." Miller stood up. "I give you one more day."

Gavriel knew that it was not a threat. It was a clarification and, to his surprise, he took it as a show of respect.

In the moonlit night, the soldiers slept around Gavriel. The only sounds were those of the faint wind and the rhythmic tap-tap of the sentry's boots on the gravel. Gavriel did not sleep. He examined the sky, conscious of the story that Chao had told him, saw planets that were much larger than in the constellations of the real world. Mercury, Venus, Mars, Jupiter, Saturn hanging in the sky. All of them orderly, aligned with the buildings on the main avenue that pointed to the Easter gate, where the sun would rise at dawn. And placed between the high planets and the low gate, a modest construction he had seen in his wanderings through the citadel and ignored. It was a limestone building over which the moon hung, illuminating it in blinding white; a smaller pavilion that suddenly took on meaning. *There*, thought the Man Under Contract, and his mind went back to the town of Zhongdien, to the handcrafted box he had bought on impulse and that slept now at the bottom of his backpack, unopen for so many months. Its lid was carved with symbols of the House of the Moon, and it proved no impulse had existed, no freedom had been granted to him. The Search, always the Search; it had ruled even the trivial moments.

That night the citadel also whispered secrets concerning the soldiers, and the figures with broad shoulders and tight jaws took on a different countenance. He knew that Mancusi had lost his three-year-old son to an obscure heart disease. He had cradled the shrinking little body almost until the end. He learned that fifteen years of soldiering have left Poul nearly blind in one eye, something he hid because mercenary work was the only way he knew to make a living. He discovered that Agudo played in a corner of his mind with the psychotic fantasy of shooting Miller in the back of the head due to an affront of vague definition, and that if he could do it without fearing any consequences, he would enjoy it with such gratification that seemed inhuman.

At dawn, after breaking camp, the soldiers formed a circle involuntarily and, for a moment, martial certainty gave way to indecision.

"Artiel?" said Miller with one hand resting on the holster of his pistol.

Gavriel pointed to the white building that, in the sunlight, stood out even more than it had last night.

"There, that pavilion. If we go down quickly, the maze will let us out."

Poul kicked at a pebble. Walker produced a sceptical hiss. But Chief Miller ignored all of this and shouldered his backpack.

"Let's go then."

They arrived at the lunar building without incident. The resolution of the conflict was accelerating, and Gavriel knew that just a few pages were left on this Search of his. Upon entering, he perceived a distinctive energy. Before the arrival of the soldiers, the citadel had been welcoming but also melancholic and quiet. The white pavilion, however, was vivifying. Gavriel forgot the hardships of the journey, and the debilitation of inanition disappeared from his limbs.

"Over there," he said, indicating the great portico that gave access to the interior of the structure.

The soldiers hurried to follow him. The hall led to a series of steps leading down, and the troop moved on to reach a hypogeum of enormous dimensions. Gavriel forced the pace, and the more alert he felt, the more soporific were the movements of the soldiers. They descended deep ramps into the earth and passed through chambers, halls and passages dimly lit by lightwells.

"Artiel … wait …" Miller said.

He was panting.

"It's there, down there. Let's go."

The certainty of the Man Under Contract was complete. Without realizing it, he was leaving the group behind.

"Artiel!"

Chief Miller aimed at his back with his gun. Gavriel stopped.

"Number Two …" Miller swallowed hard. "Number Two, you put the handcuffs on him. No more running."

Mancusi looked at his boss with empty eyes and then spoke. "Petrichor," he said.

"What? Get your cuffs out, man."

"Petrichor. Petrichor."

Mancusi dropped to his knees, trying to hold his mouth closed with his hands.

"Lemniscate," Poul said across the room.

Chief Miller looked from one to the other, perplexed.

"What the fuck are you saying? Everyone, quiet!"

"Petrichor …"[66]

"Lemniscate.[67]
Lemniscatelemniscatelemniscatelemniscatelemniscatelemniscatelemn
iscate."

Mancusi and Poul beat their foreheads with their fists, trying to get out the intrusion to which the invisible miasma of the pavilion subjected them. Miller, sweating, aimed his carbine with panic.

"Quincunx …"[68] said a third mercenary, and Miller began firing.

The soldiers' voices faded more and more as Gavriel ran down the hallways and turned corners, getting away. He passed many gates, all of very high measure. When he crossed a room, he stopped and saw one door on the far side. That one was special. He approached and laid his palm on the white metal. Behind it, he detected a remote and terrible presence. He retired in panic. Then he perceived an arrival, small but serene. Familiar.

"Maya."

"All things are here," Chao the archon had said, and here was one of them. The one that had been lost. Gavriel spoke to her as he had wanted to speak during all the years of their separation, and he almost thought to see her before him.

"Is it you? Is it really you?"

"Yes, it is me."

---

[66] As per Merriam Webster, "a distinctive, earthy, usually pleasant odor that is associated with rainfall, especially when following a warm, dry period, and that arises from a combination of volatile plant oils and geosmin released from the soil into the air and by ozone carried by downdrafts."

[67] As per Merriam Webster, "a figure-eight-shaped curve whose equation in polar coordinates is $\rho2=a2 \cos 2\theta$ or $\rho2=a2 \sin 2\theta$". The symbol of infinity.

[68] As per Merriam Webster, "an arrangement of five things in a square or rectangle with one at each corner and one in the middle."

"Where have you been? I wanted to look for you. I wanted to look for you so many times."

"But you didn't because for you another thing was the most important." Maya's voice spoke with no reproach. "And all the while, I was waiting for you here, at the end of everything. So much you disparaged yourself and, in the end, you were right."

Gavriel regained some courage and touched the huge door again.

"It's yours, Gavriel, the ductile metal."

"Maya … Is this the real you that I knew? Or are you a fragment of the blind god?"

Maya smiled as she had done once, on those nights shared on the beach where they met. She smiled then, naked and vital under Gavriel's hands.

"We are all fragments it dreams of." She pointed at the door. "Can you feel it there, on the other side?"

Gavriel could.

"It sleeps now, but it's time to wake up."

"What is it? How is it?"

Words flashed into Gavriel's mind.

Terrible. Sorrowful. Plentiful. Atrocious,

A bleakness for life. A fountain of existence.

Terrible. Terrible. Terrible. Terrible.

"I don't know. Nobody knows," said Maya. "Because the architect sleeps."

Gavriel looked at the door.

"Go in, find out," Maya said.

Gavriel tried the door. Maya put her hand on his shoulder with a soft touch he recognized.

"I wish I was with you," Gavriel said.

"I wish you were with me."

The door was intimidating.

"Maybe I should leave it; maybe … maybe it's not me who should do it."

"It's time it wakes up, and you are here. Do what you must, but remember," she said, "the architect builds. That's what it does."

"Will you come with me?"

Maya took his hand and said yes.

Gavriel doubted for the last time in his Search. It lasted for a moment and, as it vanished, it set him free. He pushed the door. From behind came the sudden screams of Chief Miller. If he asked him to stop, Gavriel didn't pay attention. An order rang and then came the loud *ratatata* of automatic weapons. The bullets riddled the body of the Man Under Contract, but it was done. The door had opened and all the shadows of the world came out to engulf them.

HIC JACET DEMIURGUS

All the shadows of the world.

Gavriel floated, huddled in the dark, and around him, all the shadows of the world were piled up like a gloomy cathedral.

Gavriel's mind was filled with fear and fascination, and words he once read appeared before his eyes: "No one is fierce enough to rouse it … When it rises up, the mighty are terrified; they retreat before its thrashing … Nothing on earth is its equal … a creature without fear … It looks down on all that are haughty; it is king over all that are proud."

All things, present and preterite, went through Gavriel.

"It ranks first among the works of God,

yet its Maker can approach it with his sword.

Any hope of subduing it is false; the mere sight of it is overpowering.

No one is fierce enough to rouse it."

No one.

No one.

From the depths, the presence approached. *I know this*, Gavriel thought. *I've felt this before*, and his memories brought him a boat in the Pacific besides the Japanese island of Ogasawara. In that infinite ocean, he had felt the arrival of the whale, like a benevolent giant. He had seen the mammalian eye and its understanding.

"Leviathan …" Gavriel said.

What approached now was neither benevolent nor understanding.

What approached now was an incomprehensible monster of sidereal dimensions.

"Behemoth …"[69]

The Demiurge was aroused, irritated by Gavriel's infinitesimal breathing, waking up from the dozing of infinite eras in which it was left after forging the world. It had the arrogance of the architect and the humility of the liar. The Demiurge was not God, but was a creator deity in its own right.

"Who dares open the doors of its mouth,

ringed about with fearsome teeth?"

Despite the maddening unintelligibility of its essence, there was something that united Man with the creative craftsman. Gavriel was facing his father, his mother, his author, his alma mater. The clay of humanity had come out of those hands that stretched out, searching, searching.

"Strength resides in its neck;

dismay goes before it."

The roaring voice had blown its breath of life into the primaeval dust. The Demiurge was the parent and the reason for existence, and Gavriel, torn between the terror and the magnitude of the deity that stole his sanity, recognized his origin.

---

[69] The Behemoth or Begimo is a beast mentioned in Job 40:15-24. An amalgam of many animal identities, all terrible: elephant, hippo, rhino, buffalo.

"The sword that reaches it has no effect,

nor does the spear or the dart or the javelin."

"Father! Father! It's me, Gavriel! I have come to find you!"

"Nothing on earth is its equal—

a creature without fear.

It looks down on all that are haughty;

it is king over all that are proud."

Gavriel perceived how other lives were extinguished in the deep shadow: Chief Miller, Agudo, Mancusi … They did not understand what was coming. They had not prepared.

But Gavriel had. He had been preparing for the encounter all his life. He had paid the price.

"WAKE UP, FATHER! WAKE UP!"

And then, in a lower voice.

"Maya … Maya …"

THE APOCATASTASIS OF THE END OF THE WORLD

Gavriel Artiel, the Man Under Contract, appeared on the morning of September 2nd in the centre of the city of Kathmandu, waving the red oriflamme of the Demiurge.

He manifested suddenly, naked and emaciated.

A moment later, a silhouette of colossal proportions formed behind him, surrounded by five others. The mould of divinity had produced those archontic presences just as it had produced the universe.

Gavriel straightened, looked upon the realm of Man, finally at peace with himself.

The figure of biblical import arrived to devastate and remake the world, and he was its herald.

Notes

This is a work of fiction. The bases of the religious and philosophical principles described in this book are real and (as far as my interpretation allows for) correct. The treatment done to justify the progress of the plot is, of course, fictitious and possibly absurd.

Cambodia and its temples, Tibet and Tasmania and their alpine courses, Ogasawara and its waters, as well as the intermediate places here described, are as per the memories of my visits.

The figure of the Demiurge as a cosmic artisan has haunted and obsessed me for thirty years. I do not believe in it as an intellectual concept but perhaps I do as a Gnostic abstract. This book is an attempt to free me from its permanent influence.

A.Asensio.
Kagbeni, northern Nepal.